N OF ORTH
SUNSET

NORTH OF SUNSET

HALEY AHERN

GFB

Published by GFB™, Seattle
www.girlfridayproductions.com

Produced by Girl Friday Productions

Cover design: Ashton Smith
Production editorial: Kylee Hayes

Image credits: cover © Shutterstock/1979713070

ISBN (paperback): 978-1-964721-58-3
ISBN (ebook): 978-1-964721-57-6

Library of Congress Control Number: 2025902719

First edition

*To my dearest parents, Tracy and Michael.
Thank you for teaching me hope is an ember
that must be constantly fanned or else one
may spend their life in the cold.*

Chapter One

I am indecisively decisive, and that, I think, I know for sure.

As I sit alone in my office, I look down on the blaring streets of Los Angeles blitzed by rain. The clunking of horse hooves pesters me as the telegraph chatters. To the days of automobiles and telephones and mansions built by gold: You have forever maimed me. Dammit—I miss those days. They spin around my mind as unproductively as the oak chair I sit upon, avoiding facing my desk and the single form situated on it. The pungent smell of ink taunts me, for I know this paper will change the course of my life. I halt and quickly write down today's date before a drop appears on the tip of my fountain pen. I have learned some things wait for nobody.

November 2, 2175.

I despise writing down all the personal information that will follow, but being an old man . . . What does it matter? Employee ID—check! Address—check! Social security number—check, check, check! I continue scribbling numbers and chomping simultaneously on my plant-free cookies. Eventually Americans found out that vegetables, like any other living organism, have a defense mechanism that harms the predator that tries to eat them. I can't believe people a hundred years ago thought vegetables were good for you. Don't get me wrong, these new "delicious" cookies probably still have a 50 percent chance of giving you cancer, but they definitely have a 100 percent chance of making you look like an asshole if you eat one. I mean, really, who buys these lousy things?

The crumbs from those baked goods scold me as they violate the form, but not as much as the young woman in the photograph on the shelf to my right. Suspicious eyes in a black skirt suit, smiling with three cowards in a gray bowling alley. From the black-and-white picture to the black-and-white form, that's all life is—that's the only way for an earnest man to live or, in my case, to have lived. The next question on the paper causes my spine to tremble. My wrinkled hand tries to move onward, but my ink smudges as if my pen were fighting back, pleading with me to reconsider the answer to the following blank line.

Age. What a weird word. *A-G-E, age.* What a weird concept.

I finally write down the unfair number of seventy-four. Only fifty years ago, I was a young man, hungry for change. Not the kind you find in a worn leather wallet, made from cheap metals that greedy bastards love. The kind that invites excitement amid a dull, meaningless life. Unknowingly, I was going to get it in its most cruel yet fair form that summer.

Chapter Two

The year was 2125, which made me twenty-four years old at the time. I'd moved to California about two years prior, living just south of Sunset Boulevard. My flat was on the twenty-fourth floor of a run-down brick apartment building with fire escapes zigzagging across the outside of the structure as if they were pacing back and forth in a panic, not wanting to live there either. Every now and then I would open up my casement window to check and make sure that my wrought iron fire escape hadn't decided to work up the nerve to flee and find better. Keeping that fire escape company was a rusted basket that hung outside my window, where the morning paper was delivered, or should I say "thrusted."

In those days, delivery methods were much more complex. Mail delivery was a young kid who passed through on a monocycle made of steel tubing with a large circular wheel attached to the back of it. I've always found machines more fascinating than people.

As I looked down on the bustling gray city streets that sticky June morning, past the crowd, I could see the mechanics

behind that opulent device called a News Cycle. Every time the
boy pedaled, the large wheel on the back scooped up a newspaper, adding it to the ever-spinning circle of articles rotating
around the steel. Gaining momentum from each manual push
of the foot, the paper eventually reached the top of the large
wheel involuntarily, mirroring my life. Once it reached the
peak, the newspaper was jolted out and landed in a rotted-out
basket in front of a rotted-out window, as if that rickety large
bike were a cannon with immaculate precision.

Hooonk!

Brrring! Brrring!

"Watch it, you pill!" An aggravated driver threw his pinky
up at the paperboy.

I watched the poor News Cycle swerve around the ear-
offending traffic of cars that were built more outrageously
than the former. The number one car manufacturer was Peellé
Automotive, and their H20-powered vehicles were the apple
of everyone's eye . . . especially poor people like me who had
to walk everywhere. Those shining automobiles' bodies resembled something of an ancient 1930s Stutz Bearcat, but with the
standard modern features that every car had in those days: a
large door on the back for passengers to enter, two headlights
shaped like diamonds, and lastly, a unique emblem that sat
on the front hood, made personally for the owner. When I
heard one of those water-powered behemoths of a vehicle, it
reminded me of my place in that achromatic city.

I had a degree from Brown University, which served about
the same purpose in those days as bringing a knife to a gun-
fight. America was in the midst of its seventh industrial rev-
olution, meaning if you couldn't contribute to society in a
significant, innovative way, your degree meant nothing. Being
a label lover, I unfortunately had to learn that the hard way.
In 2125, the Prohibition of Screen Sedatives was still raging.

Everyone says the pendulum always swings back, but I'm not too sure about that. Right across the street from where I lived was the Museum of Decline, one of America's most prestigious historic museums. On that eighty-degree morning, while grabbing the paper from my basket, I noticed they had just put up a new poster out front of that cement building.

Coming Soon! Screen Sedatives Exhibit. Smartphones: A Remote Time in American History.

After I looked at the poorly drawn version of what I assumed was a smartphone, I turned my attention away from the window to finally get my muggy Tuesday morning started. I couldn't tell if the source of my restlessness was the humidity or my latent problem, either way they both hung over me like an unpaid bill.

As I sat down on the edge of my unmade bed, with a mattress that felt like it was built for a Navy SEAL, my ramshackle fan seemed to hit cold air on everything in that room—except me. The wind-rustled newspaper told of a booming economy. We were on our seventy-third president and things had been running smoothly so far. Quality was the name of the game in those days . . . so they said. After wrestling and struggling to read the large pieces of active paper that my fan, for some reason, had taken a liking to, I decided to throw them on top of the ever-growing pile of meaningless items that filled my pigsty. Posterior to losing the first battle of the day, the morning paper, I went on to pursue a victory I knew I could win: getting dressed.

My one-room apartment might have been an absolute mess, but my clothes were perfectly neat. Little did I know I was getting ready for a day that would change my life, so I put on something that was considered the bare minimum of casual attire. I wore a dark suit with triangular buttons and a matching overcoat. It made balmy days feel intolerable, but that's what everyone wore. I found out that trying to go against the grain will leave you with nothing but a splinter.

Yes, I was twenty-four, but I had the mentality of a fifty-three-year-old man who'd just gotten the short end of the stick from a bad divorce. I was thought to be handsome—in the most conventional way possible—but for some reason, I had a chip on my shoulder. Like in that Johnny Cash folktale, my weasel of a father decided to give me the lousiest name known to man before he left my mother and me. No, it is not Sue, it's worse. I mean, for God's sake, my name is Oleander. Talk about getting cheated in life.

When I walked out the door to head to work, I passed by the framed certificate—the one I had once been proud of—that was hanging on my wall. As I slammed my hollow apartment door, I could hear the degree from Brown, which had **Oleander Briggs** stamped on it in a medieval font, clank against the drywall. For it would not let me forget about it. My name says it all. Pshhh, Oleander . . . That name says it all.

Chapter Three

A s I walked through the black-and-white world known as South of Sunset, I dodged crowds of garlic-smelling people who were walking through their reeking worlds as well. Getting to work every day consisted of a thirty-two-minute walk along the overpopulated city streets with outbursts of static buzzing from the radios in storefront windows. The radio content consisted of the same three things day in and day out: advertisements, breaking news, and lastly, music.

When the brick buildings started to shift from angular department stores and linear hotels to industrial and bulky factories, you could hear the sound in the air transform from warm jazz music to the banging and beeping of machines. As soon as I saw steam rising from the buildings, I knew my walk to work was almost over.

The largest and most intimidating factory on the block was my final destination . . . Fleur Industries, a company that manufactured gold-dipped roses—another pointless invention that made us college graduates shake our heads and say, "Why didn't I think of that?" We produced too many products for it to be a front, but still, I found it hard to believe that the multimillion-dollar building was purchased from flower profits.

When I arrived at the front of that monstrous factory, I wondered how on such a searing day something could still feel so frigid? I proceeded to walk up the cement steps and commit to going inside the building. The point of no return. My muscle memory took over from there as I strolled down the case-lined hallway, hearing each step echo behind me. The cases were filled with metal roses and the walls with quotes that would make even Romeo and Juliet chuckle:

> *Love can live forever.*
> *Give the gift of eternity.*
> *The #1 manufacturer in gold-dipped roses.*
> *Just like your love, our roses last.*

As soon as I mindlessly clocked in to work, the vibration of the conveyor belt rang, acting as an announcement to everyone that I had arrived right on time, like every other day for the past two years. I probably had the least romantic job out of all the two hundred and thirty-six employees in that factory. My post was at the conveyor belt, cutting the thorns off roses. It wasn't intolerable, though, thanks to James, my only friend South of Sunset besides my flight-risk fire escape. He worked with me on the assembly line at Fleur Industries and offered nonintellectual amusement. He was about three years older than me, but I still saw him as juvenile. He had dark eyes, thin wrists, and ears that stuck straight out—probably from being dragged by them too much as a child.

That morning, working the conveyor, was like any other. James started out with the same script that he always performed too loud and too early.

"How's the morning treatin' ya, Ollie?!" James blurted out.

"Just dandy, James, ol' boy! 'Move to California,' they said. 'The weather's great here,' they said."

"I know. It's about as muggy out as the inside of a prostitute's drawers, but think about it this way, at least we get to look at beautiful flowers all day!"

"That are gonna die as soon as they're dipped in piping hot gold." I hacked more thorns off.

James clicked his tongue a few times in disapproval. "Oleander, Oleander. Thanks to Fleur's patented technology, the roses live forever. The gold preserves them, obviously! It's science."

I began to laugh in mordancy as I thought about the sheer ridiculousness of that whole multibillion-dollar company. In that moment, I felt bad for all the poor bastards that bought these because (a) they'd really messed up with the missus, or (b) they truly believed in that rubbish. Either way it was pathetic to me.

As I contemplated if this conglomerate was immoral or ingenious, I saw a look sweep across James's face—a mischievous one, the kind where you see it and feel the immediate need to say no before even hearing what is about to be said. James, the master of whispering so loudly it defeats the purpose, asked me, "Do you wanna break one of these puppies open to see for yourself?"

"And damage company property?!" I laughed. "I like having a roof over my head. Thank you very much!"

"How can you be so sure the roses don't live forever unless you've seen it for yourself?"

I remained quiet. The man had a point that I had no counterargument for, so I just continued to cut the thorns off. While mindlessly slicing, I nicked the tip of my finger with a knife that was definitely not approved by the safety governance board.

"Dammit, James! This is what happens when you ask too many questions . . . People get hurt."

James snickered as he continued to cut the flowers that seemed more interested in what I had to say than he did.

"Could be worse," James remarked. "My pal Joey—"

"You mean the guy with the one eye that always points left," I interrupted thoughtlessly.

"Yes, that guy."

I ignored the signs that James was trying to speak. He opened his mouth a few times and had nothing but a few awkward sounds come out as I continued to recite my poor-taste joke.

"Bumped into him at a party once."

"What?! How?" James resurrected his enthusiasm.

"Well, we just couldn't see eye to eye!"

I began to chuckle at what I thought was a great punch line, but James appeared as if he were about to plug his nose due to how bad my joke stunk. He rolled his eyes and then proceeded to tell me that Joey had recently gotten a job working at the lumberyard.

"He is now cutting wood, and just yesterday—"

"Oh shit! Who the hell hires a man that is legally blind to cut wood?" I interrupted once again. "Don't tell me . . . He killed someone."

"Oh, no, no, no. Joey didn't hurt anyone. I was going to say that just yesterday they started to let him use a power saw. Imagine how dangerous it would be if they let you use one. Your finger would be"—James motioned losing a finger—"clean off!"

James cracked himself up over that one. Fair to say we had different senses of humor, although I did entertain him in his immature bliss. As I said this next line, I hadn't a clue that Mr. Walter, the manager of Fleur Industries, was walking right behind me.

"Screw you! The man is blind! I wanna know who puts these jerks in charge. Pshhh, blind man using power tools."

"I can assure you gentlemen that there's another reason I am not working the conveyor belt," Mr. Walter said, adjusting his glasses.

He tapped on his clipboard, then walked away. He seemed proud of his remark that had so cleverly justified his atrocious eyesight and disparaged our even more atrocious life decisions. Embarrassed, James and I watched Mr. Walter march toward the iron stairs that led to a lattice balcony looking over the whole factory. He had thin white hair that resembled the stuffing inside a dog toy, a three-piece suit with small pinstripes, and a personality that could only be described with one word: *neurotic*. Oh, and I can't forget his heavy Coke-bottle glasses and pocket watch.

Mr. Walter reached the top of the balcony. He looked down on all the employees, giving us a visual representation of the company's hierarchy . . . just in case we had forgotten. As he cleared his throat, all the machines were immediately shut off by some milquetoast workers. The chaotic factory that was filled with over two hundred employees, as well as conveyor belts, large cast-iron pots for smelting, and numerous other unsettlingly large machines, turned silent. This only happened in emergencies. Mr. Walter began to speak in his mid-Atlantic accent that we all assumed was phony and fabricated to make himself sound upper class.

"Good morning, everyone. I have a very important announcement to make."

When Mr. Walter spoke those words, all I could think was that the company had gone belly up and he was about to tell everyone to go home. Stopping production was not something to be taken lightly. To my surprise, his phonographic voice told of something else.

"Mr. Fleur will be stopping by the factory this afternoon, as he has meetings to attend in the area."

"That's what we sabotaged production for?" I whispered.

"Everyone put your best face forward when he is here, and if he catches anyone slacking on the job"—Mr. Walter's eyes homed in on James and me—"I am sure he will proceed . . . as . . . necessary."

Gulp.

I focused my eyes on the ceiling light hanging directly above Mr. Walter's frizzy head of hair. *Maybe if it fell at just the right angle, it'd injure him enough to stay home for a week or two.*

"Mr. Fleur is a very busy man of high caliber. Please do not approach him or try to"—Mr. Walter lifted his hands to make air quotes—"chat."

James grumbled under his breath and showed little to no respect for Mr. Walter's speech that showcased the enormous power trip he had been afforded.

"Last thing, you will be representing my tightly run ship. Thank you. You may resume your duties."

The enormous building roared once again as Mr. Walter disappeared into the offices on the second level. I could hear employees shouting to each other, acting as if this were the most exciting thing that had ever happened within these depressing walls. Of course, I was lucky enough to be standing right behind the two chattiest women in the whole factory.

"I can't believe Mr. Fleur will be coming to our location! No one here has ever met him. Let alone seen him," exclaimed the woman directly in front of me, her voice higher than her hairdo.

"My second cousin told me she's seen him! Word is he's doing a tour of all the factories across the US. She said he was an absolute doll," added in the second clucking hen.

I laughed in contempt. "Oh yeah? Getting terminated for saying the wrong thing. Mr. Walter definitely made him sound like an absolute doll."

Both women, their hair filled with enough pins and gel to build a fort for a small woodland creature, looked at me as if I'd said something that offended them personally. After that rare brief moment of silence and look of pure bitterness that those middle-aged women had mastered so well, they continued clucking in cheer again. As a matter of fact, so did the whole factory.

Am I the only person in the room that feels differently about the news or even cares that we are behind on production thanks to Mr. Walter? What is Mr. Fleur going to say about us being a day late?

My surroundings seemed as if they were in fast motion, growing louder and quicker as I reclined deeper and deeper into myself. I couldn't understand the excitement buzzing from all the factory workers that day. The naive fools jumped around, looking forward to being in somewhat close proximity to a man of great importance. I wasn't looking forward to finally putting a face to a name. Frankly, I was scared out of my mind. That man had the power to pull the plug on me anytime he chose with no excuse needed. I could look at him the wrong way and there went that month's rent, or worse, Mr. Walter could throw me under the bus. I had pissed him off just enough that morning. Unemployed, I would be forced to face my ever-nagging problem head-on—what I was doing with my life, or even worse . . . what I wanted to do with it. Nothing makes a young man clam up more than the world being his oyster.

Chapter Four

After Mr. Walter's poorly timed announcement that morning, I finally made it to the break room on the third floor of the factory. I had to clean up my crusty, bloody finger that had fallen victim to the inconvenient slice of a dull knife.

I rummaged through the dusty cabinets. "Holy mackerel!" I couldn't find a single bandage in that sterile space. I did manage to concoct a bandage out of a rag and tape to cover up my cut. The cloth was so bulky it had to be wrapped around four of my fingers rather than just the one with the nick. This forced my hand to make a *B* in sign language. As I finished securing my obnoxious tourniquet for my pea-sized scrape, I saw out the window what looked to be an automobile built for a monarch. It was a glistening silver color with a black streak starting at the rear and descending to the front tire, as if the painter had had an enormous brush that they'd swept across the vehicle with delicate precision. It was the last intimidating piece to complete the already intimidating building it was parked in front of. I stared down on the silver boat built by Zeus, struggling to see the front emblem. I pressed my forehead against the glass for a closer look and soon realized the emblem was a rose. In that moment, a dopey-looking chauffeur got out and ran around the car as if he were playing musical chairs. The driver then opened the back door to reveal a man in his sixties. The mysterious Mr. Fleur had finally arrived.

Although I was looking down on him, he walked in a way that let me know I was still beneath him. His three-piece suit looked like somewhat of a cross between what a politician and a well-paid jazz singer would wear. Mr. Fleur's flat-brimmed hat was tilted down over his face as he, without hesitation, stomped over those very same cement steps I'd tiptoed on that morning. Realizing he was now inside the building, I ran downstairs in a hurry to get back to my workstation. After all, I did not want to be the first employee he canned.

When I returned to my post, there was no fuss made about my "mutilated" hand. Not even a "What happened?" from a concerned coworker. Figures. Twenty-two minutes and thirty-eight seconds of me making roses pleasant for the human hand had passed when, finally, the man larger than life entered our section.

Mr. Fleur must have been around the same age as Mr. Walter, but there was an extreme contrast between the two men. Mr. Walter neurotically trailed behind Mr. Fleur in a way that could have been performed as a slapstick comedy show. As Mr. Fleur took off his felt hat, I could finally see his face from across the room. He was smiling and shaking hands with employees, congratulating them as if they had just won a race. Five minutes would go by of Mr. Fleur having a genuine conversation with a worker, Mr. Walter politely tapping him on the shoulder to continue, then Mr. Fleur being distracted once again by another long-winded conversation.

As Mr. Walter was going through the checklist of all the machines present, Mr. Fleur whispered in his ear.

"Okay, everyone! I need this department to line up, shoulders touching," Mr. Walter shouted in a squirrelly voice.

Oh no, am I on the chopping block?

We all quietly lined up, giving each other blank stares.

"Good. Now put your hands forward, palms down," he continued.

Mr. Fleur then walked up to each person, intensely staring at their fingertips. It all felt so ridiculous to me, but I guess when you're one of the richest men in the world, no one questions you.

"Make sure to cut your nails and wash underneath them," Mr. Fleur said to James, who was directly next to me. "Clean habits reflect a clean mind."

James had neither.

Mr. Fleur's eyes drifted in my direction as he moved in front of me. His careless, lighthearted smile abruptly turned into a look of shock as we made eye contact. Mr. Fleur looked as if he had seen a ghost. His face turned pale. His eyes then shifted from my face down to my mangled hand, igniting a look of concern. His look of concern reached my eyes once more. He turned away and grumbled "Very good" as he dismissed all the timid employees.

Mr. Walter then proceeded to gather everyone in a room that looked similar to a lecture hall. This grand room was located on the opposite end of the factory on the fourth floor and featured a run-down stage with an even more run-down podium smack-dab in the middle of it. As everyone shuffled in, I could see Mr. Fleur standing at the podium, fidgeting with papers. His hands were shaking a little. All the employees sat down in metal chairs that made the most unpleasant screech if you scooted or leaned over to talk to your neighbor.

I think it was Mr. Fleur's status that frightened me the most. Once he recited what the company was about, everything changed. Something in his eyes told me he needed us more than we needed his paycheck.

"Thank you for taking the time out of your day to be here," Mr. Fleur so graciously said. "Without you, we would not be able to make the leaps and bounds that continue to inspire."

At that moment James and I gave each other a look—we both thought this meeting was a waste of our time.

"At Fleur Industries, we believe what we are doing is greater than gold-dipped roses. We are giving people hope that some things can last for eternity. No gift says our love will stay alive forever more than a rose that is preserved in twenty-four-karat gold. Because what is the most precious thing in the world? The most valued?" Mr. Fleur asked, testing our ability to tell if that was a rhetorical question or not. I sat there in silence, knowing some fool would eventually blurt out something.

"Gold," answered one of the employees from the eleventh row.

The room got noisy with reactions once that man with an incredibly wrinkled button-up shirt broke the ice.

"Good guess, my son, but no. It's life," exclaimed Mr. Fleur with the kind of enthusiasm you didn't ever encounter South of Sunset. "And people will want to invest in something that is capable of preserving life. It gives them a sense of power and control over the inevitable. That is the eternal search every person is on."

From the row directly in front of me, a man no older than thirty-eight responded without hesitation. "How do we know that there's not a crumpled-up flower inside?"

At that moment I was thanking my lucky stars I wasn't that guy. I could feel Mr. Walter watch his tightly run ship quickly turn into a bunch of kayaks being tossed around the rapids in every direction. The employees were getting a little too comfortable around Mr. Fleur. I don't blame them; his presence had the softness of a Sunday afternoon, and his voice was as inviting as an ice cream truck jingle. Simpleminded creatures, forgetting he could lay down the hammer on them at any second. If I were him, I would have given that guy a bologna sandwich and a road map for asking the insulting question that was on everyone's mind.

"Why, you . . ." Mr. Walter walked toward that guy as if he were going to grab him by the throat.

"I understand why you may ask that, but high risk, high reward," Mr. Fleur calmly said to the worked-up employee. "Using the Fleur Atom Immunizing Technological Health . . ."

"That's a mouthful," James whispered to me under his breath.

"This patented formula preserves the life of that rose in the exact state it was in before being dipped," Mr. Fleur eloquently stated.

"Well, is it really living if it is confined in hard alloy?" the antagonistic employee prevailed.

"Are you still living if you're lying in your bed asleep? The answer is yes, my friend. Think of it that way. Except it will not continue the aging process until its coat is dissolved and removed. From there it will continue on the course of its natural life from the state it was first preserved in."

"What if I decide I want my rose to be free and continue living its life?! Can I just break it open?"

"Someone get the hook," I whispered to James. I was getting tired of the many questions that obnoxious employee had, but I could tell James was intrigued. I tapped him on the shoulder to get his attention. Being in a Fleur-induced trance, James didn't seem to hear my joke. Mr. Fleur continued weaving his web of magical spoken words as the room stood still under the same spell James had fallen victim to.

"No, that will make the rose deteriorate. It will need to be carefully injected with a solvent that breaks down the coating and removes the Fleur Atom Immunizing Technological Health from its system." That was the last response Mr. Fleur made, finally shutting up the stubborn employee.

My next problem, though, was getting James to shut up. He spent the rest of the workday mumbling deep in concentration, trying to remember that long-winded scientific name Mr. Fleur had mentioned. I couldn't tell if he sounded like a mad scientist or a bumbling idiot as he tried to pronounce those words.

"Fleur atom imu . . . imuna—"

"Now that's a good salesman if I've ever seen one," I interrupted James, putting an end to his painful interpretation of vowels.

James looked at me in a serious manner and, for once, was at a loss for words.

"Oh brother, he's even got you all starry eyed." I shook my head.

"Well, I just think that—"

As James began to rationalize with me, Mr. Fleur came into view with his unignorable large stature. He grew bigger and bigger as he made his approach.

"Afternoon, gentlemen!"

Both James and I smiled and nodded, not knowing the right thing to say back. Mr. Fleur then proceeded to motion toward my hand. "Awful bad cut ya got there, my boy."

"Eh, I guess it comes with the territory," I said quietly, sickly amused by his sympathy.

"They have ya cuttin' off the thorns, don't they?"

I shrugged and smiled, politely hinting yes.

"What do you men go by?"

"This is James, and I am Oleander, sir. Oleander Briggs."

"Well, no wonder that rose was trying to get ya. With a name like that, it saw you as a threat! Hahaha, ya know oleanders are highly toxic flowers. Just one leaf can kill a man."

"So I'm told," I snidely replied. Hadn't heard that one before.

"Well, I have this salve for you, Oleander. I carry it with me for just those types of cuts." Mr. Fleur pulled out a small glass vial that was so conveniently in his right coat pocket. He stared at it for a brief moment, as if a memory had swept across his mind, then he continued on with what he had to say. "Created it for my little girl the day she scraped her knee running through the yard. Poor baby was allergic to neomycin, so I couldn't use the regular ointment we had lying around the house. I had to create something specific just for her. I knew that little spitfire would injure herself often. Restless thing, always having mud fights in her ballroom dresses or attempting new stunts in the living room. I have made enough to last a normal, levelheaded person about fifty years! What a man will do for his daughter."

"You seem like a very good father, sir. She sounds lucky to have you," James added.

"Oh, no," Mr. Fleur replied. "I'm the lucky one. You boys will understand someday when you have kids of your own. You will do anything in your power to make them feel better, to take away their pain, give them peace of mind. You'd give them your arm and your leg if you could! They become your whole world."

James nodded as I responded to Mr. Fleur, unfazed by what he had to say. "Ohhh, I can't even think about having kids, sir. I'm just trying to get through the day."

"Hmm, that's understandable at your age."

An uncomfortable silent pause occurred, so I blurted out, "We are already behind on production today, sir, so I better be going. Come along, James."

"Hold on a moment!" Mr. Fleur's high cheekbones quickly ascended. "I'm happy someone around here noticed. Well, since your name is Oleander, you must take a certain liking to flowers."

"Well—"

"We are about to create a new collection for fall and I would like your say in it."

I remember seeing a little burst of light, far off in the distance, way behind Mr. Fleur. A flash of something. Later on, I asked James if he'd seen anything odd that day, and he said, "Yeah, a look of enthusiasm from you for the first time."

I guess I was enthusiastic, whatever that meant. How could one not be when one of the most influential men in the world had told you the following: "Mr. Walter will arrange for a courtesy vehicle to pick you up tomorrow morning at eight thirty sharp. I expect you to be standing at the front door of this here factory, ready. My driver shall not wait for any man, even if it's King Midas himself."

I responded to Mr. Fleur with a typical blank look and an even more typical "Yes, sir."

"Well then, Oleander." Mr. Fleur spoke in a tone that said he knew his words were more immortal than his flowers. "I am looking forward to seeing you . . . North of Sunset."

He walked away, disappearing in the same direction I'd seen that burst of light come from. Once Mr. Fleur was out of view, James tapped me on the shoulder to help me step down from the high horse I'd never gotten the chance to hop on.

"Wow, for once your name actually got you somewhere." James chuckled.

"Yeah, that wasn't in a trash can."

As I walked home from work that afternoon in a giddy daze, I found myself skipping and humming. This was not normal. I started to think the reason steam was rising from the towering buildings, ascending into the sky, was just so it could shake hands with the sunset. I don't know how to explain it, but the city had a warm, quiet glow about it. The same feeling as opening a new unread novel. As if you can hear the stiff paper crack and the seams begin to loosen when you turn the first page. You don't know what is in store, but you know it is just the beginning of something grand, something spectacular, something that will make your whole world open up. That age-old feeling of "Here we go!"

Chapter Five

Darkness comforted the sky as the late sun finally said farewell to the boulevard. That night after work, I did everything I could to make sure I was prepared for the following morning's voyage across town. I steamed my shirt on that rickety, decrepit ironing board. I polished the black shoes I'd put aside specifically for fancy soirees. I laid out all my hair products on the bathroom counter, which could probably have used a deep cleaning . . . seven months ago. I made sure I controlled everything I could. After all, the ride to North of Sunset was apparently so important that even King Midas could not get a freebie.

I set the trivial square alarm clock that was on my worn-down wooden nightstand. That piece of furniture had enough scratches on it that it looked as if a prisoner had once used it to count the days.

". . . and we don't know much about this new disease, but it has been reported to . . ."

Click!

I turned off the radio, which was playing the nightly

Science's Latest Discoveries program, and crawled into bed, mumbling to myself, "Eight thirty sharp, Ollie, eight thirty sharp."

The night ran away like a fugitive—clumsily and unexpectedly quick. The ring of my metal alarm clanked in the morning, waking me up in a cold sweat as if I were a warden who'd let my prisoner escape. It was still pitch black out, so I turned on the lamp that stood alone in the corner of my one-room flat. I wrapped my leather watch around my wrist and centered it.

"Dammit!" It was five o'clock in the morning, so I immediately rushed to get dressed. After sticking a chalky toothbrush in my mouth, I hopped in circles around the room, putting my respectable shoes on. That was probably the riskiest thing I had ever done up to that point. I took breaks from dangerously adding the finishing details to my ensemble to spit leftover toothpaste in the sink, leaving me with sagey fresh breath.

For the final touch, I went over to the iron bar cart that served as storage in my bathroom. On top of that table with wheels was an array of labeled glass bottles filled with cologne. I read and sniffed each one with ridicule. "Sleek Metal" . . . nahhh. "Alpha Male" . . . too greasy smelling. "Wine and Pine" . . . *cough, cough, hack!* Its musty aroma smothered me. My eyes watered as scratchy marbles trickled down my throat. I closed my eyes in focus as I tightened my upper and lower lip together. My chest stuttered a few times—echoing the aftershock of a cough. I quickly regained my composure and will to live.

Finally, I grabbed "Smoked Bourbon" with a gleam of hope. As soon as I smelled it, I realized that one was a terrible idea. The scent of an extravagant night out at a pub smacked me. Last thing I needed was for Mr. Fleur to think his employee was a lush. In that moment of frustration, a bright idea swept across my mind.

I have another bottle of cologne! That old, expensive one I bought from a French man in Sawtelle last year.

I proceeded to dig under my bed, shoving belongings and old bags around. I pulled out a heavy trunk with leather trim and metal buckles. Its cognac-brown color looked smoky beige due to the dust. Sitting on the floor like a child opening a present on Christmas, I swung the lid up. My father's old Brown sweater, which had once been soft, sat on top of the random trinkets, folded neatly in a perfect square. I unfolded the stiff sweater cautiously. It had once looked as if it could fit a giant, but it was only a medium. I rubbed my fingers back and forth along the brittle seams. A minute went by, then three, then five. A skip down memory lane got me for a moment, just a moment. I folded the sweater back up, then continued spelunking in the littered trunk. I threw some old essay papers to the side, revealing the awkwardly shaped glass bottle lying in the corner.

Perfect! A one-of-a-kind fragrance that will show Mr. Fleur I am a distinguished man with unique taste. Working with flowers, the man must have a great nose and would definitely be able to pick up on the intricate notes in this cologne, though uncultured individuals might not.

I drowned myself in that interesting concoction of fragrances, then whiffed in satisfaction. Getting caught up in my exquisite taste, I'd lost track of time. I glanced at my watch, yelled the brief yet impactful word "shit," then ran out the door, shoving my wallet in my coat pocket. The fact that I didn't fall down the spiraling black staircase in my apartment building was a miracle in itself. When I reached the heavy glass doors at the front of my building, the darkness of the morning began to lighten half a shade, stirring a great panic within me.

I ran through the city streets, dodging obstacles left and right in the dimness. From wooden apple boxes to people unexpectedly hopping out of trucks for early-morning deliveries, my performance could've won a gold medal at the Olympics. After running, jumping, and ducking the entire way to work, I finally arrived at the front of the factory. I put my hands on my knees to catch my breath, then raised my fatigued arm to look at my watch. The shaking time read five forty-five a.m. *Phew! That was a close one.*

Almost three hours passed of pacing back and forth, killing time (and avoiding dirty looks from coworkers), until it was 8:36 a.m. Looking up at the Fleur Industries building, now in daylight, I stretched my arms out.

At this point, no one is going to show up. Of course this would happen to me!

I faced my back toward the street in protest, cursing to myself about my bad luck. I pulled myself deeper and deeper into the vortex of pessimism as my brain dissected the reasons why this always happened to me.

"Taking in the glorious sight, huh?!" a deep voice shouted from the street.

I turned around, caught off guard.

It was the dopey driver I'd seen from the break room the day before. He quickly got out of the beautiful Peellé Automotive town car and ran around to open the back door in the same goofy manner. I was surprised he didn't hit his head every time he stepped out of that vehicle, due to his lack of coordination and pole-like frame. He stood by the car like a floppy-eared Irish setter. I glared at his unique appearance: a kempt mustache that could've worked on a man with a monocle and top hat or a construction worker—I couldn't figure out which one yet—and an outfit that resembled a chauffeur costume you would find in a Samhain store, for it hung off his lanky body like a damp sheet set out to dry. This man was in his twenties. His face gave that away. Forgetting my manners while staring at that strikingly odd young man, I finally remembered to reply to his question as I got into the back seat.

"Oh yes, the building looks quite beautiful this time of day. Clean and crisp. Uniform and large. Very beautiful."

"Working the factory already sucking the life out of ya, ain't it?" He laughed without even a glance back and began driving.

"How can you tell?"

"The way someone says 'beautiful' is the ultimate telltale sign if they mean it or not. It's not the meaning of the word, it's the tone of how they say it. I'm sure if you were describing a dame, the way you'd say 'beautiful' wouldn't sound anywhere near the way you described that old factory back there." He motioned in the rearview mirror.

I turned around to look back at the gray factory that was growing smaller and smaller in the distance, representing everything that tired me.

"Part-time driver, full-time philosopher, huh?"

"Full-time driver, part-time voice actor." He paused, then corrected himself. "Actually, no-time voice actor right now."

"So that's why you're so good at reading people's tone."

"So that's why you're so good at reading people's tone," he replied in a voice that sounded terrifyingly like me.

We both laughed at his spot-on impression. I continued laughing; he stopped abruptly. I noticed his nostrils flare and his face turn sour as he began sniffing the air.

"But on a serious note," he said, "what is that smell? I don't know if you had breakfast yet or not, but I'm sorry, pal, you can't eat that in here."

I looked at him, confused. *Why does he think I have food*

in the car? I started sniffing around as well, then sniffed myself and realized he fell into the uncultured category.

"Oh! You must be smelling my French cologne!"

"Escargot?"

"No, no! That's not its name. It is expensive and imported."

"Well, it has gotta have some name about cooked snail, 'cause that's what I'm smelling, Mac."

I scoffed under my breath as he continued in a cavalier tone. "Oh wait!" He chuckled to himself. "Pardon my French . . . I don't think I got your name."

"Oleander Briggs."

"Franklin Petacki. Now, Oleander, I'm going to level with you real quick." Franklin's face turned serious as I leaned forward, preparing myself to absorb important information. "When Mr. Fleur shows you around the greenhouse today, as soon as he turns away . . ." I leaned in closer as Franklin dramatically paused. "Snatch one of the flowers and rub it all over yourself!" He cackled and he shouted some more. "Better to smell like a daisy than the fertilizer!"

I rolled my eyes and sat back in a disappointed manner. I eventually laughed it off as we headed up windy, dull roads lined with streetlamps. We continued talking the rest of the ride, laughing and hazing one another. Every stop sign was followed by a shaky burnout around a tight-hedged corner.

The day I met Franklin still burns in my brain. He was the first person I had ever met who I felt immediately comfortable around. He seemed like the last guy to judge a person, no matter their quirks. The type of guy that would be friends with a clown and a pope, a gambler and a grandmother, a singer and an ex-convict, and possibly . . . me. Although he drove me around, for some reason, I envied him. He was everything I wasn't. I couldn't stand him for the longest time after that summer, made me sick to even think about him, but looking back now—boy, am I grateful for him. Anyways, back to the story before I get ahead of myself.

The large rolling unit of metal finally came to a halt at the most inconspicuous location: an avant-garde wrought iron gate with wrought iron roses spiraling around the intricate lines of the architecture. I noticed a matching iron-rose-entangled intercom in front of the gate, by the driver's window.

This must be the Fleur Estate.

Franklin reached out the window, in a way that must have been extremely uncomfortable, and rang the buzzer.

"How can I help you?" a staticky voice said from inside that little speaker.

"This is Frank here with Mr. Fleur's guest, Oleander Briggs."

"Sorry, sir, but we are not expecting any guests at the moment."

The car got quiet as my mind started to wander, thinking maybe it was all a fluke.

I pressed Franklin. "Are you sure you have the right address? Do you think Mr. Fleur forgot? Maybe he meant the day after tomorrow—"

Frank ignored me, talking directly to the intercom. "Really, Scott, really? And on the kid's first day too."

A fuzzy laugh ruptured from the speaker once more as it spoke back, "Gotta break in the fresh meat somehow." It then proceeded to make smooching noises, mocking me.

"Retire already, you old kook," Franklin shouted.

"I'll retire when I'm dead! Hooah!"

Franklin looked back at me. "That's Scott, head of security. He's older than dirt, but he can outrun and outshoot every man on his detail."

"Don't forget outwit," the speaker added in.

"Oh, and he's humble too?" I replied.

"Very." Franklin rolled his eyes.

Beeep! Clank!

The disgustingly large gate began to creak and its joints began to shift as if it were a fearsome giant that had just been woken up from a peaceful slumber. A knot looped around my sternum, lassoing me in, telling me not to proceed. I had no clue what lay beyond that gate. Believe you me, if I told myself what was going to transpire at that estate, I'm not too sure I would have gone in.

Chapter Six

The morning sun shone through the velvet ash trees, casting harsh shadows upon the monstrous gate. It towered in front of us—enticing us forward. After the clanking and beeping of the beast softened, a quiet creak grew to a crescendo. The gate slowly opened like French doors, letting us know we could now enter with its permission. The windshield framed a new world. A place I hadn't seen before, not in dreams or magazines. A glowing wish for the future, my future. It was as if an orchestra had appeared out of thin air, playing a symphony of music meant for only my ears, the strings sweeping across my soul, filling it with wonder. A place colored in vibrance.

As we drove up the decomposed granite road, I saw lush green lawns with pastel-toned gardens lined in yew shrubs. Magenta roses, vibrant periwinkles, and tall hedges carved into opulent sculptures were delicately placed across the sun-drenched estate, as if it were a chessboard for the gods. Ethereal fountains, large enough you'd think it was Niagara Falls, and Roman architecture breathtaking enough that even

I was convinced we'd flown out of crummy California. The light and airy feeling of that grand property was an experience that I wish upon every person, no matter how unlikable. The luxurious grounds resembled a Monet painting rather than a newspaper clipping.

This is surreal.

My hazy blue eyes reflected the pools they stared out on while my reflection in the window glared at me. Franklin kept driving, unfazed that everything had been completely turned upside down. The greenery made his olive-colored skin apparent and his forest-green eyes even more intriguing. He had a unique look to him.

We continued up the hill scattered in decadent plants of pink and green to eventually reach the peak. The land unfurled to reveal a long driveway leading to a peach-colored chateau with at least a hundred windows. Its round, curve-filled architecture and columns were the complete opposite of the straight and angular buildings I had become so familiar with South of Sunset. The balconies trimmed the building's exterior as if it were a pink champagne cake with royal icing. It was hard for me to wrap my head around a driveway being circular, but it was even harder to fathom a place like this was someone's home.

On the front steps of that grand estate stood Mr. Fleur, resembling a king in front of his castle. I could see his rosy cheeks and piercing cobalt eyes. The flower in his dark-blue coat pocket was white with yellow accents resembling fireflies in the middle of it. I believe it was a sloe flower. Those flowers mean difficulty, but I didn't know that at the time. All I knew was that the only difficult thing in those whole fifty acres was watching Franklin clumsily get out of the car. By the time Franklin reached my door, Mr. Fleur had beaten him to it, so

Franklin just stood by the car, awkwardly fidgeting, not knowing what to do with himself.

"Greetings, Mr. Briggs," Mr. Fleur said as I got out of the vehicle.

"Hello, Mr. Fleur. How are you doing today, sir?"

Mr. Fleur ignored my polite response as he faced Franklin. "Thank you, Franklin, for driving Oleander over here. I greatly appreciate all you do for my family."

"Oh, any time, sir." Franklin smiled as he loosened up again and headed back to the driver's side.

I was a little aggravated that Mr. Fleur had brushed me off like that and turned his attention to the driver. Talk about degrading. But all was forgiven as soon as Franklin drove away and Mr. Fleur and I made our way toward the front door.

"Thank you for making it out today." Mr. Fleur finally gave me his undivided attention.

"Oh, my pleasure, sir. May I say what a beautiful property you have here."

We entered through the ten-foot-tall doors, revealing an interior that could've been mistaken for a Roman art museum or a cathedral. I remember looking up and seeing the ceiling covered with a fresco of dreamlike clouds and angels that could've debuted in the Palace of Versailles, and gold crown molding that the forty-niners couldn't even imagine in their wildest dreams. The marble floors and glistening chandeliers gave that strange place a romantic feel. The front room we entered was extravagant in size, but still somehow warm and inviting.

"You might as well enjoy where you live, right? If my surroundings don't bring me joy, I change them," Mr. Fleur said, his voice somehow not echoing.

"That's a good outlook to have, sir. Many people don't think like that."

"And many people are unhappy."

"Touché." I looked down with a bittersweet smile. I knew I was one of those unhappy people. If I'd had half the dough Mr. Fleur had, I'm sure I would've been as nauseatingly cheery as he was.

As we continued to walk through the grand hall, I noticed every doorway looked as if it were made for a giant. Twinkling sconces with blown-glass roses lined the way, serving as a guide, like lights on an airport runway. We then entered a grand room, impossibly larger than the last. This room was surrounded by windows. A strong gust of wind filled the air with the scent of eucalyptus and freshly washed sheets. A beautiful lavender grand piano with gold trim stood in the middle of that striking yet dainty room. The lid of the piano was propped up like a car hood, displaying a baroque painting underneath it.

I found it odd that with his unlimited finances, Mr. Fleur only had one piece of art in that whole room. The painting on the piano showed a group of men standing in front of a large gate, pushing on it. They were dogpiling over one another try-ing to open it to reach the empty space on the other side of the gate, like a herd of sheep running from a predator. An ex-pression of sheer panic was on their faces as they all looked straight forward toward that open space with their axes and knives held up in their hands, each doing the same thing as the man next to him. No more than twenty paces behind them was a forest filled with lush cypress trees. Sitting underneath a tree was a lone man, separated from the mob of fear-filled men. Next to him, the mangled remains of a tree he'd chopped down with his axe lay on the grass. Across the man's lap was a wooden ladder that he was almost done carving with his knife. That painting seemed ridiculous to me.

Why wouldn't the men in the painting just look around

them and see the trees? Let alone the man building a ladder for himself?

It must have stood for something greater to Mr. Fleur, a personal message or something. I later asked him about that painting and all he could say was, "The *m* isn't just silent in *mnemonic*, it's also silent in *masses*."

Mr. Fleur was an enigma to me. As we made our way toward that piano, he went on telling me a little more about himself. "When my wife, Cheryll, and I decided to start a family, we figured Bel Air was the perfect location. You good at geography, Oleander?"

"I like to think so."

"Then I'm gonna put you on the spot real quick."

I turned attentive and my posture improved immediately as I prepared to take a test.

"When you look on a map, where is Bel Air located?" Mr. Fleur asked.

"Why, it's just north of Sunset Boulevard, sir."

"Yes, it is." He smiled. "Just north of Sunset." He motioned for me to sit down on the gold-trimmed piano bench as he stood next to me. "Now do me a favor and close your eyes."

I looked at him in hesitation, afraid of feeling stupid.

"Go on now," he insisted.

After delaying, I finally closed my eyes skeptically. With my eyes closed, reaching the limits of my trusting abilities, Mr. Fleur began to speak. "Imagine it's, say . . . ohhh, around seven o'clock in the evening and you're sitting on top of a hill watching the sunset." As he calmly spoke, I pictured myself there. It was a place with rolling hills at the height of golden hour. I was there, sitting in the ryegrass, watching the sunset. I could almost feel the soft breeze brush against my skin as Mr. Fleur continued. "The warm summer breeze is blowing, and the sky has the most exquisite shades of raspberry and lemon you have ever seen. You thought the sunset the day before was the most beautiful one you'd ever experience, only to be proven wrong today."

At that moment in the daydream, I thought I saw a woman or the hints of one being there. A feeling as if she were by my side, adding to the beauty, but I couldn't see her face. I only saw a silhouette in my periphery, sitting in the ryegrass. I then listened some more, envisioning all that Mr. Fleur spoke of.

"The sun is as bright as it can be, almost blinding. This is right before it tucks away behind blanket-covered mountains, far on the horizon. Now look just north of the sunset, up at the sky."

I tilted my head up with my eyes still shut tight.

"What's there?" he asked.

I mumbled, unsure of what the right answer was.

"Heaven," said Mr. Fleur.

I opened my eyes to see his endearing expression.

"Heaven is also north of sunset," he reinforced.

As Mr. Fleur began to walk away, I quickly got up to follow. I reached into my secure coat pocket to make sure my wallet was still there. I know . . . terrible. Mr. Fleur did not pickpocket me, in case you were wondering. After subtly showcasing my trust issues, we walked through another larger-than-life doorway that led to a back room. It resembled a laundry room without the laundry or a mudroom without the mud.

"It's no coincidence they put Bel Air north of Sunset. I like to think of it as heaven, and if I can choose where my loved ones and I get to spend the rest of our lives together, why, I'd want it to be in no place other than heaven . . . and heaven is always North of Sunset."

"You can say that again." I laughed as we walked outside, the acres upon acres of gardens coming into view.

Looking out on the property, Mr. Fleur shouted at the top

of his lungs as if he were greeting the whole world. "Heaven is always North of Sunset!"

We walked down a decomposed granite path, surrounded by flowers and hedges, as if enchanted forests did exist in this unforgiving world. I stayed timidly behind Mr. Fleur, unsure of where he was taking me next.

Chapter Seven

We strolled down a lane that zigzagged through the never-ending garden of stone sculptures and hedges in the shapes of exotic animals.

"This one's my favorite!" Mr. Fleur pointed up at a twelve-foot-tall hedge in the shape of an elephant.

"Holy mackerel!" That gargantuan plant shaded the whole surrounding area.

"I wish I could've been alive when elephants existed," Mr. Fleur said as he rubbed his chin.

"It's a shame."

"They were one of the rare creatures said to never forget." He softly laughed. "Maybe that's why they went extinct. Too wise. Luckily for you and me, kid, we never have to worry about man going extinct. We are all too forgetful to be a threat."

I smiled an uneasy smile. "Look at the past hundred years, we tried a few times and still failed. World War Three, Four, the Second Civil War. I mean I could go on about—"

"Elephants seemed like such majestic animals." Mr. Fleur continued to stare up at the inanimate hedge. "Come along,

Oleander." He fixed the sloe flower in his coat pocket, then proceeded.

I felt like a spectator at a botanical zoo of Mr. Fleur's creation. Mr. Fleur led the way as if he were a tour guide at a museum, turning back every few sentences to make sure I was still behind him and stopping at scenic resting points to give a backstory. He chatted on and on about the property and his anemoia-filled ideas until he noticed I was politely anxious to get down to business.

"Oleander, the reason you are here today is to help with the fall collection for Fleur's Eternal Roses. We are taking a great risk this upcoming season and expanding to other flowers beyond roses. This will help our consumer audience grow from just love interests buying roses, to friends, coworkers, and family who deserve recognition without the romance. Just a friendly gesture of a daisy or a lily, perhaps. You follow me?"

"Yes, sir. I think it's an excellent idea. It'll expand your target demographic, for sure."

Boy, was I a little brownnoser . . .

"For our initial launch," he continued, "we will be releasing three flower species. This is where you come into play. I will need your expertise and decision-making on the final three flowers we choose for the collection. I figured since your name is Oleander, you must already know that there are over fifty thousand different types of flower species out there. Lucky for you—there used to be over four hundred thousand just a century ago!"

At that moment I became overwhelmed by the sheer volume and finally had to come clean to Mr. Fleur that he'd chosen the wrong guy. Just because I had the same name as a flower didn't mean I cared a scrap about them. "Honestly, sir, I only know the basic ones your average Joe can name off the top of his head."

"And that is why you will be coming here every day for work instead of the factory," he stated without hesitation, as if he'd already anticipated my answer.

The fragrance of roses wisped through the air as banana leaves waved in unison, coaxing us to take a few more steps forward. Once we passed the corner, a secluded glass structure was revealed. It was a large transparent greenhouse surrounded by rosebushes and cottonwood trees that melded it with the scenery. It looked fragile enough that if you threw a pebble at it, the whole structure would shatter, creating a rainstorm of sharp sand and stone and flowerets. Framing the glass was lacy copper filigree that had been oxidized to appear dark green, making the large, paneled windows more avant-garde.

As we walked into that terrarium-like cottage nestled away from the main house, I noticed that the alluring transparent walls somehow made this structure soundproof. Up the walls grew vines upon vines of unrecognizable flowers, which made the space look almost as overgrown as a jungle. This botanical garden probably had every single one of the fifty thousand species of flowers Mr. Fleur had mentioned in a one-thousand-square-foot room. Marking the center was a pond made of stone, and inside that pool of water lay lily pads floating ever so gently, rippling with each word we spoke. The ceiling of the greenhouse was made of glass as well, with one panel directly in the center stained with every color observable to the human eye, creating a kaleidoscope effect as the sunlight projected onto the pond.

While my eyes trailed up that beam of multicolored light, I noticed a woman on the other end of that floweret-filled room. She was standing on an unsteady ladder, watering the flowers in a hanging basket with a mauve-colored tulle gown on. I watched her, intrigued, as I could only see the back of her head at that point, forgetting Mr. Fleur was still talking to me.

"I expect you to study every species of flower that would be a reasonable candidate . . . not skipping over one." Mr. Fleur added, "Learning everything from its biological makeup to its expected lifespan, the climate and conditions it needs to survive and—"

"Don't forget floriography, Dad!" the woman on the ladder interrupted, finally turning around so I could see her face for the first time.

She had bright-green eyes that mimicked the shape of a cat's. Her chestnut-colored hair was much longer than how the women wore theirs South of Sunset—it flowed down her back like a waterfall. She had the same rosy cheeks that Mr. Fleur had, but with freckles sweeping along them, spanning across to the bridge of her nose. I assumed she'd inherited those from a combination of her mother's side and the sun taking a liking to her so much. Her freckles looked as if a painter had finished with his picture, then out of pure boredom or drunken bliss, flicked paint from the end of his brush all over the artwork, laughing to himself about his unconventional genius.

After her remark, showing that there were some people in the world that did have control over Mr. Fleur, she began to rock a little on the ladder, not enough to cause a scare, but enough to make a person watching nervous.

"You beat me to it, Gloria! Now come down from the ladder, sweetie," Mr. Fleur said.

She slowly began to make her way down the ladder. Her lemon-colored heels descended smoothly until her movement was cut short.

Rip!

Her heel had gotten caught in her long dress. She tugged the side of her gown, only to lose her balance.

"Oh boy!"

She quickly clutched the ladder with both hands, regaining

her center of gravity. She sighed in frustration as her left ankle wobbled on the narrow step, allowing the other foot to wiggle itself free from the fabric. She restepped and almost tumbled to the ground. This happened three times over in different sequences. Her dress was so big that if she fell from high enough up, it might float her down like a cupcake parachute. Wearing a gown or, better yet, high heels on a ladder was beyond eccentric, but there I was, still caught in awe. As she planted her shoes on the ground, I heard Mr. Fleur start to breathe again.

Gloria Fleur was another one of the unforgettable characters I met the summer my life became a novel. She had to have been freshly twenty at the time and resembled one of those fairies in a medieval painting. She had a look about her that was timeless, but a feel to her like a ticking time bomb. After spiking everyone's blood pressure, Gloria effortlessly floated toward us.

"Oleander, this is my daughter, Gloria," said Mr. Fleur as Gloria shook my hand.

"How do ya do, Oleander?!"

"I am doing fine, pleasure to meet you—"

"Just fine? Ain't that a nail in the tire!" she huffed.

"Well, I meant—"

"You know what you need," she interrupted once more.

"Oh, come on now, Gloria," Mr. Fleur interjected. "Leave the poor boy alone."

"A sunflower." Gloria ignored her father. She then walked over to a bundle of sunflowers standing in a planter on the wall and plucked one in the most ungraceful way. I could feel Mr. Fleur wince as she ripped out the flower. He leaned in toward me and mumbled under his breath, "She killed it, now you have to take it."

We both laughed as she made her way back to us with a drooping sunflower in her dainty hand.

"They are known to bring happiness," Gloria cheered.

"I feel better already," I politely said.

"Gloria is big on floriography."

"Floriography is the ancient language of flowers," added Gloria.

"Every morning she picks a different flower for me and puts it in my coat pocket." Mr. Fleur pointed to his chest.

"Well, people always say 'Good morning' and ask 'How are you?' What is a better response than a flower that describes your exact mood," Gloria reasoned.

I shrugged, not knowing how to respond to her unique angle on saying hello.

Gloria puffed up her cheeks. "I'll put a buttercup in his pocket if I'm feeling childish and goofy that day." She clasped her hands together and posed like a damsel in distress. "A lavender to show my love." Her face fell flat. "Or even an Oleander." She paused for a beat. "To let him know I'm in a bad mood that morning and to proceed with caution."

"Oh, Glory." Mr. Fleur sighed in disapproval as I felt my smile become heavy.

Gloria's eyes locked on mine as she continued to speak with a smirk on her face. "You know that's what an oleander means in floriography, right? Proceed . . . with . . . caution."

I felt unnerved as she walked away with a smug look, humming and swinging her arms in a fatally innocent way.

"Oh, don't mind her, my boy. She meant nothing by that."

"She seems like a very sweet girl," I replied.

"She is, got a pure heart, that one," Mr. Fleur commented. "But a vocabulary as polished as an old rusty spoon."

"It's refreshing."

We walked out of that technicolor terrarium.

"Refreshing? I'm glad you see it like that, son. From an early age she's always been very decisive, sometimes even to her own detriment. She's as stubborn as an ox and will not go back on anything she says. Confident thing. Never seen her doubt herself once, that's for sure."

As Mr. Fleur rambled on about how wonderful his daughter was, I saw Gloria far off in the distance, on the other end of the lawn. She was swinging on a tree swing that was hanging sturdily from a mossy weeping willow.

"I'm telling you this now," Mr. Fleur added, regaining my attention, "because you two will be working very closely together over the next two months on this collection. She will be there to assist you and serve as a second opinion, if needed."

"I look forward to working with Gloria, sir. At the factory we always have more than one person on a job, so I'm used to working with others."

"Well . . . she's not."

I felt my jaw tense up as Mr. Fleur continued, "You will see for yourself in time, my boy."

Off in the distance, Gloria continued swinging without a care in the world. The end of her airy dress blew in the wind, trailing one step behind her, as if it were trying to catch up with her spontaneity too. At that moment, my self-inflicted stress increased to a level higher than its already above average normal. I was not a confrontational person, so I dreaded the thought of possible future disagreements. At the same time, I was thanking the Southern California gods above for nepotism. Good old nepotism was allowing a twenty-year-old girl, with no degree, to have a say in the future of a major corporation. If the new line flopped, at least the blame wasn't going to be entirely on me.

"Ha!" A laugh involuntarily came out of me at that point, thinking about how spacey that girl was. She had the type of pure innocence about her that you didn't ever see South of Sunset. If anyone was acting innocent SOS, I can guarantee you it was a front that they used to try and get ahead somehow. I was truly intrigued by Gloria.

As I was trying to figure out her odd behavior, I forgot Mr. Fleur was still going on and on about his daughter, in a performance that could've won him the Most-Biased Father Award.

"She's filled with gusto," he continued, "but don't let it fool you, son. The girl has got an incredible head on her shoulders. Last thing I'll tell you about her is that she keeps to her word, come hell or high water."

"That's marvelous, sir. Oh, forgive me for asking, but . . . is this a promotion?"

"Well, it is a step above your current position for a limited time, if that's what you're asking. I like to refer to it as a special project."

"Marvelous, marvelous." I stammered, "Oh boy, uh, what I mean is . . . would there be a raise in pay? Just because this drive alone would cost me an arm and a leg. I don't have an automobile and I don't know if it would be worth taking a cab—"

"Oh, none of that nonsense, my boy! I'll make it worth your while, monetarily speaking, of course. As for transportation, Franklin will pick you up at the factory every day for the next two months. On me."

Should I ask him to give me a hard number? No, I didn't want to take the risk of offending him and losing all of what could be zilch.

At that moment, a butler in a three-piece suit tapped Mr. Fleur on the shoulder ever so gently. "Greetings, Mr. Fleur," he timidly murmured.

"Is it noon already?" Mr. Fleur jumped a bit.

"Yes, sir. Charles Grenadine from UCLA Health is in your office right now."

"Oleander." Mr. Fleur turned to me. "Go to the kitchen where my chef, Anthony, will have lunch ready for you. On the right side of the house there will be a door. You will enter through there, then continue to walk the corridor. You should run right into it."

"Thank you, Mr. Fleur," I automatically replied.

"Are you sure you got it?"

"Yes, sir."

"Because I can repeat it one more time, if you like."

"I'm okay, sir."

"You sure?" he pressed, giving me one last chance for him to clarify.

"I'm good, sir. Thank you."

"Okay, then!" Mr. Fleur smiled. "Farewell, Oleander, I look forward to seeing what you put together."

He began to walk away, but I could still hear him talking to the butler. "Sorry, a man can lose track of time real quick when he gets on the subject of his daughter."

"Understandable, sir." The butler added, "You have every right to be proud. As you know, I have two little ones at home."

The pair got far enough away that their well-enunciated words turned into quiet murmurs. I finally slouched once again, relaxing into the person I normally was, then frantically mumbled to myself, trying to remember Mr. Fleur's directions. "Okay, so I go right of the house, then there's a door, go through that. Corridor. Should be easy enough." So I thought . . .

Chapter Eight

I had one simple task: find the kitchen. I stood alone on a concrete platform surrounded by five-foot hydrangeas, like a gladiator standing in the empty arena, taking in the peace before they unleash the ferocious beast on him.

The beautiful, silent, spacious gardens I stared out on suddenly turned into an intimidating maze I had to navigate tactfully. The land unrolled itself in front of me, never stopping, continuing to be out of reach. Instinctually, I should've been able to figure this one out, but my inability to admit that I didn't know something got the best of me. I started to walk in a direction that looked promising, only to be surrounded by ten-foot hedges that blocked any chance of visibility to the main house. Fleur Estate grew more and more complex with each step I took, falling further and further into it.

An alarm was just about to go off in my head, acknowledging I was hopeless, when I saw a group of three landscapers trimming a yew wall in the garden maze. The three men were in matching British racing green jumpsuits, resembling a pit crew, except instead of cars, their art was plants. As they

clipped and spliced the greenery, they acted as if their signa-
tures were on every piece of meticulous vegetation in this estate with a gold frame around them.

I passed by the cheery men.

"Afternoon, sir!" one shouted.

"Afternoon." I continued to walk, only to be stopped by a
dead end of hedges. After a second of disbelief, I turned around.

Should be easy to get back to the house.

I moved forward in the opposite direction, traveling through
the gardens some more. I passed by the same group of landscapers for the second time.

"Afternoon, sir," the second man said.

"Afternoon." I felt my forehead warm up a few more degrees. I continued past the men once again. I spent another
twenty minutes walking, only to hit a giant chain-link fence.

"Dammit!"

At that point, beyond frustrated, I turned around and
stormed back into the garden maze, hoping that I'd reach the
house this time. I trudged through the ever-growing garden,
walking unevenly as my feet started to ache from the sharp
leather of my shoes digging into my raw Achilles tendon.
My underarms began to sweat away the expensive cologne I
couldn't afford, and my wallet clinked in repetition, heckling
me. My walk became more lopsided as I passed by the same
landscapers again!

"Afternoon, sir," said the third and final man. They were all
in on the joke now.

"Hi."

"You looking for something, sir?" It was as if he already
knew the answer but just wanted to hear me say it.

"I'm okay, I know where I'm going. Thank you, though."

I walked off again. I had gone too deep at that point—my
pride was on the line. Scott, the old security guard, probably

watched me struggle to find my way through the garden over the security screen, whispering to himself, "Asshole."

I walked through the gardens once more—for another twenty minutes. I was confident I'd finally found the right way out when I discovered a different path to go down. The hedges ascended higher as they slowly blended into the banana leaves that created an arched roof over the dirt lane. The delicate plants shaded the way, creating humidity in each breath I took. The property was like one big humidifier for the parched summer air. The oxygen became shallower and shallower as I turned left down a split road that the high sun was projecting on. The spotlight revealed a path that grew more and more familiar as I continued on my long walk. I then saw the same three familiar faces standing in the same familiar place I had seen them three times before, smiling and laughing to themselves. I had somehow made a loop, landing back where I started.

I stared at the men. My emotions teeter-tottered on a scale that was equally balanced between frustration and embarrassment. The man on the end nudged his head toward the hedge behind him that they'd just finished trimming and that had an arched opening now, hinting to me that that was where I should've gone all along. I proceeded to walk around them like a dog with its tail tucked between its legs and entered the path behind them. All three men burst out laughing. I didn't care. I finally saw light at the end of the tunnel—I just hoped I didn't miss lunch.

I embarked up the large steps that led to the front door of Fleur Estate's main house. The front sidewalk was lined with exaggerated planters filled with baby cypress trees shaped like spirals, creating some more privacy for an already unfindable location.

"That's where I was gonna go anyways," I whispered to myself.

"Who are you talking to?!" A compact man who looked to be about sixty-seven years old jumped out from behind a planter, landing in a wide stance, as if ready to attack. Scott, the old, crotchety security guard. He was wrinkly with a shaved head and jowls that drooped like an Italian mastiff's. He was built like a brick shithouse, unlike me with a slender, average physique.

I laughed unassumingly. "Oh, no, I was just—"

"Just what?" Scott poked my chest. "Talking to plants."

I felt his eyes lock in on me, as if I were the irrational one!

"Well actually, sir, some people do. They say it's good for the plants. Scientifically speaking . . . when you exhale carbon dioxide—"

"What the hell are you doing with carbon monoxide?!" He lunged toward me, grabbing my arms and forcing them behind my back as if I were a highly dangerous criminal he'd finally made an arrest on. I squirmed in his grip while he pulled out the walkie-talkie that was on his hip. "I'm gonna need some backup here," he said in an official tone as he struggled with me.

"No, no, no! You're getting it all mixed up, you old—"

"Why, you," he growled. Scott let my arms go as he squared up, ready to kick my teeth in.

"Hi, Oleander!"

Gloria came into view right when the egg was about to hit the fan. She gently walked toward us. A sigh of relief came over me as Scott looked disgruntled and confused, wondering how Gloria could be fraternizing with the enemy.

"Hi, Gloria," I smugly replied.

She swiftly reached the two of us as we stood in an alert manner. "Oh, I'm so happy you met Scott! If you ever, ever feel unsafe . . . he is your go-to guy!"

"How comforting," I mumbled.

I felt Scott look at me as if he were a dog ready to attack. Whenever Gloria looked at Scott, his angry expression turned into a cheesy smile, only to turn back into an angry glare toward me once she looked away.

"Boy, Gloria, you are looking more and more like your mom every time I see you," Scott announced.

"No, she's looking more and more like me! The woman doesn't age, Scott! Neither will I."

"That's right, sister!"

I couldn't help but chuckle at his statement—it was worth the dirty look from him.

"I assume Oleander is looking for the kitchen. Can you please escort him there?"

"Yes, ma'am," replied Scott.

"As I'm sure you need to eat too," she said in a motherly tone.

"Oh, no, I don't eat lunch," Scott scoffed. "I survive off corn nuts and black coffee. That's all the diesel I need."

"Lovely," I said under my breath, earning another look of disdain from the esteemed Scott.

"Well, it sure looks like it works for you," Gloria said, causing Scott's chest to puff out proudly.

"Well, good day, fellas!" Gloria waved as she floated away through the front door.

Scott and I smiled and nodded goodbye to her as if we were school children on our best behavior in front of the teacher.

Scott began to walk away from me as he bluntly said, "Come on now, Pansy." He motioned me to follow.

"It's Oleander."

"I know . . . Pansy."

Scott walked around to the left side of the house as I

trailed behind him, hopping a little every now and then to catch up.

"Isn't the kitchen to the right of the house?" I asked, remembering what Mr. Fleur had said.

"Do you want me to help you or not?" he said in an insolent tone.

I threw my hands up and continued following him, asking no more questions.

We entered the house and reached a living room I hadn't seen before. The floor was covered in polished Saltillo tile, black-and-gold rugs, and cat palm plants in every corner.

"Sit down right there. I'll be right back. You move, I wring your neck!" Scott pointed to a green velvet chair against the back wall. "Oh, and good job getting through the garden earlier . . . asshole." He laughed as he walked away, soon entering what looked to be a bathroom door. I sat still in that chair, helpless.

"Dammit! This is the most important thing we can do. You can't back out now!" A deep voice projected through the house, bouncing off each wall and floor tile like a cannonball.

Alarmed, I left my post of safety and silence, walking down the hall toward the yelling. When I peeked around the corner, I saw an intriguing image. There she was, Gloria, hiding behind an open door that led to a mahogany-filled office. Her ear was pressed against the hinge, listening in on the screaming as well. She didn't see me peering in from behind her as the arguing from the two men continued.

"Are you going to respond?" screamed the first man, who sounded a whole lot like Mr. Fleur.

"I do not want to offend you, Milton," stuttered the second man, "but what you are attempting to do is too great a risk!"

"Charles! You and I both know it's worth the risk."

As I stood around the corner, I watched Gloria's back

flinch, her shoulder blades raising in synchrony with Mr. Fleur's and Charles's voices.

"You are about to throw away your and Cheryll's future, everything you've built, your lives—"

"No, I am not! We are going to succeed, as a family. Together."

"I understand you want to do everything together as a family, but there are certain things in life you just don't risk."

"Just don't risk for your daughter?"

Gloria gasped, then grabbed her hand, reminding herself to remain quiet.

Mr. Fleur continued, "I want to see her succeed in life. I want to see her have a bright future. I want to be there when she walks down the aisle, when she decides to have kids, and when she builds her own empire. I want her to be able to look at me and know I gave her everything I could so she could even have a future. At least the opportunity to succeed or fail. It's not about the outcome, it's about giving the child the confidence and the comfort to let them know you are behind them no matter what. Wouldn't you do the same for your kid, Charles?"

"I understand, but the smallest thing as a rose being preserved in gold already has us pushing science's limitations. Even your customers don't really believe—"

"Get out! Out, I say," yelled Mr. Fleur.

Charles began to stammer as he backed up. I couldn't believe how serious the men were about this new collection of other flowers. Poor Gloria had to overhear that. Charles made it sound as if the collection would fail if Mr. Fleur got her involved.

"I know you are an expert in health and science and are a great friend," Mr. Fleur stated, "but not only do you come here and insult my business, but my priorities as well!"

"Well, I-I just—"

"You have five seconds to go through that door or else I'll put you through it myself!"

At that moment the audience dispersed: Gloria scurried to the right, Charles rushed out the office door, and I ran back to that green velvet chair my butt was supposed to be glued to.

Chapter Nine

Scott came back to the green chair ten minutes after the mysterious arguing in the office subsided. When he saw me, he sighed, as if he was disappointed I was still sitting there, not giving him an excuse to tear me apart. He led me to the kitchen without saying anything except "Here is the kitchen . . . asswipe." He opened the door and motioned sarcastically for me to go in.

Danish butter and crisp sourdough billowed in the atmosphere as I entered the sage-green kitchen that looked as if it were built to house a sixteen-course meal, twenty-four seven. The copper range hood echoed the laughter and hollers of the thirty employees standing in line as the pots and pans clanked. The eighteen-hundred-square-foot kitchen's floor was shielded in checkerboard tile that had a few cracks around the outskirts. With the amount of foot traffic that kitchen probably endured, it was surprising the whole floor wasn't shaped like a salad bowl.

"Got smoke in your engine or are you going to get in line?" A maid motioned to me as I stood in the middle of the kitchen, staring at the floor like a dolt. The noise abruptly stopped as everyone curiously glared in my direction.

"Oh," I replied.

The chattering continued once again. I inched my way around the fifteen-foot pink-marble island, squeezing between employees to reach the end of the line. Everyone was so cheerful, talking about their vacations or families or what was on today's menu. The crowd shuffled in and out like the conveyor belt at work—the more that went away, the more that came in. I was in the middle of the line, pretending to read a sign on the pastel wall across the way, when I saw a familiar face . . . Franklin!

I desperately waved to him in hopes he'd see me. He finally caught my overpronounced wave and gave it right back, but in a goofy manner—a goofy manner he had somehow perfected. He shuffled to the back of the line, each step he took matched with a "Hi, Frank" from a face in the crowd. I looked over my shoulder to see he was in the back of the line, but luckily it was moving pretty fast.

In a few minutes, I reached the front, where a chef was giving each employee a paper sack filled with a freshly made sandwich. He handed me a bag and I politely thanked him. Franklin was in the middle of the line by then and I had no one to talk to and nowhere to go. I stood a few steps to the right of the chef and watched the employees move forward swiftly. Franklin still had a handyman and a maid to go before he received his lunch.

Slam!

A man who looked to be in his sixties stumbled into the kitchen, stammering to himself. He had a cut above his eyebrow. He frantically rushed through the kitchen as he patted his head with a handkerchief.

"They are so out of touch with reality! That man is

dreaming, ha! I tried to warn him, but he just has to refuse reality! Throwing it all away for some—"

The room turned silent as the staff stared at the hysterical man. That must have been Charles, the guy from UCLA Health, who had been arguing with the boss. He looked shaken up about something—maybe the cut on his face? *What if their altercation wasn't just verbal?*

Charles scurried his way through the leftover employees and made an exit out the side door. He almost tripped, hitting his hip bone on the corner of the sturdy island. The conversations commenced again once he left, but no one said a word about him; they continued on about their superficial hobbies and interests.

"Well then," I murmured to Franklin as Chef Anthony handed him a sandwich.

"You will get used to it." The chef rolled his amber eyes.

"Where should I sit to eat this?"

"It does not matter, as long as it is not in here."

Franklin sucked up a big chunk of bread that was dangling out of his mouth, like a goat mowing down a tin can.

Chef Anthony threw him a look of disapproval.

"Well, that's my cue," Franklin stated as he wrapped up the other half of his sandwich. "Time to take ol' book britches home, anyway!" He shoved the crumpled-up bag in his coat pocket and headed for the side door. "Wish me luck!" He waved his bony hand and proceeded out the pistachio-colored door.

"Bye, Frank," I replied a few seconds too late.

I lingered by the chef, waiting for someone to show up and say, "There you are!" Nothing. Nobody. No direction on what was next or what was expected of me. The kitchen began to clear out as the silence loomed. If I hung around any longer, I'd stand out like a tree in the plains.

I swiftly exited the side door everyone seemed to use. My

head throbbed an uptight beat as I guessed and stepped and stepped and guessed my way through the stone courtyard on the side of the house, continued down the cobblestone, and eventually reached the front of the house.

There in the middle of the front lawn was a stone fountain with swans elegantly tilting up toward the sky, streaming out water. From elephants to mazes, that fountain stood out more boldly than the rest. The pair of birds were mirrored halves of one another, perfectly symmetrical in height, towering at around twenty feet tall. The afternoon sun backlit the fountain, creating a misty effect as the water shimmered in the air. All the statues and rosebushes watched me in contempt as I walked over to the fountain, drawn to it. It was extremely visible as well, so it was a smart spot to park myself for the first day, especially if someone needed to find me. Correction—it was vital.

I sat down on the ledge of the fountain and began to unwrap my sandwich, along with the Mr. Fleur and Charles brawl.

Could it really have been about putting Gloria in charge of the new collection? Fleur Industries is such a big corporation. Is there an enormous amount of pressure on this new line or is it all a front?

I stared out at the profligate grounds.

There must be so many moving parts to the gold-dipped roses. If the roses really stay alive under there, like they say they do, the science behind it must be so complex to make that possible. Again, if that even is possible.

I took a bite of my sandwich and tried to work out why Charles had been so flustered.

"Ooof!"

A sharp splash of cold water struck me in the back, causing me to jump. I turned around and saw nothing. I examined the water, watching the remnants of a wave. Proof I wasn't imagining things. The pool began to grow still, slowing down with each wavelet, until . . .

Skip, skip, splash!

I held my sandwich up to my chin, coddling it as the liquid leaped up to my clean shirt. It was a pebble that had caused the disturbance.

"Hey," I shouted.

I walked around the grand, yet ironic, sculpture of the swans to see Gloria Fleur standing on the other end of the fountain . . . skipping rocks.

"Oh, I'm sorry! I didn't know you were on the other side. Did I get ya?" A giggle rose on Gloria's lips.

"Uh-huh, sure." I turned around and headed back to "my side" of the fountain, using the one napkin I had to dry off my chlorine-scented shirt.

"Honestly, I didn't mean to get ya! I was just skipping some pebbles and—"

"I don't know if anyone told you this, and I hate to be the one to break it to you"—I turned around to face her—"this is a fountain . . . not a lake."

"And?"

"Everything has a purpose. Fountains are made for pennies, lakes are made for skipping rocks, and ladders are not made for high heels." I looked down at her yellow shoes against the kelly-green grass.

"Who says?"

"Me. Nice little stunt you pulled back there."

Gloria tilted her head, beautifully showcasing her spacey disposition.

"On the ladder," I clarified.

"Ohhh."

"Nearly gave your father a heart attack."

"Oh, he's normally not much of a risk-taker, but lately—"

"Oh, I'm sure he's got his hands full with you, you trapeze artist." Gloria laughed as I continued talking. "Stuff like that is right up your alley, huh?"

"Stuff like what? What do you mean?" A smile of intrigue swept over her.

"Taking risks without thinking them through, maybe? I don't know . . . you seem like the type of girl that likes to sink the whole ship just to get to swim." I began to chuckle.

Gloria's face turned scarlet as the corners of her mouth became dead weight. In that moment, I could almost see the heat radiate off her.

"What nerve! I have to! I have no other choice. I can't control what other people choose to do because of—"

"Whoa, whoa! I was only kidding with you—"

"That's not something to kid about. Who told you, anyway?" Gloria feverishly looked around. "How do you even know about—"

"Well, your father was just—"

"Ugh!" Gloria stormed off toward the house. I walked back to my spot and sat on the fountain.

Was it something I said? Why is she so oversensitive? All I did was joke about her dangerously teetering on a ladder.

I sensed there was more to the story than everyone was letting on, from Gloria turning irate to the scuffle in Mr. Fleur's office to even the staff not saying a word—money makes people mad, and these people were nuts. Luckily the one person on that property with common sense was back, Franklin. He had just dropped off Charles Grenadine and pulled up to the front of the estate. As Gloria marched up the steps, sobbing, Franklin jumped out of the car to meet her. I was far enough away for them not to notice me staring, but still close enough to hear their conversation. Gloria was hysterically crying as Franklin comforted her.

"Did you tell him?" she interrogated him.

"Ohhh, I would never," he defensively replied.

"Well then, my father must have—"

"You and I both know your father would never say a word, especially after only knowing someone for less than twenty-four hours."

"You're right, you're right. I think I'm just really emotional right now, given the circumstances. I just, I just—"

Gloria began crying even more hysterically than before.

"And you have every right to be," Franklin calmly said as a woman no older than fifty came running out the front door at level ten. I assumed that she was Gloria's mother because of her unique identical features. Same dark hair and an Irish-looking nose.

"Oh, shhh, shhh. It's okay," said the woman as she hugged Gloria. While Gloria's chin nuzzled into her shoulder, the woman looked at Franklin and mouthed, "What happened?"

"Hi, Mrs. Fleur," Franklin said. "She's just having a tough—"

"Franklin did a terrible Kermit the Frog impression, that's all, Mom," interjected Gloria. "I just can't stand to see Kermit be misrepresented like that. Being blamed for something he can't control. It's not his fault he's got a raspy voice, those are just the cards he was dealt in life. I'm sure if that poor little frog could change it, he would. He'd probably want to be a rain dove with a beautiful melody to sing—but that's not the cards he was dealt, that's not even close to the cards he was dealt!"

"You are so right, Gloria," said Franklin. "I will be sure to never do my lousy Kermit the Frog impression again. Kermit already gets enough guff for marrying a pig."

Gloria sniffled as she laughed at Franklin's joke. Being a bystander from afar, I was beyond confused by this whole conversation.

"Thank you, Franklin. I've got her now," said Mrs. Fleur as she walked into the house with a shook-up Gloria.

I sat on the fountain, feeling like a chump, until Franklin came over.

"Ready to go?"

"That's all?" I replied.

He nodded, then proceeded to walk with me back to the same vehicle I'd arrived in.

The car ride home started off extremely uncomfortably. I didn't know what to say or if that was going to be the end of my time at Fleur Estate. I did make my boss's daughter cry on the first day, and on top of that, I didn't lift a finger to do work, only to eat their food.

"I'll pick you up same place, same time tomorrow, pal," Franklin said, his voice just as affable as it had been that morning.

"Oh, really?"

"Of course! Mr. Fleur likes ya. Sooo, how was your first day?"

I soon realized there was nothing wrong and that that must have been a normal occurrence with Gloria. "Oh, it was great! I think this collection will be wonderful. The property is outstanding. I can't believe—"

"The Fleurs are colorful characters, huh?" Franklin interrupted, insinuating I should cut the crap.

"Very," I responded as we reached the gates to South of Sunset. The vibrant world faded away as the dull city showed its ugly head. I had to get through one monotonous night there before I could return to the Fleur Estate the following morning. I began to crave it like a junkie looking for their next fix.

The secrets, the wealth, the fresh air . . . It was all so alluring. The place was a siren song, engulfing my mind, beguiling me to discover its fortune.

Chapter Ten

I remember sitting in my muggy apartment that night, absorbing all that had occurred that eventful day. North of Sunset made South of Sunset look even more dull and drab than it already was. No color, no curves, no round architecture, just angular buildings and streetlamps lighting up the pitch-black night. Inside, there was only a slight glow of gray coming from my jagged desk lamp, and my room reeked of detergent and damp paper.

When I sat at my writing desk, I put down the sunflower Gloria had given me, its brilliance gone. With my glasses on, showcasing my pure concentration, I read a book about the different meanings of flower species, which I had picked up from the public library. I scanned each line, my wrist sticking to the desk as I lifted my arm to turn the page. It must have been at least eighty degrees that night, which meant my room was ninety. The Fleurs were probably in a delicate slumber over in their five-hundred-fan castle surrounded by a jungle of transpirational cooling plants. Overheated and aggravated, I tried my best to study.

An ear-piercing police siren came from outside my window. "Can I ever get a moment of peace and quiet around here?!" I rambled to myself as I slammed my window and latched it shut. I then proceeded to walk away from my desk, grumbling, "Well, while I'm up . . ." I shuffled into the mildew-harvesting bathroom and headed toward my swanky bar cart that had all my well-thought-out colognes sprawled all over it. I took the French one I'd worn that day, that had earned its spot on the infamous cart of unpleasant smells, and angrily tossed it in the trash.

I scoffed. "Escargot . . . pshhh."

I made my way back to the desk, mentally prepared to continue with work. Once I sat down in my creaking oak chair, I began to make a list in alphabetical order of all the flower species that sounded intriguing. Hours passed and I was finally on *M*. I read the floriography of the flowers out loud, then wrote the names on a list if they were a reasonable candidate, meaning they looked appealing, were hearty, and didn't mean anything morbid. I had to be picky, to say the least, since Mr. Fleur wanted three chosen out of fifty thousand.

Magnolia: nobility and a love of nature.

Marigold: grief, despair, and jealousy.

I crossed off *marigold*, knowing I didn't need to add to the lousiness of the world. The next one I found to be very intriguing . . . a morning glory. Dozing off at that point, I figured it was time to nap the sack. The busy city streets turned quiet, with only a yell here and there. But the volume level of the bustling crowds soon rose again along with the sun.

The following morning my world was illuminated once again when I arrived at the Fleur Estate, driven for the second time by osmium-foot Franklin. The gardens just as green, the hydrangeas just as vibrant, and Mr. Fleur just as loud, leading me to hear another conversation not meant for my lower-class ears.

It happened when I was walking up the front steps, taking in the rosy morning. To the left of the front door was a large Palladian window that belonged to Mr. Fleur's office. I saw him peer out the window, gently moving the large curtain, which was adequate for a Broadway stage. He cracked open the multipaneled window, letting the seventy-five-degree breeze flow in as Gloria came swinging through the mahogany office doors. She had an olive branch in her hand as she approached Mr. Fleur.

"Mornin', Glory," cheered Mr. Fleur. "Hmm, that doesn't look like a flower to me . . . Changing it up I see."

"I'm sure you already know what this stands for," remarked Gloria.

I saw her put the branch in his coat pocket, leaving it ungracefully sticking out in an awkward manner. I positioned myself to the right of the window so the pair could no longer see me. I attempted to casually wander, skimming through the pages of the floriography book in my hands, disguising my deliberate eavesdropping.

"Peace! Boy, is this good news," exclaimed Mr. Fleur as he decoded the olive branch along with Gloria's suspiciously high mood.

"I felt like doing something out of the sweetness of my soul today."

"Oleander just pulled up a moment ago."

I dropped my book when I heard my name mentioned. The pair quickly snapped their heads toward the window. I held my breath, pressing against the wall, not ready to give up my position just yet. They immediately went back to their conversation.

"I'm sure he will be relieved when he sees you are choosing to be peaceful today," joked Mr. Fleur.

"That man couldn't be relieved even if he tried!" Gloria

crossed her arms. "He's about as optimistic as a flame in the snow!"

"Glory."

"Okay . . . I'm goin', I'm goin'!"

"Whoa, whoa, hold on a second," Mr. Fleur countered.

"Yes?"

I quickly peered in to see her impatiently brushing her shoes against the emerald art deco carpet.

"Remember, just because someone isn't the same way you are, that doesn't make them a bad person. People were made to have different outlooks on life for different reasons. That's how the world keeps turning. We wouldn't want a bunch of erratic Glorias running around with the codes to the bombs, right?" Mr. Fleur laughed.

"I guess so." Gloria shrugged, her face offput.

"Same way we wouldn't want a bunch of Oleanders running around as therapists for the seriously depressed."

"Oh, Dad!"

My heart dropped into my stomach, finally hearing what I wasn't supposed to as Mr. Fleur went on.

"Come on, now. That boy has not one ounce of empathy, but that's what you need for this project. Someone who will keep you on track, completely focused, and not get too attached to anything."

I should have been bothered by his insults, but I was flattered. Mr. Fleur thought I was perfect for the project due to my extreme discipline. How did he know that, though? I'd only spoken with him twice in my life.

"Why, that's an awful thing to say!"

"It's not awful, it's just the way he is. Same thing as me saying you get attached to things too quickly. For instance, your mother told me you were crying about Kermit the Frog yesterday?"

"Oh, no, no. I just think you have him pegged wrong."

"The frog did marry a pig—"

"No! Oleander!"

He just laughed at her. Gloria throwing a tantrum about something must've been a daily occurrence. She'd started the argument about my negative disposition in the first place, and I was glad to see her not like the consequences.

Mr. Fleur spoke once again to Gloria in a cool and collected manner. "Calm down, Gloria. I know you're passionate and all, but I am not making any judgments about anyone. All I'm saying is don't forget what his name stands for."

"I know, Dad . . . proceed with caution."

I did not like the way that conversation ended, but at least my character wasn't slandered. So what if I was focused? So what if I came off as dull to these people? I was there to get a job done and I wasn't going to let a loose cannon ruin that for me. I hadn't been afforded the opportunity to live in luxury, like some people.

Realizing the time, I trudged over to the elegant greenhouse tucked away in a corner meant for solitude. Ironically enough, that corner was going to be where all my stress occurred. I sat on a concrete bench inside and began reading more about flowers. I spent a lot of my days that summer reading. I had gone to Brown and was well versed in many things, but this job was a whole other niche. Before I was hired by Fleur Industries, I'd had no clue a whole multibillion-dollar market existed just because of flowers. Nowadays, I can examine a seed and tell you right off the bat what type of flower species it is. Hell, I can even name all fifty thousand by heart, but let's get back to the days when I was a handsome young man in a sharp black suit that didn't know the difference between a ranunculus and a rose.

I spent about thirty-two minutes reading, until an abrupt

swing of the door caught my attention. I assumed it was going to be Mr. Fleur since he'd greeted me yesterday, and I hoped he'd give me some more direction.

I turned around and said, "Mr. Fleur, it's so nice to see you," only to realize it was Gloria. I sat back down and mumbled, "Oh, it's just you."

That ruffled her feathers. She'd lampooned me, so I thought I'd do the same.

She adjusted her sour face to a look of peace, then softly joked, "I know they say you begin to look like your parents and all as you get older, but I hardly think my figure resembles my father's quite yet."

Gloria slowly guided her hands down the outline of her long cream-colored dress, accentuating the sides of her chest and all the way down to the curves of her hips. She moved in a slow manner, knowing that my weapon of words was no match for her unbeatable weapon . . . being a femme fatale.

"Yeah, I've never seen your father with such a nice pair of—"

Gloria gasped.

"Heels!"

"Well, you haven't seen him on a Saturday night when he's had enough scotch to drown—"

"No way! Your father actually puts on heels?!"

"No! It's a joke." She laughed as she added, "You really do have a bad sense of humor."

"I do not! Anyways, I'm not here to make you laugh."

"Too late."

"Come on, let's get started."

She sat down next to me in protest as I opened up my floriography book and pulled out a handwritten list that I used as its bookmark. I would rather have used that proudly written list than dog-ear my book pages. I was poor, which made me understand the value of things. I began to fib to Gloria about how I'd stayed up all night doing my research on the different species of flowers. As soon as I mentioned that I'd narrowed it down to fifty-four possible species, Gloria shouted, "Fifty-four?! That's narrowed down? Can I see the list?"

She swiftly grabbed the perfectly folded paper from my hands before I could answer. I tried to reason with her, as if my paper were a hostage and I the desperate father, stuttering and stammering, knowing the situation was out of my control at that point. I quickly said that I needed to finish reading the book before I could narrow the list down any further. I tried to explain to her the complexities of these plants and what they needed to survive. I assured her that, luckily, I'd studied biological science at Brown University, and that understanding this sort of thing was beyond her capabilities.

In that moment, she ripped the pen out of my hand, to its surprise, and began scribbling and crossing out names on my perfectly written list.

"Gardenia, no. They are far too sensitive about water intake and temperature. Orchids, no. Their biological makeup varies far too widely between each one. Azalea, no. Dahlia, no. Iris, no. Violet, no."

"Hold on!" I shouted at her. Gloria ignored me and continued in a mocking tone, as if she were humming a song. She kept recklessly crossing flowers off the list.

"No, no, no, nooo-no-no. No, no, no. Nooo, nooo, no, no . . . nooo—"

"What are you doing?"

Gloria slowly looked up at me and batted her eyelashes. She softly said, "You wouldn't be asking me that if you knew the biological makeup of all these flowers. Half of these aren't even compatible with the Fleur Atom Immunizing Technological Health formula."

"Well, that's why I'm reading this book, to learn about—"

"Well, that's why I'm here, so you don't have to read the book."

"But you—"

"Page twenty-seven. And next on floral symmetry," she said in a radio voice.

I began mumbling to myself, turning to page twenty-seven as she continued reciting my book word for word.

"Actinomorphic flowers are bilaterally capable of division by any longitudinal plane into essentially symmetrical halves, which can increase—"

"How do you know so much about this?"

She threw the violated list back at me and sighed. "Then there were eight!"

I glanced down at my list to see only eight flower species still left on that paper, as if they were the last men standing after a tumultuous, blood-filled battle.

"I'm withering away! Let's get breakfast," shouted the loose cannon, ready to create another war zone.

Chapter Eleven

Gloria led the way out of the greenhouse as I awkwardly trailed behind, trying to catch up. Contrasting with her father, who had kept stopping and turning around to make sure I wasn't being left in the dust, Gloria didn't bother to look back once. She created the dust, waiting for nobody. Not even the sound of my voice made her turn around as she forced conversation, asking me my opinion on pigs flying.

"Pigs flying?!" I lifted my tone and still no head turn.

"Yeah! I listen to the *Science's Latest Discoveries* radio program every night and—"

"So do I!"

She finally spun around. "Last night they mentioned the first pig has been born with the trace of what could be wings."

"I missed last night's episode."

"Did you hear Tuesday's episode?" Her posture became uneasy.

"No, I haven't had a chance to listen this week with this whole new project."

"Oh, okay good." She relaxed and continued walking toward the front of the house, not mentioning another word.

I saw Franklin standing by the Fleur family car, proudly staffing his post, like I'm sure he did every day. Same goofy stance, same dopey suit, and same foolish demeanor. As we walked by him, he leaned against the car, puffed up his collar, and tucked his chin into his shoulder. In a New York gangster accent, he said, "Don't look now, Glor . . . but I think you're being followed."

"Nah, nah, Frankie boy. Don't get your socks twisted. It's only Ollie-baby," she replied in the same tone.

"Ahh, Ollie-baby! Why didn't ya say so? I didn't recognize ya with that goofy grin on your mug."

I laughed.

"Ahh, nah, nah. His face is stuck like that now. Gave 'im a good right hook in the greenhouse." Gloria winked at me.

The attention she gave me left me uncertain that she saw me as just a coworker. I had to be very strategic about how I dealt with Gloria. Last thing I wanted was to get fired by Mr. Fleur for being in a compromising situation with his daughter or even him thinking I wanted to be. Gloria already teased and taunted, probably trying to seduce me, trap me, get me laid off—all for making her cry yesterday.

When Gloria and I entered the grand kitchen, it was almost unrecognizable without the crowd of opinion-filled employees lined up to get sandwiches. The Renaissance-inspired kitchen was practically empty with just Gloria, Chef Anthony, me, and some handmade croissants. That blunt chef from yesterday transformed into a highly enthused, patient creature once Gloria approached him.

"Good morning, miss! How high is your head today?" Chef Anthony said.

Gloria raised her chin and stuck out her elbows in a masculine stance as she announced, "Higher than the Empire State Building! How high are you keeping your head today?"

"Keeping it higher than Mount Everest!"

"Darn it! You have me beat, but I'm glad to hear it."

Gloria then turned to me as Chef Anthony handed me a beautiful porcelain plate with a buttery croissant on it.

"How high are you keeping your head today?" she asked, giving me a leading look, hinting to play along with Chef Anthony's funny little game.

"Higher than the ladder you almost nose-dived off yesterday!"

Gloria squealed with laughter as Chef Anthony looked politely confused. The sweet smell of hazelnut reached me as he handed me coffee in a matching porcelain cup with a sleek black stripe lining the rim. Gloria and I turned away, each with a plate in one hand and coffee in the other, all set up for a day of who knows what.

"Chef Anthony is such a dear. Ya know, his last boyfriend used to be mine." Gloria smiled sincerely. "Before he met Anthony, of course, or should I say . . . tasted his cooking. I should've never brought him to the kitchen. Serves me right." She shrugged. "We were never in love anyway, I guess."

"His cooking that good?" I looked down at the glossy croissant positioned on my plate.

"Just promise me you won't fall in love with him too when you try his food."

I tittered at her request.

Maybe she romanticizes everyone? Could've been her style of complimenting—by admiring or appearing enamored. No wonder everyone was under her spell. Mr. Fleur did the same thing.

"I don't hold anything against Anthony, though. Never been the jealous type."

I didn't know why she was telling me all this, practically spilling her guts to me as we made our way outside. We forged through the never-ending gardens, taking a new path I had not trekked before. Gloria carried her plate and cup carelessly, and coffee ran down the side of her mug with each turn she made. Boiling-hot French roast splashed her fingers, but she didn't even flinch. I didn't know how anyone could not react to that with an "ouch" or yelp.

Does she not feel it?

That was the only plausible reason I could think of, because once we sat down, the coffee burned my tongue to the texture of sandpaper. We finally decided to dine at a round Victorian bistro table with two dainty chairs nestled under a willow tree. The set resembled faded white Chantilly lace. If Gloria were the love of my life, I would've proposed to her there. It was romantically secluded, and the sun shone through the tree, creating a sparkling effect on the dew-covered grass. The grand tree complemented Gloria's eyes in the most astonishing way, but unfortunately . . . I felt nothing. Not a hint of a flutter in my heart when her eyes locked on mine and not even a caterpillar in my stomach that could eventually grow into a butterfly. Nothing. I was not one to romanticize, unlike her.

Gloria clasped her hands together and rested her chin on her fists, showcasing her interest along with the coffee-stained sleeves of her cream satin dress. She asked me to tell her a little bit about myself and I asked her why. I didn't like being interrogated by anyone. At that time in my life, I believed people asked questions to get answers they could use against me in the future. It was hard to fathom that there were some rare souls in this world that asked because they genuinely cared about what you had to say.

"Well, we are gonna be working together for a while, and with a colorful name like Oleander, I'm sure you have a pretty colorful life!"

"My life is anything but that."

"I find that hard to believe."

"I'm dead serious. My life is pretty black and white. I went to school, got a degree, found a job—that's all there is to it."

In the blink of an eye, she looked disheartened, but then she quickly became enthused once more. "What about your family?"

"What family?" I shot down that optimism real quick.

My father left when I was a child—to be precise, eight years old. I don't blame him, though; my mother was a lot to handle. She had a personality that was very . . . out there—an eccentric who was hard to control. I think my father grew tired of having to hold her on a tight leash, so he just let go. I'm sure he realized after the fact that in his attempt to set her free, he was really the one who was free now. My father stopped holding the rope only to let the world hold a tighter rope on my mother. Cleveland, Ohio, was no place for a person like that. She had little to no education and was always claiming that she was a tormented artist. She had the tormented part down, but the art . . . That was up for interpretation.

One day when I got home from school, I saw her out front in the snow, painting our house. Looking back now, that was actually the last day I was zealous about life until I arrived at the Fleur Estate. She was painting it a vibrant yellow as the snow flurries came falling down on our white-picket-fenced yard that afternoon. She asked if I wanted to help her and, being an easily impressionable eight-year-old, of course I joined in on the reckless painting. The neighbors thought she was a raving lunatic and so did my father when he arrived home that day in his hand-me-down Tesla that had belonged to his grandfather. That might have been one of the very few electric cars that were left in those days. Luckily his father was just as anal-retentive as his father before him, so the car was still in fairly good condition, along with its charger. Most electric cars were wiped out by 2050 due to the crash of the power grid. No one could charge them, and they harmed the environment more than helped it. The grid was restored years later.

Anyways, when my father got home, I remember seeing the snow melt as it hit his forehead. The snow dissipating on his hot head could be seen by any nonaffiliated spectator, but the steam coming out of his ears was only visible to my mother and me. My father's eyes shifted to the paint all over us and the messy cans on the grass. He walked into the house without saying a word, then walked back out ten minutes later. He calmly got in his Tesla without even a glance in our direction. His car did not skid off in the snow or screech on the asphalt. He just slowly drove off, floating away into the distance, never to be seen again. My mother spent the next ten years preparing the house for his return, for she then had the tightest leash holding her . . . hope. I recollect having had an ounce of hope as well, since my father had left the only things that were of value to him: his watch, his old Brown sweater, and lastly, me, his only son. He just had to come back for all those things.

My hope soon disintegrated from an ounce to a milligram to nonexistent as my ninth birthday rolled around the following year. My mother had also disintegrated to nonexistent by the time my eighteenth birthday rolled around. I got out of that crummy little town in Ohio and earned my place at Brown on scholarships. I only told Gloria my backstory starting from Brown on.

"After graduating college, I moved to the West Coast because I was told things were so great over here."

Gloria reassured me that they were, but comparing her experience of California to mine was like comparing how a polar bear felt in the desert versus a lizard. Gloria, the lizard.

She had all the money in the world, luxury cars, designer dresses, and a chef that would go out and grow fields of wheat for her just so her sandwich could have the freshest bread. Gloria's life was the definition of living in luxury, but she argued with me that none of those things were important.

"That all means nothing in the scope of life," she mumbled with a half-eaten croissant in her mouth.

"Okay. Well, what's your story, then?"

"I went to school for as long as I could stand it. Left when I was sixteen."

"Left?"

"Yeah!"

"You mean dropped out?"

She smiled and chuckled to herself a bit as if she'd heard that response as many times as I'd heard I'm named after a toxic flower.

"You say 'dropping out,' I say 'diving in.' Same thing. There's nothing school can teach you that books can't."

"Oh yeah? Because a high school dropout would decide to read history books in their free time."

"Yeah!"

"Tell me a little US history, then."

"Be more specific. How far back should I go?"

"One hundred years."

"2025? Bold." She then went on to recite what she knew. "History shows we hit rock bottom in 2025. The market crashed and so did the average human IQ. The addiction to screen sedatives was a nationwide problem until the US went cold turkey, might I add, involuntarily. Technology and artificial intelligence got cut off due to the multiple civil and world wars we endured many years after the crash. We've been building from the ground up since."

She was right, America had been building from the ground up ever since. In 2125, we were at peak human advancement. The terabytes in our brains had increased by 2.5 percent since the year 2025. People were paid more back then by the government to stay at home than work. Word is that everyone was so weak and lazy that they had gotten themselves in the ultimate predicament . . . tough times. Born into those tough times, the following generations became tougher than nails with wits sharper than knives. They didn't rely on screen sedatives like their parents before them or this imaginary highway I learned about in school called the Internet.

Gloria continued talking about the dark nostalgia that those times evoked in one's spirit. "Sounds like it was quite a strange time in the world back then. Nothing was tangible and items were made to break. There was excess everything! I heard people were very unhappy too. I think it's because everything was at their fingertips, so they appreciated nothing . . . not even human interaction! I know I'm spoiled, but if I want to get ahold of someone, I have to either call them on the telephone, mail a letter, or make a trip to see them in person. I love any opportunity to strike up a conversation with a stranger. I heard folks back then could send messages or photographs to others in the blink of an eye, even if they were on the other side of the world! Isn't that wild? You wanna know one of the most famous sayings from the '020s?"

"Hmm, I don't know," I admitted.

"I hate people."

"'I hate people'?" I laughed at how ridiculous that phrase sounded.

"Yeah! Apparently, people back then didn't want to leave their homes unless they had to, and the common American greeting they announced when they got back inside was 'I hate people.'"

"And people wonder why the American empire fell." I laughed some more.

"Well, of course. Besides the bad judgment and soft tyranny, how can a society run on things that don't actually exist? I mean, just look at screen sedatives. Ironically enough, back then they fooled the public and called them 'smartphones.' They served as tranquilizers for the human brain and gathered all your personal information. People carried the weight of everything they'd built throughout their whole life in a little breakable rectangle that fit into the palm of their hand. Back then people made money just off their looks, as well . . . Isn't that mad?" Gloria ranted.

I played along with her enthusiasm for history, and every once in a while, I would say phrases like "an absolute travesty" or "how horrific" when she raged on about something she thought was appalling. Amid Gloria's comedic frustration toward an era our parents weren't even alive in, she turned serene again and smiled at me.

She softly said, "You could've made a living off your looks. Back then, you might've been richer than me."

I wished that were true for our time. If you didn't contribute, invent, or create something of use to society, it didn't matter how nice a mug you had . . . people would still rip you a new one. Looks became a serious problem in the '020s. It got to the point where people were going through medical procedures to change their appearance. They would spend all their money to have foreign chemicals injected into their faces, as if the money they spent was an investment in their career. Talk about an odd time. I'm sure that was the normal beauty standard back then. In school we learned that 1920s beauty was inspired by Egyptian culture and that 2020s beauty was inspired by lizards. People would undergo operations to make the shape of their face skeleton-like, resembling a lizard skull, and inject their lips with serums to make them stick out all scaly as well. It might have been some sort of spiritual thing to be able to see into someone's brain because people would up-turn their noses with knives and needles, so their nostrils were visible head-on. People would also try to imitate lizards with the way they talked. An old 2020s accent sounded like a cross between lisping certain letters, especially S's, and smacking the gums between sentences, since no one in those days could fully close their protruding mouth.

"I have to say, we have become much more sophisticated than the '020s. Everything isn't artificially produced nowadays and is built to last," Gloria proudly boasted as she sipped her coffee. Every time she took a sip, her eyes shifted from mine down to her mug in a humble manner, as if she needed to focus on not spilling. It was very endearing.

"If you don't have to manually work something, it is not technology, it's an insult to your capability," I added in, show-ing I was well versed in history too. "If people are too lazy to crank a few knobs or have to keep ripping paper out of their typewriter because they can't spell worth trash, they are below average, my friend." I told Gloria that I believed soci-ety would become more and more manual as time went on, making human intellect and physical abilities more advanced. Looking back, I was right. I mean, that was the government's goal, anyway, in banning screen sedatives. Humans had be-come so reliant on objects that they'd become unable to rely on themselves.

"I bet ya those people in 2020 stayed in school," Gloria de-fiantly shouted, stoking the fire.

"Why do you have it out for school?"

"I hated it. I'd rather be working in the real world."

"Yeah, because this is the real world."

"Anyways, since 'dropping out,' as you say, I've been helping my father with his scientific research and technology."

"Oh, nice! For the gold-dipped roses?"

Gloria leaned in with a sly look on her face, as if she were about to tell a secret, getting closer to me with each breath she took. Her chin tilted down toward the ground as her eyebrow raised with mischief. "You know the goal isn't to just preserve roses, right?"

"Well, yeah! That's why I'm here, you guys are expanding to other flower species." I laughed uncomfortably, wondering how she could be so bright, yet so vapid.

"Beyond roses?" Gloria laughed back. "Beyond flowers! Using the same technology that preserves those flowers . . ." She paused and stood on her chair, hiking her dress up to her knees and putting one foot on the table. Gloria posed like an old war hero as she raised one hand up to the sky. I hunched over the table, embarrassed by her lack of couth. I hoped no one would see me sitting there as she stood on the small table like a madwoman. Luckily, I could only see Franklin in the distance, smiling as he passed by, but that didn't matter; he was used to Gloria's antics as well. I was worried Mr. Fleur would appear.

"What are you doing? Get down, Gloria . . . please?!"

"Fleur Industries is about to attempt what no one has ever successfully done before. Bum, bum, bum, bummm!" She bent down and now had both her knees on the table, her face too close to mine. I tucked my chin into my neck, trying to create some space between our faces. She softly whispered, her eyes locked on mine, "Preserve human life."

I stood up in shock, rattling my chair a bit as I moved it

to the side. I began to step backward. "If this is another one of your bad jokes, Gloria, I'm going to—"

"I'm serious!" Gloria climbed off the table. "We have the technology to preserve human life. Come on, let's find my father and he can tell you all about it himself."

Gloria grabbed my shoulders as she pushed me through the gardens. "In shock" was an understatement. I don't know what was harder for me to believe that day . . . the legitimate possibility of preserving human life or that this girl had no sense of personal space or boundaries. If I breathed a certain pitch, she was close enough to tell if the note was sharp or flat. Either way, I yearned to know more.

Chapter Twelve

Gloria and I abruptly swung through the front doors of the main house and practically ran into Mr. Fleur. I noticed he had a newspaper in his hand, and he noticed I had a Gloria in mine. I quickly pulled my hand out of hers as Mr. Fleur gave me a look of intrigue that rode the line perfectly between positive and negative speculation. He brushed off what he'd just seen and went on passionately expressing his disapproval of the newspaper's headline. *The Sunset Times* read of young adults arrested for selling screen sedatives in East of Sunset.

"It's so frustrating to see these kids wanting to bring back something they never even experienced. My parents lived through the height of screen sedatives and the prohibition. My father served in World War Four," Mr. Fleur explained. "After the imaginary highway called Internet was cut off in America, the population did not know what to do with themselves. There weren't even newsstands for them to get any information at that point!" He smacked the paper against his hand.

"That sounds terrifying, sir. Gloria and I had a question for you—"

"My mother was a model on the Internet, influencing people . . . whatever that means. I was no older than eight when she lost her job. Everything fell apart. That's why you can't become reliant on one thing in this life." Mr. Fleur looked directly at Gloria.

"Oh, I'm not! You know that. Yes, I'm working on the flower collection and helping with scientific research for Fleur Industries. But on the side, I've been practicing my singing," Gloria defensively stated.

"You want to be a singer?" I asked.

"My great-great-grandmother was one back in the day, so it's in my blood," she said.

"She was also a floozie," Mr. Fleur countered.

I could tell Gloria wasn't serious about the whole singing thing. With no limit on spending, she probably changed her career as often as her socks, or the topic.

"Well, it's good you're thinking about your future," Mr. Fleur replied to Gloria. "Many people don't." He motioned at the paper once more. "Our infrastructure can't even handle smartphones, so I guess it doesn't matter what these dopes are doing. It's more the idiocracy of it all! My mother couldn't get a job after the Internet crashed. She had no artificial intelligence to make a resume and no way of finding the answer to any question she had. Books were gone, libraries destroyed, and many other places for finding the truth had been eliminated. More than half the country fell out of work and out of love just as quickly. People were forced to face each other and all the uncomfortable issues that went along with that. They were no longer able to drug themselves numb with screen sedatives. I remember the day the police came to our door because of the Cellphone Buyback Initiative. My father was registered as not having turned in his smartphone, almost got arrested. Our family was in shambles, like the rest of America. That was the start of the Sober Awakening, which I'm sure you kids know about. Shortly after, prohibition laws were passed to ensure that never happened again. Society has been fully cleansed, thank goodness. I am the first generation of Purists in my family, Oleander, my parents were Generation Alpha and their parents before them Generation Z."

"I'm technically the first Purist, since you were alive for eight years before smartphones were completely abolished, Dad," Gloria stated.

The government had banned smartphones before I was alive, so the subject didn't interest me much or affect me at the time. All I knew was history repeats itself. It comes down to the age-old question: Should the government outlaw something because it is bad for the people or let the people make their own decisions? I think that is one of the most controversial questions, which no one can fully answer. After all, the government should protect their citizens from harming themselves or each other, but at the same time, the point of living in a free state is to make those decisions yourself. To take risks when it matters.

"Dad! Tell him about how we have found a way to preserve human life!"

Mr. Fleur wiped his chin in disbelief and sighed. "I was right about you not having the codes to the bombs, Gloria."

"Bombs, sir?"

"Oh, no, just something Glory and I were joking about earlier." Mr. Fleur laughed.

"Ohhh, so she was joking," I said.

"Not about preserving human life," Gloria countered.

"Oh, no, she's right about that, son," Mr. Fleur interrupted. He began to walk away as he said, "Follow me."

Gloria, Mr. Fleur, and I walked down a hallway I hadn't trekked before. The Fleurs' house seemed as if it were ever growing, almost as infinite as their gardens. There was something so profound about that estate. There was always a new room I hadn't been in or a new hallway that would suddenly appear out of thin air. It was always different and large, but somehow still familiar . . . like home. Grand, abstract, colorful, and warm.

Mr. Fleur led the way through the house as Gloria and I followed anxiously behind him for the same reason, to prove each other wrong. I didn't know what to expect as we entered through maroon-colored doors that looked as if they were designed by the same man who'd built Odysseus's Homeric galley. On the other end of those elaborately carved boards stood a theater. Row upon row of plush velvet seating covered the floor with row upon row of steps spanning from the back door all the way down to the stage. As I looked up toward the ceiling, I saw a balcony running across the perimeter of it, transporting me back to the days of vaudeville. Completing that campy yet opulent room was a large stage at the front with curtains that matched the ones in Mr. Fleur's office.

Bewitched by the room's charm, I didn't realize Mr. Fleur had already begun to walk down a row of chairs. I quickly rushed after him and took a seat directly next to him. Gloria circled around the front of the theater, then walked back up the steps to sit on the other side of Mr. Fleur. I assumed so I'd undoubtably notice her. It was beyond unnecessary for her to make a whole loop to go around, but Gloria was not a woman who valued "necessary." When she took her seat, their butler immediately rushed over with a bag of hot buttered popcorn for her. I mean, I can't make this stuff up. She softly grabbed the large bag and coddled it like a small babe on her lap. Mr.

Fleur then twisted his head in a forced manner and asked the butler to have someone start the picture.

Are we going to be watching a movie?

I was very excited and unsure about the whole situation. I had only seen a motion picture twice in my life, once when I was seven and another time in college. I detested motion pictures. They were for people who were too vapid to read—like my mother.

The green velvet curtains slowly opened as a screen descended on the stage. I saw two men in the corner of the stage, one using a pulley system for those heavy curtains and the other cranking a lever that dropped the screen. Those two nameless men disappeared as the lights went down, making the whole room unnervingly pitch black. Mr. Fleur was gone too, for I could not see him, even though our shoulders touched. Soon his face formed in my vision again as specks of light shot across the room. Steadily picking up, those flashes turned into a solid beam projecting from the back wall onto the screen.

We were going to watch a film, not one of fantasy and heroes, but one of an unbelievable truth.

Chapter Thirteen

The black-and-white screen read, *Fleur Atom Immunizing Technological Health and the Human Body . . . presented by the M. W. Fleur Foundation for Science, Engineering, and Medical Research. In collaboration with Charles H. Grenadine, MD, PhD, UCLA Health; Robert C. Burton, MD, Director of Science, USC; and Milton W. Fleur, MD, PhD, DO, Fleur Industries Inc.*

I recognized the name Charles, the man from UCLA who'd been arguing with Mr. Fleur yesterday. I knew it had to be greater than flowers for an argument of that level. A rose then jarringly appeared in the center of the screen, with nothing around it. Just an empty gray frame with a gray rose standing straight up. A voice came from the screen, a narrator as you'd call it, to explain to us what was going on . . . in case we were already lost.

"This is a rose, part of the Rosaceae family. When still rooted, its lifespan can be up to thirty-five years if taken care of."

The screen then split in half as the rose moved over to the

left side of the frame. On the right side of the screen appeared a blank-looking man standing in a hospital gown . . . poor bastard. I'm sure he was paid well for that. The narrator came back to clue us in, again, in case we were lost.

"This is a human, part of the Hominidae family. Its life expectancy can be up to two or three times that of a rose."

"I made this video when I wanted to be a director. That's Clarence. He's a sweetheart," Gloria said.

The line between the split screen then disappeared as the man reached over and picked up the rose, which happened to be in the same room. I was sitting on the edge of my seat, waiting for a big scary monster to jump out. I understood why her interest now was singing. The scene was so empty and sterile, to the point of unsettling. Still, I sat there in the dark, figuratively and literally, waiting for the narrator to continue his robotic speech.

"Both reproduce, respond to thermal stress and sunlight levels, and carry out physiological respiration, whether it be through photosynthesis or a large inhalation. Both organisms have the same basic needs: nutrients, H_2O, and air . . . whether it be O_2 or CO_2."

The screen split in half once again, the rose on the left side alone and the man on the right. The flower on the left got watered as the man on the right took a sip from a glass. I suspected he had to have been drinking something other than water to get through that video. The narrator went on to explain that many factors varied between those organisms, but their means of survival did not. Soon the man and the rose disappeared on the black-and-white screen, and a building I knew all too well cross dissolved into frame.

"This is Fleur Industries," said the voice. "A worldwide corporation that preserves roses using its patented gold formula with Fleur Atom Immunizing Technological Health."

A few oohs and aahs came from Gloria's direction.

The inside of the factory appeared on the screen, and there it was—my workstation. I watched that colossal conveyor belt rolling along as consistent as the 405 River. Mother Nature and the machine, never ending, always building and destroying in a constant vicious cycle. At that moment, I wanted to point at the screen and shout, "That's where I work! I stand right there," like a starstruck fool, but that would have been a completely useless statement, since the room was already aware of that information. I just remained silent and let the sterile video continue on.

"This advanced technology was discovered and backed by the M. W. Fleur Foundation for Science, Engineering, and Medical Research. Using this technology, which has been proven successful for roses, we will be moving forward in its use for the preservation of human life," stated the narrator.

I gasped as one of those overmanufactured world-renowned Fleur gold-dipped roses was shown on the screen, glistening in all its metallic glory. The rose soon faded out with another hokey cross dissolve to show a man in a lab coat. He might've been ten to fifteen years younger than Mr. Fleur, as his hair resembled the color of cracked pepper more than salt. He had a stick in his hand, which reminded me of my professors back at Brown, and stood next to an elementary-level diagram of the human body.

"Now, to better explain, here is Dr. Burton with a diagram showing you how the process works."

"He's the best," whispered Gloria.

Dr. Burton pulled a lever that released a bunch of black marbles through the glass tubes in the diagram, almost like a children's table game. They ran down the fake intestines on the display board.

"The black dots represent the formula consumed by the

subject," Dr. Burton announced, speaking for the first time. His voice had a unique bent to it, similar to the accents you hear in West of Sunset, better known as BFE. He must've overcome his rough upbringing to find better education somewhere else too. It was entertaining to hear him explain the sophistications of science in his hillbilly accent, I'll give him that. Ten points for production value got added to that terrible film by throwing in an eccentric desert rat scientist.

"Once the formula is consumed, it will make its way down the esophagus into the stomach, dispersin' from the small intestine through capillaries to all the other organs of the body. Eventually submersin' every cell in the system with the Fleur Atom Immunizing Technological Health. Think of this as a pause button. It stops the system from continuin' but keeps the organs vital."

The screen showed the two other assembly lines in the factory that ran parallel to mine, one that had people injecting the serum into each flower, then the other that dipped the roses in gold. That black-and-white film showcased pretty accurately how drab and dull factory life was. Each person was a cog in the machine. The screen transitioned back to Robert C. Burton, the continental cowboy scientist who made the name Fleur Atom Immunizing Technological Health sound even funnier and more ridiculous than before.

"When everythin' is preserved internally, the subject will be dipped in a gold solution that protects its exterior shell so nothin' can disrupt or disturb its preservation process. They will be protected for however long the designated holder or holders see fit. The Fleur Atom Immunizing Technological Health serves as a pause button, our reversin' formula serves as a play button. When the designated holder decides it is time for the subject to continue in its natural agin' process, the subject will be restored."

The video cut back to that same shot of the gold-dipped rose. It was picked up and put in a bucket filled with a solution. The gold melted away like it was wet paint—for all I know, it probably was—then the lifeless rose was pulled out of that tub. Luckily, they didn't film that poor paid actor doing the same thing. The screen split in two one last time to show both the rose and the man being injected. He was lying in a hospital bed. Once poked in the arm, he woke up as if it were a miracle. Terrible acting, I have to say, very unbelievable.

"After just one injection, the formula will be dissolved gently from the system and the subject will wake up with their last recollection and physical form bein' the same as they were the day they were preserved," said Dr. Burton in his deep, twangy voice.

In that moment, the reality of it all set in—in the most disturbing way. I looked over to see Mr. Fleur watching the video with a warm smile on his face, glowing with pride, while Gloria chomped on her popcorn, reacting to certain cues.

The narrator's voice spoke once again on the screen as different impersonal laboratory clips played. "And that's the process, folks! Thanks to the strides made by the M. W. Fleur Foundation for Science, Engineering, and Medical Research, the first three humans will be volunteering as subjects to undergo the preservation process on August 31 this year."

Mr. Fleur nudged me and whispered, "Just about two months, my boy."

I congratulated him quietly, not knowing what else to say as I continued watching what was supposed to be an uplifting video but came across as a macabre tragedy. The screen then showed a nuclear family playing in the park. Carousels were spinning in the background almost as fast as my head, and children were eating ice cream while laughing with each other. Those were definitely paid actors, for I had never seen anyone happy to the point of it being painful to watch.

The narrator began to say, "If the experiment is proven successful," but I didn't hear the rest of that sentence because Gloria shouted over it, "If successful?!"

She then threw popcorn at the screen like a riled-up audience member at a bad play.

The narrator continued, "This will open up a world of possibilities in science, leading many individuals to continue on the path of life . . . only to reach heaven when their time is up." The screen faded to black.

I sat there in silence, caught up in all that had been presented in the picture show. As my thoughts spiraled out of control, loud clapping and cheering from Gloria snapped me out of it. After hissing at the screen a few times, commenting, and cheering throughout the film, Gloria got up like a satisfied critic that had just endured a roller coaster of emotions. She then went on raving about how incredible this experiment was going to be. Mr. Fleur stood up and I followed as we scooted out of the row of chairs.

He said, "I know you probably have a lot of questions, Oleander, but I got a board meeting to get to. Collect all of your thoughts and I will be able to answer every question you have about this later on."

"I'm very busy working on the fall collection, sir, so another time works better for me as well."

Boy, was that a lie. I was not about to tell him that I'd had my ass handed to me that morning by an entitled twenty-year-old girl who'd scribbled out all my hard work. I mean, talk about discouraging. Something that would take you years to research, let alone understand, Gloria could just explain off the top of her head. The worst part of it all was her delivery of facts. She spoke about complex biological nuances the same way she spoke about ice cream. It was as if she just suddenly remembered she was craving rocky road, then continued on with what she was saying before. Something that seemed so important to you, so big, all of a sudden turned into the size of a pea. Besides that, how could I have even focused on the difference between daffodils or lilies after I found out about the whole human guinea pig experiment? Preserving someone's life, pshhh.

Do people really hate living in this era to the point of freezing themselves for later?

Mr. Fleur walked out of the theater as Gloria led me toward the stage, luring me in. She had her arms wrapped around her half-eaten bag of popcorn as we clumsily stepped up onto the grand stage. The large screen had been pulled up, and the men who controlled the curtains had turned off the lights. I walked to the side of the stage and turned the lights back on, shining a spotlight on Gloria. In that moment, she set her popcorn down on an abandoned piano. She took a seat on the torn leather bench as she rested her head, dramatically gazing up at the ceiling. Her face caught the light as if she were a Hollywoodland movie starlet.

She recited her lines in a Shakespearean tone as she remained in character . . . Well, for the most part. "Oleander, oh Oleander . . . whatcha thinkin'?"

Her improper enunciation of phrases was probably from teaching herself grammar. It was the one tone Franklin couldn't mimic. Thinking about it now, I don't think anyone could. It was what made Gloria Fleur the charming Gloria Fleur. That and her ability to pick up cues of one's emotions without a word being spoken. Being hypersensitive, she could tell I was in my head, so I quickly walked to the center of the stage to seem more present. I switched my focus back to her as I recited how I felt.

"I, the Great Oleander, think people are fools for believing life is going to be better in fifty years than it is today."

Gloria walked over to me, acknowledging her cue. "Well, the Great Oleander"—she rolled her eyes—"it will be for some."

I swiftly grabbed her and dipped her in a dramatic manner, intensifying our ridiculous scene as Gloria squealed with laughter.

"How do you know?! How are people going to willingly volunteer? What man in his right mind would do that to himself?"

"They're not doing it for themselves, they're doing it for science," Gloria shouted as she broke free from my hold and projected out to the audience. She looked back at me in a serious manner and softly said, "Ya know, for a greater cause."

I'd heard "for a greater cause" too many times in history class to count, and trust me, it never ended well. I didn't say that to Gloria, though, I just continued to pry instead.

"Well, my fair madam Gloria, how is this going to happen—"

Gloria frantically ran around the stage, grabbing my arms and tossing them. "How do you have time for all these questions?!" She jumped up on a wooden box and shouted, "Time is ever fleeting! Passing on too quickly . . . like an overfed goldfish."

She was being absurd at that point, like a child performing outlandish charades, yipping and dancing around. She didn't just take something and run with it, she flew with it. I tried to reel in the conversation by asking more questions about the experiment.

"How in Sam Hill did your father convince people to be test subjects?"

"Aren't you supposed to be busy working on the fall collection, the Great Oleander?"

I rolled my eyes.

"Come on. I must schedule the cars to be washed."

"Cars?"

Gloria nodded and smiled as we walked out of the theater.

"I don't even have one and you have multiple. Boy—"

"Trust me, it's no fun when you have to be the re-fur-ray between your parents over it."

"Do you mean 'referee'?"

"Oh, yes." Gloria's cheeks blushed. "My father brings home cars as one does groceries."

"I guess he can afford to."

"Affording something versus purchasing it should be treated the same as thinking versus saying it. Just because you can, doesn't mean you should. Kind of like his upcoming experiment."

Chapter Fourteen

My mind whirled like a tornado of doubt as I anxiously waited to find out more about Mr. Fleur's dangerous scheme. Gloria remained careless, stomping through the gardens that afternoon as the sun dipped lower in the sky. Summertime felt different at the Fleur Estate. The hot, dense summer air that swarmed you South of Sunset magically turned into a refreshing summer breeze that brushed your skin ever so gently. It was as if Mother Nature delicately tapped you on the shoulder, just to remind you she was still there. But unlike Mother Nature, Gloria had not learned the art of subtlety. In that moment, she was gripping my hand as she dragged me down another path. I think she made it a point to take a new route to the greenhouse each time.

Gloria had a sophisticated yet childlike understanding of what it was like to be human. For her, clothes were meant to be lived in, hair was meant to fall out of place from running faster than your feet could handle, and gowns were meant to have a muddy line along the bottom from being dragged through dirt-covered trails. That was Gloria's signature: a dress that cost more than a year's rent for me with dirt stains all over it, showcasing how out of touch she was with the value of money.

The sand-colored decomposed granite crunched a little as we made our way past a small building the size of a hut or quaint cottage. The paint on that structure matched the same shade of rosy peach that the Fleurs' main house was covered in. Stone accents and columns matched the main house as if this small building were a mini replica or guest house. The door was wide open, revealing the oddly contradicting interior of that Roman shack.

"Hold on just a moment, Gloria," I whispered.

First thing I saw was the back of Scott's head. He probably had been purposely shaving it since he was twenty years old to appear tough. First thing I heard was crunching, not from the decomposed granite Gloria and I walked on, but from Scott snacking on corn nuts in that small room. His back was to us as he sat at a desk inside. A large wall covered in screens lit up the room. Those screens were all shapes and sizes, some small and circular, others large and rectangular, and some medium sized and octangular. Scott had a cornucopia of security screens monitoring every inch of the property, including the spot where Gloria and I stood in front of his security command post.

At that moment, I thought we had been caught, but we hadn't. Also, if Scott saw us lingering out front of his post, there was nothing we could've realistically been booked for, anyway. I think I just feared Scott, not because of his power or from respect, but because he was so irrational and kooky that he would kill me and cover it up just because my face aggravated him too much that day. Gloria and I were blatantly visible on a triangular screen that hung on the top left side of the wall. Luckily, Scott was facing right, talking to a deep, familiar voice.

Lanky mustache-man Franklin was on the right of Scott, speaking to him like an old relative. What I could make out of their conversation was that Franklin was explaining to Scott that he was in a creative slump with his voice impressions. Scott kept violently crunching on his corn nuts as Franklin spilled his guts.

"Lately my impressions haven't been very, uhhh—" Franklin paused for a moment as that small triangular screen came into his line of sight. His face turned confused as he squinted his eyes, trying to put together what he was seeing.

"Personal." Scott finished the sentence for him.

Franklin's concentration was broken from the screen that had us on it. Gloria's back was turned away from the security command post as she pointed in the direction of the greenhouse, then to an imaginary watch on her wrist. I abruptly pulled her back against the wall of the hut, concealing us from that particular camera. She looked shocked. She threw up her hands and played along as if it were a spy mission. When in reality it was my guilty pleasure of listening to other people's woes.

"Uh, yeah . . . personal. My impressions haven't been very personal lately."

"Well then, Frank, you need to spend more time working on them."

"Pshhh, I wish. Problem is I don't have time, Scott."

"Well, if it was that important to you, you'd make time for it."

I peered into the shack, trying to get a better read on the situation.

"Scott, I didn't think I'd be working here full time for this long. That's the issue."

"No, it's not. You're the issue."

"Thanks." Franklin tapped his foot as he examined the

screens behind Scott. I watched his forehead wrinkle as he noticed we had mysteriously disappeared from his view.

"When your father passed away, no one forced you to take
his place full time . . . You offered." Scott regained his attention.

"Temporarily, until they could find a driver they could
trust." Midsentence, Franklin's voice turned from defensive to
solemn.

Poor Franklin, staying at a dead-end job until they could
rehire. I was sure the Fleurs were in no rush to hire someone
else. Why would they? They trusted Franklin, he was reliable,
and lastly, he knew how to handle Gloria's volcanic temper.
They didn't just need a driver; they needed a part-time babysit-
ter for that one. Franklin was stuck, hopelessly and utterly
stuck. Trust is not given, it's earned. I was already untrusting
with barely a dollar to my name, so I couldn't even imagine
how jaded the Fleurs were . . . excluding Gloria, of course.

"Frank, it's now or never. The Fleurs have known you your
whole life. Why would they voluntarily replace you? You've
been wreaking havoc on this property for as long as I can
remember."

Gloria remained pushed up next to me with our backs
against the security command post exterior. She was giggling
away as we listened in on Scott rambling about a time when he
had hair and Gloria and Franklin were no older than five and
eight.

"I was patrolling the grounds fifteen years ago when I
heard a high-pitched scream come from the gardens. Once
I reached the gardens, I saw little you, with the same goofy
ears, and little Gloria, with the same troublesome giggle. Little
Gloria was crying because you'd thrown a mud pie at her, ru-
ining her princess dress. I was fuming that day, but could feel
only so bad because when I went to grab you, Gloria threw a
mud pie right back, missing your face and getting me right in

the knee. I ended up dragging you two yipping children out of the garden and back to your parents. Little Gloria scurried back to Mr. and Mrs. Fleur, unfazed of course, while you returned to your father, who was anxiously waiting at his chauffeur post."

"I remember that day." Franklin smiled.

"Your poor pops. I had never seen a man's face turn so pale that it was almost transparent. Wow, that was all the way back in 2110. He thought he would be fired because of your inability to behave."

"Oh no, but the Fleurs were so understanding."

"Still are," Scott replied.

Gloria rolled her eyes at me in an embarrassed manner, as if she were trying to brush off Scott's and Franklin's deep compliments to her family's character. She walked away, for she had suddenly lost interest in our spy mission. It seemed as if the conversation we were eavesdropping on turned sour to Gloria as soon as her name was mentioned. She quietly wandered off as I stayed behind, still pressed against the wall, trying to figure out more pieces to that asymmetrical puzzle.

"They're the reason I stay," Franklin said in a serious tone. I could not see him, but Franklin's voice sounded how I imagined watering eyes looked as he continued his melancholy sentence by saying, "They need me."

I found it odd at that time in my life how genuine Franklin was. It was as if he had lived the lives of many men who had been on many treacherous journeys. Franklin and I were around the same age, both in our early twenties, but I couldn't understand how he seemed so worldly. Looking back as an old man, I realize that I may have graduated from Brown, the school of prestige, but Franklin had graduated from life, the school of hard knocks.

"Are you gonna keep standing there or are we gonna get work done?" Gloria shouted from afar.

My face felt slapped with heat. I ran toward her, creating scuffs in my recently shined black shoes. By the time I caught up with her, my perfectly neat hair was falling over my forehead in a disheveled way, and my freshly pressed suit resembled what your hands look like when you've been in a swimming pool for too long.

I huffed loudly. "What'd you do that for?"

"What do you mean? Do what?"

"Don't pretend."

Gloria smiled. "Oh, I just try to lower my antenna when it starts picking up too many channels, that's all."

I held the door open to the greenhouse, then motioned for her to go in. After all, she was still the same girl that Scott had mentioned in his story—always starting fights.

"Looks like I gotta keep *you* focused." She laughed as she walked in.

I bit my tongue and made nice, reminding myself what professionalism should look like.

Chapter Fifteen

That evening after work, I sat at an empty table in the South of Sunset public library, located just a few blocks from my jail cell of a dwelling. On hot summer nights, the library was filled with the smartest yet poorest people that side of the boulevard. It had multiple air-chilling systems that left you teetering on the line between cooled down and bone chilled. I always got a kick out of watching the panicky parents with fussing children storm through those heavy wooden doors as if a stampede were happening outside. Each one would be sweating profusely and loudly sighing as they wiped their brow. After a moment of weakness, they would muster up the grace to subtly pretend they'd gone in there to actually read something. Then, in ten minutes tops, the children would have their coats back on and the group would be out the door once again.

Yes, I was there to escape the heat as well, like the rest of the cattle, but I did feel the desire to brush up on my biology. The large coal-colored bookshelves towered over and surrounded me like the colorless brick buildings of the city. The abundant amount of gray novels filling the library's airspace reminded me of all that humankind knows. Yet all the people on the ground level, roaming around, reminded me of all that humankind was ignorant of. I could spend my whole life reading every novel and textbook in that sacred place front to back, and I still wouldn't be able to answer life's many questions.

I huffed to myself as I flipped through the pages of an anticlimactic nonfiction text. *I can't believe that Gloria had the nerve to say she has to keep me focused . . . Pshhh, me?! I am a well-oiled machine, accomplishing and overachieving every task thrown in my direction. Nothing can distract me. Not Gloria and her striking beauty. Not that mind-bending experiment. Nothing in the slightest bit.*

I quietly boasted to myself about my honorable capabilities as I continued to scan pages. My mindless page flipping came to a complete stop as a sound swept through my ears, striking my eardrum like an alarm. It was a lullaby—an eerie one. I quickly spotted the direction it came from. A small child across the library was playing with a music box as her mother roamed through the aisles of malleable truths. She had the wooden device placed on the table as she clumsily cranked the metal knob, filling the library with a twinkling melody. As I stared at the music box, I noticed a ballerina in an elegant arabesque posed on top. It was daintily spinning around and around, growing larger and larger the more I stared.

The dreary world around me began to blur as the metal-prong notes became almost as unnoticeable as my own breath. My head grew heavy as I watched the ballerina made of fine china slowly look more and more like Gloria Fleur. She spun around on that machine the same way Gloria did in my mind. Constantly performing a dance of wits, only stopping once her handler paid no more attention to her. She waited on the turn of the crank so she could react in the only way she knew how.

As I blinked my dry eyes multiple times, I forgot to open them back up on the last blink. Soon I found myself in an empty ballroom with beautiful chandeliers and yellow lights resembling the stars in the sky on a clear night. That tinny lullaby grew louder and louder as it filled the air of that unsettling, warm venue. I stood in the middle of the vast floor as I tried to gather what I saw twenty feet in front of me. *Gloria?* It couldn't have been, but it was. She was in a lavender dress made of tulle, posing in a beautiful arabesque like that dusty ballerina. There she was, placed on top of a large wooden music box with an even larger brass crank on the side of it. She began to spin, showcasing her phenomenal ability to transform from a loose cannon into an elegant, feminine being. I walked toward her slowly. Each step acting as a drum beat to the percussionless tune she mechanically turned to.

"Gloria," I whispered as I reached the foot of the extravagant pedestal she was effortlessly placed upon.

I looked up at her, trying to find an answer to what I was experiencing. Her unique beauty grew more and more intimidating the longer I studied her features. Gloria's rosy painted cheeks and emerald eyes slowly tilted down at me as she spoke in a slow-paced manner. "This is as close as you'll ever let yourself get to me," she said in a serious voice, not matching her normal sarcastic bent.

"No." I reached my arms out toward her.

The space between us expanded quicker than the flash of a strobe light. Pushed by inertia, I ended up on the opposite side of the room. It was as if the floor had moved under me. Gloria was now a hundred feet away, still spinning . . . unfazed. I attempted to walk back to her, but to my surprise, each step forward led me further away. A switch flipped inside me as I began to run toward Gloria, swiftly going from a hurried jog to a full-throttle sprint. The harder I exerted myself, the larger the space between us grew. I finally stopped, catching my breath on what felt like a backward escalator. Gloria was far off in the distance, no less than thirty yards away.

Her voice projected throughout the ever-growing ballroom of haunting lights as she announced, "It's like you said . . . you're a well-oiled machine."

I noticed my position in the room had changed as I looked down to see my feet attached to a metal platform. I was stuck on the music box now, endlessly spinning, trapped on this mechanical contraption. I dizzily looked up, and I could see the back of Gloria's dark chestnut-colored hair as she slowly walked away from me. Free.

"Gloria! How did I get in the box?!"

She continued walking, as if I were a muted radio.

"Gloria! How do I get out of the box?" My heart started to pound.

"Think." She didn't even turn her head.

"I'm trying to think outside of the box! I'm trying. I am trying!"

Gloria just continued strolling away, as if she had tunnel vision, wanting to walk out of that room or, even worse, go anywhere that was away from me.

"Help! Help!" I was paralyzed by that large, overpowering platform that had me by my ankles. "Wait, Gloria! How did you get out of the box?!"

"I never have to think outside of the box because I never let myself be put in it."

"But you were just—"

She continued walking away, leaving me alone in that expansive ballroom with nothing but hardwood floors and the sound of my own gears.

"Gloria! Gloria, wait! Please don't go! Gloria! Help me! I'm stuck! I need help!"

Soon an unrecognizable force shook my body as if an earthquake had occurred on the world that my shoulders held up. The tight grip that rocked my arms from side to side affected my vision, leading me to see a blurry version of the library. My sight sharpened as I realized what had happened. Drool covered my textbook, and the earthquake was nothing other than a panic-stricken librarian shaking me awake.

"Sir?! Sir! Are you alright?"

"What?"

"Oh . . . um, you had your face down, sir. And . . . um, you started mumbling 'Help,' and, and—" she stuttered.

I rubbed my face in disbelief, finally having control over my actions once again. I must have fallen asleep and dreamed about Gloria. I don't think I could've fully deciphered whether my vision was a dream or night terror. Yes, I was terrified, but on the other hand, I'd experienced levels of emotion far beyond what I'd known. I didn't just notice Gloria's irrational behavior and strange beauty—I admired it. I understood its value and didn't want to lose its presence. Instead of her soul being a two-dimensional idea, it engulfed me, covering my soul like a quilt. Every fiber was soft to the touch, warming a person who never knew they had been freezing for years. Gloria's mind was similar to the stitching that ran through a blanket, so detailed and thought out. You overlooked it, thinking it was unnecessary, not realizing it was what held the comforter together. I caught myself midthought; the librarian was still standing next to me, trying to figure out if she should be concerned for my well-being or hers.

I looked up and asked her, "What time is it?"

"It's, it's seven—7:54, sir."

"Seven fifty-four?! P.m.? A.m.? You gotta be more specific with me here."

"A.m., sir."

The librarian flinched as I aggressively stood up, shoving all my belongings into the most disheveled pile. My shirt was a mess, my coat buttons mismatched, one sleeve rolled up, and my tie as crooked as a politician. I cursed to myself as I ran out the door, dropping books throughout the library as the quiet bookworms tilted their heads to see if an eccentric really did exist.

I didn't have time to run home and get cleaned up, I just had to go to work as is. I believe I did the most running I had ever done in my life during that summer. Boy, I'll tell ya, the fear of getting fired will definitely put a little fizz in your pop. I had never missed a day of work before, and I was not going to let that be the day.

Chapter Sixteen

I ran directly from the monotone South of Sunset public library straight to the factory without even glancing at my reflection in the storefront windows. I had tunnel vision to get to work on time. Once I reached the factory, I saw the Fleurs' black-and-silver town car parked out front. Franklin looked like he was talking to himself in the driver's seat, making animated facial expressions. He was probably practicing some offbeat character for an audience that would never get the chance to hear him. I ran over, already late, and hit his glass window in a desperate attempt to win some time back. I startled him midsentence and he looked over at me like a deer in headlights. He immediately got the hint to stop daydreaming and unlock the car door. I jumped into the back seat as if he were my getaway driver and I the last robber standing in a heist gone sour. Franklin asked me what happened as he examined my disheveled, grungy appearance and my half-undone coat.

"I was up all night studying and—"

"Well, I would've done a lot more . . . 'studying' back in

school if I knew that's what the kids were calling it. Ay, ay." He laughed as he clumsily reached into the back seat and poked me in the arm.

I swatted away his lanky arm and motioned for him to hit the road. Franklin finally turned his head around and did his job . . . driving.

"Hey, at least you're smelling better than the first day I met ya," he joked.

I laughed along, hoping he'd change the subject.

"So, who's the lucky lady?" Franklin asked out of the blue.

"Franklin, it's not a lady," I answered, realizing he must've seriously believed my unkempt appearance was due to a wild night with an even wilder lover.

"Ohhh, okay, okay. I see, pal. That does make a lot more sense now. Ya know, Chef Anthony was saying he thought you were cute and—"

"What? No."

"Whoa, whoa. No need to get elevated here. I'll just tell him you're already seeing someone, jeez. I'm sure your man is very grateful to have a loyal guy like you around."

"My man?! What? Franklin, I'm not seeing anybody. Guy, gal, no one."

"Well, you and Gloria seem like you're getting pretty cozy."

"Gloria . . . pshhh. I could never. She's about as appealing as a cold steak."

"A cold steak, huh?" Franklin's eyebrow raised, creating a ripple in his forehead. As we entered the Fleur Estate grounds, he laughed as if he had seen it all. "Well, congratulations, my friend. You're the only young man who's ever set foot on this property and not found her beautiful. Seriously, I commend you. You are one lucky son of a bitch."

"Oh yeah? She's got a bunch of suitors, huh?"

"What do you think?"

Gloria came into view as she walked out the front door wearing a tangerine-colored dress. She floated down the steps to the driveway.

"Great, must be over a hundred, then!"

"I thought you said she was unappealing."

"Physically she's alright, but personality, ohhh—"

"Trust me, I know. I'm the one who has to drive around the poor fools that try and date her. People want someone who is their mirror image, but never a mirror. Gloria's a mirror. She shows them their true selves. Makes them look at an unbiased, unfiltered reflection. Most fellas don't like that. Time and time again, a guy falls for her, thinking she's beautiful, then runs like the wind when he realizes he got more than he bargained for."

"Ha! You can say that again."

As I said that, the door was swung open by the subject of our conversation.

"Say what again?" Gloria's chin stuck out as Franklin and I turned silent for a moment . . . like two fools.

"That you have a great, uhhh . . ." I stammered, unsure of what compliment to give Gloria to assure her we weren't bagging on her. My eyes began to scan, and Franklin luckily finished my sentence.

"Personality," Franklin shouted.

Gloria immediately looked down at her chest, examining the area I'd recklessly stared at the other day.

"So that's what they're calling them now? Just yesterday Oleander called them heels."

I immediately felt a knot in my throat as Franklin looked at me. "Cold steak, huh?"

I hurried out of the car as Franklin obnoxiously laughed at my expense. He drove away as I went through the front door with the not-so-oblivious Gloria.

"Is that what you had for dinner last night?"

I just mumbled, trying to find my footing once again.

"Cold steak?" Gloria clarified.

"Ohhh, yeah. I wasn't feeling very well this morning. That's why I look like this right now. I didn't have time to get ready." I laughed in relief.

"Aw, well, that's okay. Come upstairs, I am sure my dad has an extra suit for you somewhere."

"Oh. Well, I don't know if I feel comfortable—"

"Come on, quit your moping. I insist."

"Well—"

"Well, what? You got a problem, don't you? Well, I got a solution."

I followed her up the stairs, not knowing what to say. Not only was she forcing me to cross the line of professionalism, but she was also involving Mr. Fleur by offering up his wardrobe. Nevertheless, I took the bait, letting life be in control of me.

After tiptoeing up the spiraling staircase and walking down a large corridor lined with oil portraits, we ended in front of a large wooden door with gold trim. In the middle of the door was a placard engraved with the initials *GEF* and hand-carved ivy surrounding the edges. This was Gloria's room. I've still never found out what the *E* stood for, maybe something pretty like Elenore or Evelyn. They might as well have made her middle name Explosive or Extreme or Exactly Everything Exciting on Earth. Any of those would have suited her just fine.

As we entered her room, it served as a visual representation of Gloria Exactly Everything Exciting on Earth Fleur's mind. Fabrics upon fabrics were thrown all over the incredible suite, as if her clothes were part of the decor. On one wall stood a vanity with sparkling perfume bottles and lotions sprawled across it. If inanimate objects had opinions, my swanky bar cart would definitely have thought that exquisite setup was out of its league. The oval mirror on top of the vanity was surrounded by vibrant coral-colored amaryllis flowers. Those mean self-esteem, pride, and confidence. Maybe I ought to put those in front of my mirror nowadays when I get ready for work, as my wrinkles have me resembling a Shar-Pei. Reflecting back, I wish I would've appreciated everything I was so self-conscious about as a young man.

Gloria's room made my pigsty look tame. She scrambled around her nest, picking up a green shoe here and a turquoise robe there, shuffling items into piles to make herself feel better. "Sorry, it's kind of a mess right now. Well, actually, it's always a mess, but uhh . . . ya know, it's hard to find time, and uhhh . . . oh! Where are my manners?! Have a seat. Um, stay. Just . . . ya know what, I'll be right back and uhhh . . . yeah! Okay!" Gloria frantically rushed out the door.

At that point I was trying not to shit myself. It was the first time I had ever seen Gloria nervous or even the slightest bit awkward. I had no idea what she was going to try and pull. Worse than that, Mr. Fleur could walk in and see his employee sitting on the edge of his daughter's bed. Talk about unprofessional. Oh boy, if Mr. Fleur saw me—I should've started writing my will right then and there. I stood up in a panic, not knowing what to do about the predicament I was in.

Oh, this is bad! This is really, really bad!

I paced back and forth. I grabbed my forehead and finally rallied myself to walk out the door. My plan was to leave and say I left my notepad at home, then I'd clean up and come right back. It wasn't foolproof, but at least it was a step in the right direction. But due to a step in the wrong direction, I passed by Gloria's decadent vanity. The young man in the reflection had wrinkled clothes, greasy hair falling in front of his face, and skin as clammy as someone who'd eaten a Carolina Reaper. I could not leave her bedroom looking like that. If anyone saw me, no story I told would suffice. All I had was Franklin as a witness to my pre-Gloria sloppiness. I had to wait it out and hope for the best. My life at that moment was in Gloria's careless hands.

After a few minutes passed, the cavalry finally arrived. Gloria had a dozen ties wrapped around her neck and a pile of rich-looking suits draped across her forearms. She announced her heroism as she laid out the suits on her designated pile chair.

"Did you stop by the shoe department while you were shopping? Enough time has passed that I started growing gray hairs!"

"Trust me, me taking a while isn't the reason for your gray hairs . . . sweet Oleander." She softly laughed.

"Sweet?" I could feel myself growing nervous. I was in uncharted waters.

"Well." Gloria paused as she walked toward me. Her focus locked in on me as she came closer. In the blink of an eye, her face turned from enchanted to shocked. "You're sweating like a pig!"

I felt my breath grow heavier and heavier the closer she came. I was tormented by what I should do.

"Are you feeling okay?" She sighed as she sat next to me.

"Yeah, I mean, no! Umm—"

"It must be that cold steak Frank was talking about earlier."

"Yeah, you're right. It definitely is the cold steak!" I smirked on the inside. I knew the true meaning.

Gloria stood back up and rushed to the bathroom. I could hear the faucet run as she huffed in concern. She came back into view with a wet rag in her hands and a dry smile. She sat back down next to me and placed the cloth on my forehead gently as she said, "This should help."

The mildew smell of the rag Gloria's hand pressed against my forehead was familiar, like a day off school. I felt taken care of. Even if it was on false pretenses, I sure felt better.

"How does your head feel now?"

"It's okay."

"Are you still warm?"

"I don't know—"

Gloria removed the damp towel and placed the back of her hand on my forehead to check. "It's hard to tell." She pulled her hand away, then grabbed my head with both her hands and pressed her lips to my forehead, double-checking my "fever." I'd just had a cold rag on my head, so she couldn't legitimately feel if I was a bucket of ice or boiling water. She'd touched my face because she'd wanted to. As she pulled her mouth away, I caught myself in a daze.

"You don't feel like you have a temperature," she stated.

I didn't listen to a word she said, I just leaned in to kiss her as if it were inevitable.

Gloria jerked away from my face in horror, offended by my lewd attempt to attach my lips to hers. "Whoa! What are you doing?"

"Oh, oh . . . I am so sorry! I thought that you wanted to—"

"What?! Catch whatever the hell you have? No thank you!" She stood up straight as an arrow, aggressively pointed to the stack of suits she'd delicately laid out, and shouted, "There are five suits on the chair to choose from, the navy is my favorite. Have at it!"

Gloria marched out the door in an angry manner and slammed it behind her, leaving me in disbelief on the edge of her bed. I was mortified. *What have I done?!* I had to calm myself down and stick to the one battle I had a history with: getting dressed. I went with the advised choice and put on the navy suit. The option of neckties ranged from black pinstripes to wild pink paisley. I went with a plain red tie that, in hindsight, made me look like a political candidate, but in that moment, it felt like the best option. After all, I was going to be on trial by Judge Gloria for my heinous crime.

I then went into her bathroom and turned on the gold swan-shaped faucet. The soft water ran through my fingertips, slowly warming to the temperature of a perfect day. Even the water North of Sunset was different—even the water was different. I damped my hair and slicked it back the best I could with my mitts. I went underneath Gloria's sink to find nothing in there, no hair gel, no combs, not even bamboo paper. For the girl who could have everything, she had nothing I considered a basic necessity.

I looked in the mirror.

Good enough!

After ten minutes of double- and triple-checking that I looked presentable, I walked out of Gloria's bedroom, keeping my head on a constant swivel for peering eyes. I tiptoed down the stairs, ready to freeze if I heard the rustle of footsteps. Luckily, not a soul was in sight.

Once I reached the main level, I rushed through the house, trying to find the quickest way to the greenhouse. Not looking where I was going, I bumped into Gloria . . . the last person I wanted to see. She smiled at me with her mischievous grin, rolling her mood over as well as a trained canine.

"Well, look at you! You must be feeling better."

"Oh, I am. Thanks for helping me out . . . nurse." I smiled back, not sure if Gloria was over the incident upstairs or playing nice since we were standing right in front of Mr. Fleur's office.

She nodded politely and began to walk past me. I noticed a flower in her hand, an odd flower. I stopped her, knowing that the flower was the cryptic key to her mood that morning.

"What do you have there?"

"Wouldn't you like to know." Gloria smirked.

I cocked my head sideways as I took one last peek at the flower dangling desperately in her hand, just as I was. I tried to scroll through the files in my head of all the flower species that were similar to that peculiar-looking one, as Gloria continued with her facade.

"You look sharp, but I kinda liked you better before."

"What? When I looked like a mess?"

"Yeah, it was endearing. Showed me you're actually human."

"Human?"

Gloria walked away, swinging the flower in her hand as she went through Mr. Fleur's office doors while I stood in the hall. As those large wooden doors swung more aggressively than the poor plant in Gloria's grip, I saw Mr. Fleur sitting at his desk. He and I made eye contact. He scrunched his forehead as he looked up at my coat. He seemed confused and borderline appalled when he noticed what I was wearing. Soon, the door shut, giving me an opening for a swift exit to safety.

As I walked away, I could faintly hear Mr. Fleur say, "Is there a reason Oleander is wearing my suit, Gloria?"

I quickly headed for the greenhouse. I would wait there in solitude for the guards to throw me out rather than feel the wrath of Mr. Fleur himself. After all, my life was in Gloria's hands. She could make up a lie and save me or throw me under the bus faster than a snap. Having little to no control over the situation at that point, I decided to try and decode the flower that held Gloria's mood for the day. I skimmed through the pages, trying to identify that magenta flower that still had moments to live.

"Aha! A red catchfly!" I rejoiced to myself.

After figuring out what the flower was, I put down my first

textbook and rummaged through the never-ending stack on the greenhouse floor. There it was. The key. The book of floriography. Growing more impatient, I couldn't move my fingers as fast as my head wanted them to go. I flipped page after page, frantically grabbing too many at a time and having to go back to make sure I didn't miss it.

Found it. Red catchfly. Meaning: I've fallen victim to . . . youthful love.

Youthful love? I shut the book in a panic.

Chapter Seventeen

I sat in the flower-covered greenhouse that late morning, baffled, as the sun grew higher in the sky. My senses felt heightened and a knot suddenly appeared in my stomach. I don't know if I can fully explain the feeling of knowing that someone considers you in the highest regard, but to put it bluntly, it was exhilarating. Out of everyone on this tragedy-filled planet, I was the one who did something for her. I affected her in the soul, the place where the most historic events in someone's life occur. The sun beat down on my back through the clear glass as I foolishly spaced out due to an overdose of flattery.

Gloria roared through the greenhouse door, acting the same way she always did, showcasing her teeth as bright as moonglow. She continued on as if nothing had changed, but she seemed different to me. I stood up to greet her in a gentlemanly manner, but to my dismay, my pants did not get the message. Being a few sizes too large, my trousers started sagging, so I had to hike them up above my waist.

"Hi, Droopy Drawers!"

I laughed it off as we both sat down on the concrete ledge inside the greenhouse, with only a few books between us.

"I hope your father is not mad I'm wearing his suit."

"Oh, no, I explained everything to him."

"Everything?"

Gloria began to laugh. "Well, I guess not everything."

I sighed; my faith in Gloria's judgment had been mildly restored.

"Again, I am incredibly sorry. I completely read that whole situation wrong," I admitted.

"No, you read it right."

Now, I've never been one for eye contact, in fact, in my younger years I avoided it, but in that moment, that was all I wanted. As if I had been starved for human connection and Gloria's eyes were the first I'd had the honor of looking into after many lonely years. I stared and stared, longing for that connection, but did not receive it. For Gloria just began turning the pages of her book, pretending that she had not just professed her love to me. There I sat, once again, like a fool, waiting on the go-ahead from the Ice Queen of Sunset Boulevard.

Gloria began talking business once more, rambling on about the cosmo flower species and how incredible they were. I sat there with my scuffed-up shoes facing her, still staring, waiting for her to justify her comment. My shoulders pushed two and a half inches back the moment Gloria looked up at me.

"You taking notes?" She motioned to the pen in my useless hand.

"Huh? Oh." I started writing in calligraphy one level neater than a caveman as Gloria continued.

"So, as I was saying . . . cosmos are very resilient flowers. They bloom even in poor soil conditions and can handle multiple climates. They're kind of pretty little things."

I chuckled. "Resilient, pretty little things. Reminds me of someone I know."

"Anyways." Gloria looked down as her face turned the color of a pink azalea.

Gloria's humbleness was one of the many admirable qualities about her. She knew who she was and was sure of herself. It was as if her wisdom was a secret and her strong morals were an unspoken code of ethics. She was far above the rest of us and we knew it. Hell, she knew it too, but would never let on. In that moment, Gloria's and my relationship switched from foes to friends.

After that emotionally monsoonal morning, the days passed like a drunken vacation on the coast of a foreign land. Our time spent together started out as mornings of focused hard work and departing in the early afternoons, then eventually our responsible mornings turned into croissant breaks, gallivanting around the property, and me leaving just as the sun set after eight o'clock in the evening, accompanied by a disappointed look from Gloria. The flowers placed carefully in Mr. Fleur's coat pocket also progressed, switching as quickly as the summer rain. With every "Mornin', Glory," Mr. Fleur spoke, his heart probably broke a little more. Innocent lilies meaning "I am walking on air" soon turned into threatening lavenders pledging loyalty and devotion.

After all, Mr. Fleur had predicted his fate the first day I arrived at Fleur Estate, when I'd sat at that Renaissance piano and he'd described a sunset on a golden hill. All that he'd mentioned in that moment was exactly what I experienced later on, one evening with Gloria. We sat on a hill as we watched a sunset with the most exquisite shades of raspberry and lemon, and it proved to be the most beautiful sunset I had ever experienced. The vision of a silhouette holding my hand that I'd had in that daydream turned out to be Gloria as she sat beside me one day after work. We watched the sun tuck away behind the blanket-covered mountains as bugs started to come out and dance. I woke up the following morning with bug bites sprinkled across my arms like constellations, but I never said a word to Gloria. For she wanted to dance with the bugs that evening, floating around and stinging where it hurt the most. She begged me to dance with her, but I turned her down due to my immense self-consciousness masked by my more immense desire for the perfect self-identity.

"I don't dance, Gloria."

"Well, I do." Gloria continued twirling, not missing a beat or a partner.

The fondness I had for Gloria grew like a pleasant jazz tune you'd hear broadcast over the radio. It was captivating enough to leave on, warm in sound, and the entire melody played out before the lyrics even started. This left me feeling like I already knew it. Gloria would say she loved music with her whole heart, but I found that hard to believe. Everything that evoked a positive reaction from her now had her whole heart . . . including me. Maybe she had nineteen hearts? It was easy to believe that with the way she loved things that brought her joy. Same went for the things that brought her grief; she despised those things with her whole heart—the kind of deep-rooted hatred that one hopes is never sent in their direction.

Gloria's body served as a location for all her nineteen "whole hearts," as if each one was a large estate similar to the ones in Bel Air. They were separated, unaware of their neighbors, built with immense love and care. Every large property was unique and grand in its own way. My heart was more like an overcrowded apartment building. Each room compartmentalized, only allowed to take up so much space. Gloria should've been evicted from that place a long time ago, but there she was, trespassing in others' apartments that weren't hers, jumping on their couches and drinking their champagne.

There are some things that will always be around, and champagne is one of them. I turn down drinking nowadays since my intestines are looking more like Swiss cheese, but back in those days I said yes to any form of indulgence. People have known for hundreds upon hundreds of years that alcohol is poison, so why do we still drink it? Maybe because we fear missing good times or maybe because it is the earliest form of keeping people at peace. Yes, you will get fools in a drunken rage or experience a bar fight now and then, but throughout time it has been the ultimate peacekeeper. You can get rid of many things, but alcohol isn't one of them.

Of course, the government has tried other tactics of keeping civilians at peace, but all of those backfired far worse. Medicines created by pharmaceutical companies was a big one two hundred years ago, then a huge operation in the 2050s happened, shutting down every major pharmaceutical company of the time. We still have medicine, of course, for only those who truly need it. A second tactic, which I learned about in junior high, was screen sedatives. The initial goal of smartphones was to turn the people complacent, losing motivation or self-esteem so they wouldn't rise against the government. The government would constantly throw ridiculous material in front of their faces so when the outrageous truths appeared, exposing the government, no one paid attention to them and wasn't even shocked. After that experiment was cut off in World War Four, the population decreased quite a bit after the tragic death of the Internet. The future looked uncertain to those whose income or well-being was dependent on the Internet. Overnight: savings lost, jobs lost, passions lost . . . purpose lost. I can relate to those post the Great Crash.

Feeling lost and unsure of the outcome is like water that never stops spinning down the drain.

Since I brought up spinning, let's talk about the one who was the best at doing it out of control, especially in places she shouldn't. The beautiful heiress, Gloria "Everything" Fleur.

Chapter Eighteen

The summer matured as time sailed by easily and unapologetically. Our project of testing and researching flowers was handled either not efficiently enough or too efficiently, because we had a lot of free time on our hands as we waited for results from the different experiments. Gloria, who could afford everything, was the best at buying time.

"Why did your parents name you Oleander?"

"I don't know."

"Ohhh, I don't buy that. I'm sure you've asked them the very same question." Gloria stepped up to a hand-laid stone wall that stood on the far end of the property. She grabbed my wrist, guiding me along the perimeter to an opening in the wall.

"Well, to be truthful, they gave me ever-changing answers as the years passed. I still don't know the real reason. At first, it was that my father wanted to name me Alexander and my mother disliked the commonality of it. So her compromise was giving him 'ander' and I guess 'Ole' was the only thing that went decently with it, besides *S-L*. Another theory is that she started painting a lot of flowers then too, so I think everything followed in suit. That's how my mother operated . . . on a day-to-day basis."

"That's the only way to operate."

"That's how it feels lately." I sighed.

"I'm taking you around this way, it's a far better view."

As we reached the other end of the wall, the hill sloped down to reveal a hundred acres of rose fields. Rows upon rows of crimson streamed like blood on the land, looking like the five red stripes on the American flag, except it was landscaped with hundreds. An overpoweringly floral fragrance filled the air—like a women's department store.

"This is one of the locations where we grow the roses. Too bad we can't grow humans the same way for the experiment." Gloria laughed as she nudged my arm.

I curled my lips politely in a half smile at her morbid joke.

"Onward . . . the Great Oleander!"

We shuffled horizontally down the dirt hill, Gloria in front of me. Three green specks moved through the rows in unison as we made our way to the foot of the hill. Gloria tapped my shoulder and we headed down a row.

"This is my best-loved place. I come down here to hide away from life's responsibilities."

What responsibilities?

"Some days, when I'm feeling unbearably lonesome, I lie in the dirt," Gloria said as she crept down so the flowers were above her head. She moved her flattened hand along the ground. "I run my hands along it. Even though it holds rocks, it feels like satin on your palms. Then, when you come to think of it, you're walking on satin. That makes life not look so bad. And the people below it are just sleeping under a satin blanket. Makes it sound a whole lot comfier, huh?"

"Let's be a little more light, why don't we?" I wanted to

change the subject. Her talking about death made the flower field we were standing in feel like a celebration-of-life ceremony.

"You're so right! We're the follies of Sunset, darling!" She lifted her arm in a ballet-like pose as she began to twirl down the field, humming loudly enough for the three jokesters in their dark-green jumpsuits, whom I'd met my first day, to look up for a moment. They went back to work, unfazed, but my shoulders caved in as I looked around to see if anyone else had seen us.

"Da da, da da dum. Dum dum, da da da! That's a tune my great-great-grandma wrote. I found the sheet music in her belongings." Gloria continued to sing the unknown folk song from a hundred years ago. "Cotton candy sunsets. Blues, pinks, yellows, reds. Smell of popcorn in the aiiirrr!"

"Gloria, shhh. You need to calm down."

"The rides never lasted long, the sugar melted on our tongues, but kids like us . . . ha! We don't care."

I continued walking behind her as she sang her melody about carnivals and a Ferris wheel world.

"Please, Gloria."

"Oh, come on! You're no fun!"

"I can have fun!"

"Uh-huh." She continued singing, "The man with the top hat would sing out loud 'Come watch the acrobats fly!' I laugh 'cause they never fall, love's not like that at all . . . There's not a net every tiiime!"

"There is such a thing as time and place, Gloria."

"No such thing. Right now is always the right time and place!"

She continued dancing as I gave her a look, pleading with her to be serious. Well, I got what I asked for. She abruptly stopped and threw up her hands in frustration.

"That's the issue with people nowadays! When they want

to dance, they get stiff as a board. When they want to sing, they stay silent. When they want to smile, they keep their lips straight."

She faced her whole body to me. "When they want to tell someone how they really feel, they do anything in their power not to say the word *love*. How does that even make sense?"

"Well, I think a lot of people are afraid." I avoided eye contact.

"Of what?"

"Love . . . getting hurt."

"But that's not love!"

I sneered at her ignorance. *Can someone really be this unaware?*

Maybe Gloria was oversimplifying love or maybe I was overcomplicating it. After all, it is a language far and few in between have successfully translated. For some it's like gambling, they would bet all they have on a promising hand in hopes that they'll win big. As time goes by, their soul's fortune is chipped away dollar by dollar, and soon they hope to just walk away with a number close to what they started with. That was my opinion of love, but Gloria had a very different outlook on it.

"Heartbreak, betrayal, whatever else people say stinks, should not be grouped in with love! It may be disguised as love at the time, but that's not what it is at all. Those terrible things happen when it's not love," Gloria shouted as she moved through the roses.

"Well, imagine you love someone and it doesn't work out."

"Imagine you love someone and it works out for the rest of your life! That's a possibility too, ya know." Gloria stretched out her arms, resembling a California condor.

I shook my head. "Okay, okay. It's just hard to fathom."

"Not really." Gloria gazed directly at me as she tilted her head sideways a bit. She looked as if she were a new puppy that had just gotten in trouble. She was upset and confused as to what she had done wrong leading up to that point. She looked deeply hurt and tortured by my skeptical words, but at that time, I didn't think twice about it.

Gloria reached over to pick a rose.

"You don't wanna do that!"

"Why not?" Her tone grew bitter.

"Well, you don't want your pretty hands getting all cut up from the thorns," I sternly said.

"These pretty hands?" She showed me her dirt-covered palms.

I grabbed the handkerchief out of my coat pocket. "Let's fix this. You're a disaster." I wiped the dirt off her hands as her face lost its resentful demeanor. "Trust me. My job at the factory is cutting those bad boys off."

"Hands?"

"No, you fool. Thorns. Almost lost a finger last month." I roughly finished wiping her hands and sighed. "You should take better care of things. They'll last you much longer."

"I don't care about stuff lasting long."

"It shows." I walked away.

Gloria timidly followed me back up the hill, holding her dress up so it didn't drag in the dirt. As we trudged across the uneven ground, my footing slipped.

"Dammit!"

I immediately folded my body forward, placing both hands on the ground to catch myself. Once I felt steady, I slowly came to a standing position once again. I lifted my hands and turned them inward to see my palms. They were covered in dirt.

"Ha! Hahaha!" Gloria crossed her arms over her stomach.

"Not a word!"

Her cracking up halted, and she continued to walk up the hill. I was behind her, wiping my hands and grumbling to myself. The sun began to set as we reached the front steps of the house. The dry air brushed my throat, making me realize I hadn't drunk any water that day.

"I'm curious. Do you really think it's hard to fathom love lasting?" Gloria's direct question was uncalled for.

"Ya know, my head is really pounding. I think I better head home." I looked at Franklin, who was standing by the car on the other side of the driveway. I waved him over. Gloria gave me a farewell, sprinkled with a look of concern, as she headed into the house. Her head was down and she fidgeted with her hands, concentrating as if she were knitting with invisible yarn. Once I met up with Franklin, he greeted me in a less-enthused but still-kind manner.

We spent the ride back to South of Sunset talking about the recent auditions Franklin had gone to. Over the past month that I'd spent playing cat and mouse with Gloria, Franklin had ignited his desire to get back into voice acting. The rides home got progressively more interesting each day as his characters started to take form. From the trials and tribulations of old French ladies to Italian nighttime mechanics, Franklin kept me entertained. Sometimes he would even get close to crashing the car because he'd gotten so into using both his hands as acting tools. But Franklin almost driving us off a cliff was the least of my worries.

Chapter Nineteen

I remember the next day turning into a miraculous one, but it started out bland like any other. That's how some of the most memorable days start. Gloria and I spent the morning eliminating a few more flower species from the list. We weren't at the final three yet, but we were getting awfully darn close. My clothes were already sticking to me that morning as the humidity rose to 70 percent. The job was fairly easy, but what made it difficult was all the distractions. Hell, life was one big distraction. When I would try to reel Gloria in to complete a task, her focus would last thirty minutes tops. When I would try to finish the work at home, police sirens would go off outside or my neighbors would be having a party. If I tried to go somewhere public, like a library or café, to get work done, strangers would either disrupt my train of thought or the walk there alone would tire me out. Maybe I was incompetent and unable to focus due to others' irresponsibility or maybe others were the incompetent ones, running around life as if they were circus acts, performing for attention.

"Gloria! Oleander! Shake the dust off your bones. Let's go to the laboratory!"

Today's performance was by the boss himself. Mr. Fleur came marching into the greenhouse with no hello or explanation as Gloria and I sat on a ledge, sifting through the photographs of each flower coated in gold.

"What's happening?" Gloria asked. Even she was caught off guard.

"What isn't?" Mr. Fleur waved his hand quickly. "Come on, come on!"

We both got up quickly and stiffly and followed him outside. He wore a Payne's gray suit with a peony in his pocket. Those flowers mean a whole lot of different things, all positive, though, like wealth and romance. Gloria was lovely that morning, so it made sense. I sometimes wished Mr. Fleur would give her a flower; he was much harder to read—all smoke and mirrors, but I wanted to believe every word he spoke was rooted in truth.

"I'm taking you kids around the back, behind the garage. Franklin is going to meet us at the back gate."

"Why?" Gloria asked.

Mr. Fleur's eyes narrowed at Gloria for a millisecond, then he continued walking. We reached the front of a twelve-car garage covered in ivy with walnut-stained garage doors. We didn't stop there, though. We traced along the perimeter of that building until we reached the back, where Franklin was waiting with the town car.

"I tried, Mr. F. I really did try to get him to—"

"Franklin, is the back gate open?"

"Oh, yes, sir." Franklin nodded cowardly as he got in the vehicle.

Mr. Fleur was acting mysteriously vague, sitting shotgun

while Gloria and I stepped through the back door, taking our expected seats. We exited out the back gate and looped around to the street. As we drove past the main entrance of the Fleur Estate, I saw a man standing by the front gate—waiting. That strange figure lifted his chin, trying to peer through the closed gate. His head quickly snapped in our direction, too late, as we passed by. He stared for a moment, then he turned back to face the gate; his silhouette grew smaller and smaller in the rearview.

Franklin drove us further north, up a large green hill. When I looked down on the Fleur Estate from afar, the aerial view revealed a sea of green sprinkled with pink, and fields of scarlet running behind it.

"That is one of the many rose farms we have," Mr. Fleur stated, pointing to the red.

"Wow."

"Dad owns probably no less than three hundred thousand acres of rose farms across the country," Gloria boasted.

"It is true, but a lot of my wealth isn't from roses," Mr. Fleur admitted.

How did he get rich? Who was that guy at the gate? Where are we going?

The brakes creaked as we reached an art deco tollbooth.

"Seventy-five dollars, sir," said the polished man inside the booth.

I watched Mr. Fleur hand Franklin a wad of $10,000 as he said, "Here you go. Tell him to keep the change."

The toll worker's copper eyes almost popped right out of his head like two pennies when Franklin's bony hand slapped the cash in his palm.

"Thank you, sir! Thank you, sir! Thank you! Thank you!"

We left the man rambling in his little green booth as we drove onto the Sunset Bridge. Mr. Fleur looked out his window, toward the 405 River below. "This city is building back up too fast."

After reaching the other side, we took a windy path carved through the mountain range as if it were a scurrying mouse, frantically turning and running back and forth. That was the nicest I had ever seen Franklin drive, no burnouts, no drifting in the town car—just proceeding slowly with both hands on the steering wheel.

We stopped in front of a large brass gate that read *Fleur Industries*. This was the place—Mr. Fleur's extravagant laboratory. A smile crept up on Mr. Fleur's face, as if his inner child peeked through, proud of all that he had accomplished. As Mr. Fleur sat in the passenger seat, silently gloating to himself, Franklin rolled down the driver's window. The car was about one foot too far from the buzzer. Franklin reached out his lanky arm toward the buzzer, his wrist bent in the most uncomfortable-looking way. He finally pressed it.

Beeep.

"Welcome, Mr. Fleur. Franklin, you're good to come in." The voice over the intercom was opposite to old Scott back at the Fleur Estate. The voice was calm, polite, young in tone, and lastly, likable.

The gate opened in a less elegant way than the gate at the Fleurs' home, but it was still an exciting experience. The front of the building was white with sky-blue glass windows and balconies covered in tiles that curved around it. That enormous structure's architecture was very New Formalism, popular hundreds of years ago. It looked extremely familiar to me.

I remember! It was one of the first things I saw when I entered Southern California. I took the ferry down the old 405 River one day and saw it to the right of me, high up on the hill.

It stood out because it looked awfully different than the buildings I had seen on the East Coast; it was very outdated to say the least. Interestingly enough, the inside was as up to date as a new puppy. As we walked through the doors of Fleur's buzzing laboratory, flashes of lab coats passed by us every minute. This operation was far larger than I'd anticipated. I should've expected it, knowing how the Fleur family operated. Mr. Fleur had bought that large building twenty years ago, when it was about to be torn down. He said it was a decrepit mess that was destroyed during World War Four; he'd bought it directly from the city. Mr. Fleur had this knack for fixing things that were broken, whether places or people, that's where his real purpose lay. He explained to me how over a hundred years ago that laboratory had been a beautiful art museum for folks to stroll around in.

"It was founded in 1953 by an oil tycoon that turned part of his ranch home into a museum where people could admire his art just as much as he did," Mr. Fleur said as we walked down the wide lobby. "Years later, in the twenty-first century, people started going just so they could go on screen sedative binges. My grandmother told me they would show up in the late afternoon, take photographs and film themselves at the museum, then leave. Very odd. Soon, the museum had to do something about it, as it was getting out of control. There was no way to manage crowds of people blocking the exhibits just to take photos of themselves. The museum tried to ban smart-phones in the building, but once that rule was passed in museums across America, not enough people showed up to cover costs. Without their devices, they couldn't boast about their extremely cultured day on the Internet, and there was no point in them paying money to view items they could see online for free."

"That is so sad," whispered Gloria.

"Only people that truly wanted to learn about art and history went, but the government shut that down real quick. They turned all the museums and historic buildings in California into shelters for the homeless."

"I thought museums were a new thing in the US?" I didn't know they were around a hundred years ago. In college we were taught that America had just started building museums twenty years ago, finally following in Europe's footsteps of curiosity closets. I wondered what had happened to the housing shelters. I'd only seen a homeless man once in my life, as a child somewhere in the Midwest. *Where did they all go?*

Anyways, I learned years later that the shabby, run-down apartment building I lived in at the time used to house homeless people in the 2040s. Decades before that, it had been a beautiful luxury Sears department store filled with 1,360 roller-skating employees. Time changes so much, but that didn't concern Mr. Fleur. He worked in the business of stopping time.

We walked up spiraling stairs, the glass ceiling towering above us. I told Mr. Fleur that Gloria and I had narrowed down the choices of flower species for the collection to five. He congratulated me on our progress and reiterated the deadline of September 1.

"We will definitely make the deadline, sir."

"*Deadline.* Ugh, I hate that word! It's so gruesome," interjected Gloria.

Mr. Fleur and I looked over at her, wondering where all that bottled up rage had come from.

"Ya know that term came from prisons, right?" Gloria asked us.

"No."

"It was a line they'd draw, and if a prisoner crossed it"— Gloria held up her hand to make a finger gun—"Boom! He'd get shot by a guard!"

"Thank you for that lovely fact, Gloria," replied Mr. Fleur.

"It's true."

We laughed at Gloria's strange ways, and headed through a pair of large golden doors. We slowly walked down a carpeted hallway that had windows running along the left side of it. The windows looked onto rooms filled with scientists performing tests and serums and bottles all over the place. From flowers sprawled on tables to research groups taking notes while interviewing people, that place was dysfunctional.

"Right now, we are in the testing stages to perfect the formula that dissolves the Fleur Atom Immunizing Technological Health from the system," Mr. Fleur said, as if he were trying to make an excuse for the chaos.

"The process must be just as extensive as the name," I joked with him.

He laughed. "Well, typically, yes."

"They started working on it only five months ago and are almost finished. Isn't that incredible?" Gloria smiled.

"It's very impressive," I replied, making sure Mr. Fleur heard me.

"We've fast-tracked the process due to the pressure of circumstances," he said.

The medical field was a very competitive industry, and still is, so I understood why Mr. Fleur was rushing to complete that experiment. The last thing he would want is someone getting hold of his technology and winning all the fame.

"I won't tell a soul," I said to him.

"Thank you. We are trying to keep this under wraps for now. Ya know, liability reasons. I'm sure you understand. That's what that man was doing at the front gate, trying to snoop. We don't want anything leaking before we are prepared."

"Oh boy, if word gets out about this, the demand will be through the roof," shouted Gloria.

"Or there will be an uproar," I murmured under my breath.

"Well, that's expected with anything you do, Oleander. High risk, high reward," Mr. Fleur said.

"Oh, the reward will be priceless," Gloria said as scientists waved to her through the glass.

"Oh, I bet." I added, "There are a lot of loonies out there that would pay to see flying houses or a time when smartphones make a comeback. Pshhh, like the Prohibition of Screen Sedatives will last."

"Well, recreational purposes are not the primary reason for this," Mr. Fleur responded.

"Maybe eventually," said Gloria.

I turned to face both of them, letting my mouth run wild. "I'm sure if you guys can do this, you can create the technology to make humans live forever. The line would be around the corner for that."

"Yeah!" Gloria egged me on.

"If you invented that, you'd probably make double, even triple what you're making from this. Being preserved for a later time . . . great. But living forever? Untouchable," I enthusiastically stated as Gloria giggled.

She was amused by my idea, but Mr. Fleur was not.

"No, no, no! I am not doing this to make money. Living forever would upset the world dynamic far beyond our comprehension. Even if I had the technology to make it happen, I would never go through with it."

"Well, I would," I replied, pushing back a little.

Mr. Fleur shook his head at me in disagreement and looked me in the eyes. "Oleander, listen carefully to what I'm about to say. Okay?"

I nodded, letting him have the stage. I remember word for word the exact speech he gave me that day.

"You wouldn't be on the search for eternity if you felt you'd lived your life to its fullest and done all you wanted to do in your ninety years. That'd be enough, right? You'd be satisfied."

"Well—"

Mr. Fleur raised his finger, motioning for me to let him continue. "You wouldn't want to live forever if you hated your life either. If every day was a living hell, why would you want to endure more of it? So why are humans constantly on the search to live forever?"

Silence.

He continued, "It's because they're creatures of habit. They fear the unknown. They don't like change."

"Well, they like a certain type of change." Gloria rubbed her fingers together, symbolizing money.

Mr. Fleur laughed back. "Yes, they are also greedy. People think one more dollar, one more minute, one more day, one more year, maybe even one more life! Just one more go around, that's all I need to get it right. Ya know, to win!"

"Don't I know it," I whispered.

"But what is winning?" Mr. Fleur continued. "It's an internal battle. You know that! If we can't find peace within, peace we will be without. People blame the world for their misfortune, forgetting they make up the world. They are their surroundings. Everything they say and do causes a chain reaction. Even their thoughts alone affect their external circumstances. The mind is a translator between you and what's around you, remember that."

The mind is a translator, pshhh. I think there is only one way to translate certain things. I've said it before, and I'll say it again . . . life is pretty black and white.

Chapter Twenty

That night, after touring Fleur's chaotic laboratories, I had plans to meet James, my neglected coworker and even more neglected friend, at a café right down the street from where I lived. Although there was an enormous amount of light pollution in South of Sunset, due to all the glowing white storefront signs, the sky looked darker there. It was as if that side of town was in a black hole. There was never a star in sight, only a pitch-black sky arced over a gray city. When I first moved to SOS, I'd thought the town was so large, so vast, but after traveling in a Peellé, I soon realized how close together everything was. South of Sunset was a vacuum and all the crumbs and scraps living there had no way of escaping.

Being part of those specks of dust, James and I liked to hang around on the lively side of town, where the sidewalk resembled a stampede of wild animals. Our neighborhood was the last decent place in all of California young people could afford, so it was filled with constant activity and a buzzing nightlife. Of course, there were scammers on every corner or someone bootlegging smartphones down an alley, but there was always a happening spot you could stumble upon any night of the week.

The café James and I frequented was one that few would go to, due to its terrible coffee and greasy flapjacks. Lovehandle's Café was cheap and open till all hours of the night, so it suited us. It was the type of place you'd call an "out-of-towner." That was the slang we used for an unsavory restaurant all the locals knew to avoid, thanks to its almost inedible food and more intolerable crowd. There would always be a group of drunk buffoons inside, having their midnight cravings; a token quiet man sitting alone, looking as if he murdered people for enjoyment; and lastly, James and me, sitting at a bistro table out front.

As we sat, isolated from the dangers inside, we watched the sidewalks flood with men in suits bought with emergency funds and women in their most prized hats, which they'd probably had no business buying in the first place. They passed by us as if their day were just beginning, although it was already nine o'clock at night. As James and I sipped on our brake-fluid coffee, we talked of the innocent and not so innocent.

"Don't get me wrong, Milton Fleur is a genius, but boy, oh boy, is he on a high horse," I scoffed.

"It's 'cause he's rich," James added.

"You're probably right. He told me that thoughts affect your external surroundings. Ha! He should see it over here," I said as a group of yipping teenagers ran out of the café, being chased by the fed-up café owner.

"Bet he's from old money too. Never had to work a day in his life."

I rolled my eyes. "The apple doesn't fall far from the tree."

"Yikes, got a Mr. Fleur Jr. over there?"

I took a deep breath in and sighed. "Yep . . . a Gloria Fleur, but it's not too bad."

"Hopefully she's at least easy on the eyes."

"Luckily."

"Well then, you're winning, my man! You get some eye candy and a life of fortune. Sign me up!"

"Jeez, James, it's not like that—"

"I think I'm gonna change my name to Tiger Lily and see where that gets me."

I just sat back and let him go off on his tasteless tangent, nodding every once in a while and sipping my coffee strategically when he said something offensive. I've heard that people find their people, but I was just a person stuck with another person who would at least show up when I called.

"And you haven't tried to get with her?" James asked.

"Well, I did . . . kind of."

"Kind of? Kind of tried or kind of got with her?"

"I got *to* her."

"What the hell does that mean?!"

I just shrugged as James continued on with his crude comments, not knowing how to read a room. I played along, not wanting to be confrontational or judgmental as I joked with him about women. I felt guilty about what I was saying. My words had more gravity to them and so did my reaction—or lack thereof—to his. I would have normally been fine with James obscenely rambling on about dames, but for some reason, it felt wrong. Gloria was the first girl I'd known who cared about me, so it seemed very careless of me to talk about her like an object or a folly. Gloria was in a whole other lane compared to anyone else, but I wouldn't explain that to James. I couldn't. I was fearful that he would call me a fool or make fun of me. Looking back now, I don't know what I'm more ashamed of: worrying about James's opinion of me or not saying how I truly felt about Gloria. I was tormented by Gloria and my own life.

The stress of external forces pushed and pulled at my

brain, as if South of Sunset and North of Sunset wrestled with each other in a territorial battle for my subconscious. The left side of my brain was where South of Sunset lived, black and white, linear and logical. Everything there was what it seemed, a fact was a fact and up was up. That realistic ideology was ingrained in me from a very young age. As my life progressed, I grew more jaded and buried myself further into the left side of my mind. The gray grew comforting, and the system society had made me a prisoner to felt like a refuge from myself . . . my true self.

On the right side of my still not fully developed brain lived North of Sunset. A glowing world filled with promise and what-ifs. When I caught myself daydreaming, I often found my subconscious yearning for this place. It was a warm, colorful world that led me to fear my potential. I only touched the surface of the right side of my mind, as if it were a vacant swimming pool that I would dip a singular toe in, pulling it out of the water before really feeling the temperature. I was afraid to dive in. But I did not fear drowning, I feared finding out I knew how to swim all along. Years upon years spent out of water would've been washed away by the old "If I knew then what I know now" euphemism. There was a sense of guilt I felt when I was tempted to explore the right side of my brain, as if I were turning my back on what I knew.

I dove into the left side of my brain headfirst, learning the ins and outs of its pragmatic knowledge. I was safely confident in my abilities on that side and possessed no reservations for wanting to discover more. For everything I could discover would just be built upon my prior beliefs. The foundation was laid down strongly on that side. If I were to continue exploring the right side of my mind, the foundation would have to be torn up and rebuilt. No one is ever ready for that within themselves. To many, truth can be as sacred as religion, never to be questioned and never to be talked about. It's an answer to the unanswered for the people who never even asked the question.

After all, we will never know the full truth until we've experienced every aspect of one's story, which is utterly impossible. Even a simple conversation with a trusted confidant couldn't be fully interpreted or understood. For example, the following morning when I arrived at Fleur Estate, Franklin shared some unnerving news.

Chapter Twenty-One

Stormy weather was a-brewin' this morning before you got here," Franklin stated.

I looked up at the sky from the black leather back seat of the "Oleander delivery vehicle." There was not a cloud in sight and humidity must have been negative 15 percent, considering how dry my knuckles felt. I looked at Franklin, cross.

He clarified, "Within the family, I mean."

I squinted my eyes, looking at every window in that castle of secrets as we drove up, but not a silhouette was to be seen.

As Franklin and I slowly cruised up the long driveway, he continued to salt the boiling water. It seemed as if Franklin was proud that he knew more than me, showcasing the idea that seniority triumphed over intimacy. "Well, this morning I was picking up my sporting catalog that gets mailed to the Fleurs' address." He paused for a moment, then decided to clarify. "I told Mr. Fleur croquet is fun once, and the following day he got me a subscription to *Croquet Connoisseurs Monthly*. Been receiving it for three years now. I haven't had the heart to tell him I know almost nothing about it and only played croquet a few times as a child. I just pick up the catalog every month and thank him when I give him his morning paper."

I stared at Franklin, waiting for him to let me hear the music instead of the mumbling of the lyrics.

"Well, anyways, as I went inside to hand him *The Sunset Times*, I overheard his normal"—Franklin adjusted his facial expression to achieve a spot-on Mr. Fleur impression—"Mornin', Glory!"

I laughed involuntarily at his impressive talent.

"Not long after that, he started shouting, 'What is going on?!' Mrs. Fleur then asked if they needed to contact their publicist. I stood back, not getting involved in their private life. Then, come to find out, Gloria gave Mr. Fleur a hellebore flower."

"Ohhh, that flower means scandal," I interrupted.

"Yeah, so the mister and missus didn't take that very well." Franklin chuckled.

"Who would? What was Gloria thinking?!"

"She's smart, very tactful. Gloria then mentioned that she'd taken a liking to you and that was the scandal."

"What? She told them—"

"Mr. and Mrs. Fleur started laughing. Everyone knows that Gloria sees God knows what in you."

I jokingly hit him on the arm, relieved yet unsettled.

Why did Gloria try and cause a blowup before breaking the news that we could become an item? Does Mr. Fleur not like me? In comparison to a huge family scandal, maybe I'm tolerable?

"That's when the coast was clear. I handed Mr. Fleur his newspaper and bantered about croquet. It was quite funny to watch Gloria overestimate their reaction. She was very serious and got upset with her parents when they started laughing at her ridiculously obvious confession."

"Welp, here we are." I didn't want any more belittling to take place.

Getting out of the car, I nodded farewell to Franklin as he waved effortlessly. I was a tad bit perturbed by that whole discussion, as if I was made a mockery. As a young man, my ego was much more fragile. I had no strong character or sense of self yet. Maturity is when character replaces ego. Some people are born with strong character, making them mature for their age. The majority of us build our character as we experience the triumphs and tribulations of life. Then lastly, there are a few that never let their ego be replaced by character, leading them to be forever immature. I landed somewhere in between the last two.

I speculate that Mr. Fleur was born mature while Franklin was still growing into it. Some of us come out older and some come out wiser. I got the former, but not the latter. Wisdom can be earned similarly to money. To earn wisdom, you must feel humiliation smack its clammy hand on the back of your head every once in a while, and trade many of your days to have it in your pocket when needed. Like the rest of us, I learned that Mr. Fleur had had to trade many of his own days to earn wisdom that was equivalent to his net worth.

The stormy weather had cleared inside Fleur Estate by the time I entered the house that morning, as the whole family was off to a late start in their morning routines. Gloria roamed around the living room in her worn-out yellow terry cloth robe while her parents sipped their coffee, chatting about more disturbing news headlines. They flipped and flopped between subjects, bringing me into the discussion here and there. This was a huge leap for me at the time, leading me to feel more worthy of their trust. The Fleur family finally put out the cigars that created all the smoke and covered all the mirrors as the mister and missus talked of their past.

Mr. Fleur reminisced about the day he met his better half as we sat in the living room that lazy midsummer morning. He fawned over Mrs. Fleur, saying, "She looks the same as she did thirty years ago."

Her thin cheeks turned a rosy shade of pink as she blushed in the same way Gloria did. She then said, "We met in South of Sunset, when it was still bricks and brooks."

Mr. Fleur grabbed her hand tenderly, then looked over at me. He said, "I was working in the market at the time."

"You worked in stocks, sir?"

"How old do you think I am, Oleander?" Mr. Fleur laughed. "The stock market hasn't been around for sixty years or so. I was working at a grocery store."

My demeanor changed, I couldn't believe my ears. My whole perception of Mr. Fleur shifted as I realized he had gotten where he was without generational wealth. He was a poor man from South of Sunset who'd worked at a supermarket, lugging boxes. If they'd met thirty years ago, Milton Fleur must have been at least thirty years old at the time. *How is that possible?*

I abruptly asked Mr. Fleur, "How did you go from that to this?"

"Hard work. Right, Dad?" Gloria answered.

Mr. Fleur smiled as his eyes shifted into the distance, reflecting on his astonishing journey. He tilted his head as his focus came back to the three of us sitting around. "Well, hard work was part of it, but the real reason is I let go of time frames. You are always told at a certain age you have to accomplish this or you're too old for that or whatever nonsense people feed you! When in reality, there is no age limit for success or for change. When I realized that, I let go of my self-doubt and went to college at thirty-five. My family was dirt poor and I had little to no education growing up, but I didn't use that as an excuse. I was given this life to make the world a better place than when I entered it, and I plan on doing so, no matter what."

"And you already have," Mrs. Fleur said as she squeezed his hand.

Mr. Fleur smiled at her, then looked at me. "That is why we are following through with the human preservation process, Oleander. It's not for yahoos who want to see the future. It's for the terminally ill, and this is their only chance at having a future. With science progressing at such a fast rate, new cures are constantly being discovered."

"So, if someone is terminally ill, they can preserve themselves, then come back when a cure is found to treat them?"

"Correct." Mr. Fleur nodded.

I sat there in awe as Mrs. Fleur looked away.

"Mama, don't cry," Gloria said.

I heard a sniffle come from Mrs. Fleur. She sat still with her head turned away. "I'm sorry, I'm just so proud of him. This is a major thing for a lot of people, ya know. Especially children."

"She gets very emotional about that sort of stuff," Gloria whispered to me, and then pursed her lips in a goofy way.

I quickly chuckled at her response, then addressed Mr. and Mrs. Fleur. "I'm sure the parents of those children will be very grateful for what you are doing here."

The pair smiled at me. After being taken by emotion for only a minute, my left brain kicked in once again, realizing all the logistics of that procedure. "Pardon me," I hesitantly said. "What will happen if the child is very young and the parents are older? If the cure is found in sixty years, won't the parents be long gone?"

Mr. Fleur fixed his posture very slightly, and his tone shifted from personal to business. "That's a very good point,

Oleander. The parents have the option of being preserved too, so they can be with the child."

"That's smart, but what if they don't want to? Knowing my parents, if they were perfectly healthy and I was ill, they'd wish me the best of luck."

"That's so sad." Gloria looked at me.

The room got quiet for a moment, then Mr. Fleur responded to my unfiltered comment. "Well, if that happens, the board at Fleur Industries will assign a chain of designated holders, also known as legal guardians, to be responsible for that child when they come back. Again, we hope the parents join the child so that's not the case."

"Yeah, but I think for a lot of people, it's easier said than done."

"To risk their life for their child?!" Mrs. Fleur snapped.

"Well, yeah, to risk their life for anyone."

"Oh, no, no, no. Not for a parent!" Mrs. Fleur continued. "That's what family is for. You stick together through thick and thin." Her anger subsided and I soon realized it wasn't directed at me.

Her unwavering concept of love was profound. The more I talked to Mr. and Mrs. Fleur, the more Gloria made sense. She was raised with love, unlike me; I was raised with water and occasional food. I had this complex feeling about Gloria; I was almost jealous of her fortunate bloodline. My family used to be all in one place and in each other's hearts—one day, we all moved out.

"Boy, I wish I had parents like you two growing up."

"I gotta say, I'm pretty lucky." Gloria smirked.

Mrs. Fleur cocked her head a bit at Gloria, put off by her comment.

"She is," I stated, reinforcing the obvious.

Gloria continued to make her point, gloating away. "Well, of course I'm lucky. I'm surrounded by those who love me and genuinely care. I get to spend my days doing what I love, and I know the work I'm doing here is greater than myself. One day, I'm going to be a singer! What more could I ask for?"

"I don't think it's possible for you to be given more," I said in a snarky tone.

Gloria's eyes widened as she looked at me. "Well, no one's life is perfect. I'm not given everything."

"I'll believe that when I see it," I said as I looked down at her $15,000 slippers that had grass stains on them and her robe that could be nicknamed "Robe-kill" due to how dilapidated it was.

After our informative talk in the living room that slow Friday morning, Gloria and I got off to a late start with work. I didn't care, though. We finished up our normal six o'clock workday around nine at night. We would normally part ways around sunset, but that night was different. The fog started to roll in as the moon turned less translucent in the sky. We strolled through the gardens that warm July night, the brass lamps illuminating the decomposed granite paths. I hung my black coat over my right shoulder, as Gloria stayed close to my left. The hedges that looked vibrantly green by day turned into a rich dark green, one shade lighter than black, at night. The flowers in the garden stood still, as if they were sleeping, only to sway a bit in the breeze of our footsteps walking by. The Fleur Estate was beautiful during daytime, but at night . . . it was enchanting. Gloria was wearing a gown that matched the color of the stars that night, and her hair remained undone.

She trailed next to me as she said, "Believe it now?"

"What?"

"That money can't buy everything."

I shook my head and continued strolling with her. "No, I don't."

"Well, money can't buy this." She stretched her arms out and motioned around her.

"Yeah, it can."

My comment stopped Gloria in her tracks. Her forehead scrunched up as she stood there waiting for me to clarify. "If I had a hundred million dollars, I could buy these gardens, easily."

She laughed. "I don't mean the gardens, I mean this." She pointed to me and then to her, implying we were an "us." She continued strolling. "This moment. The two of us right here, right now." She took a deep breath in. "The night air, the foggy paths, the pearl-colored moon."

I slowed down and looked up. "It is quite beautiful."

Gloria then turned around and smiled at me shyly. "And you, just standing there . . . with that old book you always carry around."

I looked down at my hand. "*Encyclopedia of Flowers.*"

"Yeah, that's the one!"

"Well, I gotta keep you honest." I laughed.

Gloria smugly said, "I don't think the reason you carry that book around is to fact-check me, Oleander."

"Is that so?"

Gloria then changed her tone as her eyes interrogated me. "Yeah, I think so. Don't take this the wrong way, but"—I immediately felt my guard come up, unsure of what she would say next—"I think you carry it around to make it seem like you're doing more work than you actually are."

My heart began to pound. "We literally worked all day, Gloria. You know I'm a hard worker. What are you talking about?"

"I know that, but you are still here. We aren't working right now, but you have that book in your hand. It's almost ten o'clock."

"Okay, Gloria, what are you getting at?"

"It's just . . . I think you use that book as a front."

"A front?!"

"Well, yeah. I think you keep it around as an excuse for why you're with me. Ya know, like that's the only reason you're around me, for work. You're too shy to say you actually like me."

There it was—the reason for her leading comment about my book. It wasn't the book that upset her, it was all that it stood for. After many years and life experiences, I have figured out, the hard way, that's how women operate. They get irrationally upset by a simple book or a plain shirt or a tattoo. It isn't the inanimate object; it is all that it stands for. Us men get through each day hanging by the seat of our pants, while women are more calculated, overthinking every move. For example, say a man has a tattoo, it can be blue and unnoticeable to anyone else in the room, but his woman will have a fit over it. Why? Well, it's not the design or what it says, it's what it stands for. Every inanimate object that belongs to a man shows his real intentions, and women know that. That tattoo may be a stupid decision from his youth or a promise to a past lover to be with them forever. He may tell his woman it means nothing, or she's being foolish, but she knows everything that little smudge of ink holds. It symbolizes all the reused promises he initially made to someone else. It is no longer just a mark, it's the shadow of another woman she will always be second best to. How was my book similar to that tattoo, you may ask? It was held under the same principle. It carried much more than words, it carried my actions, thoughts, and intentions.

"Well, Gloria, I was originally here to work. We need to get this job done. We don't need people speculating or thinking I have more nefarious intentions. You know I like you, isn't that good enough?"

"No! It's the fact that you care if anyone else knows you like me or not."

"I don't care!"

"Yeah, you do! You care a whole lot about what other people think of you."

"No, I don't!"

"Oh yeah?"

A moment passed and the grounds grew quiet. A disheartened look swept across Gloria's face as her eyes shifted to the ground.

"Yeah. Look! I don't care who sees us," I finally blurted out.

I grabbed Gloria, unapologetically crossing the line that defined us as coworkers. On that pale moonlit night, on that foggy lamp-lined path . . . I kissed her. It was not the type of soft kiss you see lovers exchange on a picnic at the park or the gentle type that happens in the midst of a slow waltz. It was the type you see at train stations right before a long wave farewell to another land or the type that occurs in hospital rooms before a long wave farewell to another world. It was the kiss of a desperate man trying to save all that was about to be lost. Not one of want, but of necessity.

As I pulled away, I didn't fear Gloria's reaction to my inappropriate statement. I knew that's what she had been wanting from me all along, a passionate display of affection on my part. Why did I wait so long? Well, honestly there was no sense of urgency until she had the look of defeat. When Gloria finally decided to speak her mind, it showed her last attempt before giving up on me. I could see the uninterest in her eyes melt away as I laid one on her. The spark was back that made Gloria, Gloria "Exactly Everything Exciting on Earth" Fleur.

"Gloria, I really like you," I pleaded.

Her face turned solemn. "I really like you too. I'm sorry for assuming."

"It's fine. Just don't do it again."

Gloria's eyes shifted toward the ground as her face tilted sideways a bit. Her hands clasped together as if she were slightly embarrassed about her assumptions. Although they were true, at that age I had a breakable ego that ensured I left the conversation with my dominance known. Her demeanor turned soft again, but in a different way than I had seen before. Gloria went from sharp and blunt to hesitant. She stayed fairly quiet for the rest of that stroll, and I carried most of the conversation. I could see the gears turn in her head as she analyzed all that had just occurred, but I knew I was safe. After all, I'd kissed her, and acts of fearlessness were how Gloria interpreted love.

We reached the front of the house later that night. The planters glowed with a vibrant yellow hue. Franklin wasn't out front, but I saw the town car far off in the distance, just entering the gates once again—slowly and cautiously.

Gloria reached for my hands and said, "Hey, what are you doing tomorrow night?"

My mind went into a frenzy as I began to panic. *Now that I've kissed her, is she going to cling on to me like a suction cup?* I feared I'd opened a can of worms, remembering what Mr. Fleur had said in the past about Gloria getting attached to things too quickly.

I cunningly avoided the trap and responded, "Well, I'm planning on going to the golf course with James tomorrow. I'm not sure how late I'll be there. Why?"

"Well, tomorrow night my family and I are attending a science gala in celebration of this upcoming endeavor. It's a very high-profile event that is by invitation only for those involved in the process. I was going to ask you to be my plus-one, but—"

I quickly regretted my premature answer. "Oh, wow, that sounds amazing!"

"Yeah, we'll see how fun it is. Gonna be lots of doctors, scientists, and philanthropists there. Don't know how long I'm going to want to stay."

"No, that sounds so fun! It would be a great opportunity for me to network."

Gloria gave me a brief look of disdain that she immediately fixed. She replied, "Yeah. So do you want to give me a call tomorrow to let me know if you can make it or not, depending on what time you finish golfing?"

"Oh, no, it's fine! I can go. What time should I be here?"

"Seven o'clock," Gloria hesitantly said.

"It's a date." I smiled and said, "See you then!"

I walked to the car as Franklin pulled up. As I reached for my door, it opened before I could even grab the handle. I know what you're thinking . . . no, Franklin is not that quick. Franklin was still putting the car in park as the door swung open, revealing a man in the back seat. I knew that man, but he looked at me confusedly as I blocked him from getting out of the car. After snapping back to reality, I immediately moved to the side, letting the person with the familiar face exit the vehicle. An ominous familiar face.

Chapter Twenty-Two

Islowly switched places with the older man as I sat in the back seat of the town car that night. Gloria stood by the front door as the cedar-scented man approached her. I forgot to close my car door as I sat on the edge of my seat, watching their interaction.

"Good evening, Sam," greeted Gloria.

"Why, hello, Gloria," the man enthusiastically replied.

"My father's been expecting you. Come on in."

After the front door closed on Gloria and that handsome older man, I closed my car door so Franklin could take me away from that castle of secrets. The man I'd exchanged places with was none other than Samson O'Donell, one of Hollywoodland's biggest actors at the time. He must've been in his late thirties, as silver streaks had started to run through his jet-black hair. I wouldn't necessarily say he was too old for Gloria, but she was definitely too young for him. A man like that would break Gloria's childish wonder in a heartbeat, due to his reckless lifestyle. I didn't know much about his personal life, but I assumed all movie stars were the same. As I've mentioned before, I detested motion pictures, they were for people who were too vapid to read. My mother loved the movies, taking me to one as a kid without telling my father. To be frank, I'd never actually seen one of Samson O'Donell's motion pictures, but I recognized his sculpted face and even more sculpted name from the numerous billboards he was so blatantly blown up on. He was practically the king of Sunset Boulevard, so why wouldn't he aim for the queen?

As Franklin quickly sped away from the house with me, I sighed. "I should've asked for his autograph."

"Oh, thank goodness I drove away when I did. I just saved your ass, my friend!"

"What do you mean?"

"Mr. O'Donell is there to meet with Mr. Fleur for a possible business venture. The last thing he wants to be seen as is a vain Hollywoodland actor."

I was intrigued by the unspoken etiquette of the elite. "Really?"

"Yes, he wants to be seen by Mr. Fleur as a businessman so he will invest."

"Doesn't it give him more legitimacy if he's famous?"

Franklin busted out laughing, showing he had the upper hand no matter the subject. After a solid thirty seconds passed of him keeping me waiting, he finally spoke. "Those actors couldn't lick the dirt off these people's shoes, even if they tried. Yeah, they're flashier and get recognized by the general public, but they're still maggots compared to the people North of Sunset. Take someone like Mr. Fleur or Charles Grenadine for instance, no one would even do a double take if they passed by, but little do they know, most of those huge medical buildings around the country have their families' names on them."

"So that's what most of his fortune is in?"

"Yeah, pal. Medicine, medical research, all that state-of-the-art health stuff."

"I did find it hard to believe that he made all that money just off flowers. I hadn't even known what Mr. Fleur looked like until he came by the factory at the beginning of the summer. I'd been working there for two whole years and had never seen him before!"

Franklin softly whispered, "Yeah, they're very private people."

"Oh, I'm sure they've got their secrets."

"Well, everyone does." Franklin remained quiet the rest of the ride.

The following day was a Saturday in late July, and the sun shone extra stark in the gray sky South of Sunset. My morning was lived as if it were the B-side of a record, unappreciated and filled with noise. I spent the first half of that day getting ready for the gala that I believed could possibly change my life. After taking a lukewarm shower, I hand-washed my clothes and prepped all the ornamentations that would make me appear worldly. As my black suit and undergarments hung outside my window, humbly drying, I scanned the three newspapers that were left in my basket from the busy days before.

I wasted time as if it were my mission that morning. I was wound up so tight with anticipation for the gala, I walked to the window every five minutes to figure out if my suit was dry yet. Once it was damp yet wearable, I put it on and finished dressing the part. At four thirty, I departed my rickety living quarters and headed for the streets of SOS. Although the factory was only a half-hour-walk away, I took two hours to mosey on over there. I stopped to get coffee at Lovehandle's Café, then afterward went to a food kiosk on the street corner to eat a slice of pizza. By the time my "errands" were done, my suit was dry and so was my mouth from all that unnecessary caffeine and spicy pie.

I always found it amusing to wander around South of Sunset on a Saturday dressed to the nines. It was truly like holding a social experiment. In quiet little cafés or on mellow sidewalks, folks would stare at me, trying to figure out what my grand plan was for the evening or, even better, how they could receive an invitation. Youth and boredom will forever be enemies, so when someone looks like they've got the key, people jump with curiosity fueled by envy. Speaking of curiosity, Franklin always knew how to capture mine.

When I arrived at the factory, Franklin was sitting in the car with his eyes heavy. He looked exhausted, unlike his usual chipper self. He went to get out of the car to open my door, but I just motioned for him to stay put. I got in the back seat, and he began cruising onward.

"Sorry for being such a brute today, I barely got any rest this week," Franklin grumbled.

I knew I had been staying at the Fleur Estate way past my work hours, but I redirected the attention to another individual. "The actor was there pretty late last night, huh?"

"You should've been there. Talk about an interesting night," Franklin said.

I didn't respond, as I had no reason to let Franklin know how much I desired his knowledge on the inner workings of that house. Franklin pressed a little bit more, trying to read me.

"Aren't you the least bit interested in what transpired between Samson and Gloria?"

"Between Samson and Gloria?" I jumped in my seat. "Wasn't he there to meet with Mr. Fleur?"

Franklin turned his head around as we stopped at an intersection. "Yeah, but the greedy bastard figured he'd kill two birds with one stone."

Franklin held out the line just far enough to hook and reel me in. I couldn't tell if he was testing me or just had loose lips; either way, I pathetically begged for more information at his mercy. Franklin rolled his head around one time and cracked his neck. He took a deep breath in, then began telling the story of last night's events.

"So, after I dropped you off, I was beat! When I arrived back at the Fleurs' house, I immediately limped to the kitchen to get a hot cup of coffee before my last drive of the night. As I was pouring the joe, I heard Samson leave Mr. Fleur's office. They exchanged goodbyes and a cordial 'I'll give you a call later to discuss more.' Mr. Fleur told him Gloria could show him the way out. It was late and all the other staff had gone home. Mr. F then headed back into his office to hop on a call from Europe, I assume. I slowly walked around the corner, leaving my coffee behind, making sure Samson wasn't waiting on me to leave. Then, I noticed him walking over to Gloria, who was reading in the living room, so I hung back. She didn't even look up at him when he approached her. Samson enthusiastically asked her, 'What are you reading?' And Gloria replied, 'A book about America during the Second Civil War.' He stood awfully close to her as he said, 'Well, that sounds like a very intelligent book. You don't strike me as that type.' Gloria replied, 'What? Intelligent?'"

I laughed with Franklin as I waited for him to relay more information about what had happened. He looked focused once again as he continued, "Samson started to lose his cool and stammered, 'Sorry, that came off wrong. I don't mean that, it's just, you're very pretty.' The man turned clumsy! So then Gloria responded, 'Ya know, for having to read lines, you're pretty bad at coming up with your own.'"

"Damn!"

"I know. From there, Samson said to Gloria, 'Well, aren't

you confrontational? I stand corrected, that book does suit you.' She kept looking down at her book and replied, 'Glad to hear you stand for something.'"

"She didn't hold back with this guy, did she?" I was happy Franklin and I had a common enemy.

"Samson then asked Gloria if she could show him the way out. She adjusted her spectacles and looked up at him. Her eyes shifted to the door that was no more than twenty feet away, then back to him. Gloria's expression was priceless, she looked at this man as if he were stupid. She told him the door was right there, and he still stood there smiling. After an awkward moment of silence, Gloria sarcastically said, 'Do you want me to walk you to it?' Samson laughed and shrugged, goofily saying, 'Oh yeah, that'd be great.' Talk about not getting the hint. Gloria mumbled under her breath, 'Actors,' as she got up from her chair and walked him out. As Samson was complimenting Gloria on her 'sweet' behavior, I realized I should've been waiting by the car. I ran out the back door and got to the front just in time. As they walked out the front door, Gloria said to Samson, 'I should've said stage right and you might have understood.' He laughed the most intolerable, forced laugh. Thank goodness billboards don't have sound. He then shouted as they walked down the steps, 'Hey, you're funny!' I remained by the driver's door as they continued conversing. Gloria replied to Samson's obnoxious laugh with, 'Well that's a relief! You found out I have a sense of humor and I'm intelligent? Wow, it's like I'm an actual person or something.'" Franklin continued driving slow enough to not hold back on the details.

"Then Samson crossed the line! He grabbed Gloria by the arm and said, 'Well, I know you are beautiful. What are you doing tomorrow night?' Gloria pulled out of his grip and avoided eye contact as she said, 'I'm busy.' Samson, whose mommy and daddy probably never told him no, replied, 'That's okay, what about next week?' Gloria took a step back and said, 'I'm busy then too.'"

I smiled, feeling a tad bit flattered that Gloria had prioritized me over that shmuck.

"Samson asked her about the following week and the week after that. Gloria finally shouted, 'I'm forever busy!' Samson grabbed Gloria's arm once again, more aggressively than before, and said, 'Oh, come on, baby! You don't find me attractive? Is that it?' She immediately smacked his hand off her and said, 'You are a revolting individual!' Samson then threw up his arms and said, 'How so? I've been nothing but a peach to you!'" Franklin's head swiveled around. "Now, this is where you come into the equation."

I sat up, not knowing where this was going.

"So, after Samson said that, Gloria reached max elevation as she shouted, 'You're more like a sour grape. Anyways, I don't care if you're a peach or an absolute butter cake to me. You're not Oleander Briggs, and if you're not that, I don't want you!' You're not Oleander Briggs," Franklin quietly repeated, looking straight ahead. The sound of the wheels beneath us came to the forefront as silence filled both our mouths. Franklin shook his head in an unnatural manner and forced a smile on his face. "So, get a load of this . . . Samson replied, 'Oleander, what a stupid name.'" Franklin laughed.

I laughed along, unfazed by all the turmoil my name caused.

"Then Gloria replied, 'Oh, and he's a stupid man too, but he has my whole heart. Look up, it's night! So, unfortunately, I cannot give you any more time of day. Goodbye.'"

I sat there in silence, hesitant and unsure of the whole situation I'd been thrust into.

"Samson rolled his eyes, huffed, then got in the car. He didn't talk to me the whole ride home." Franklin chuckled.

I didn't say anything and just laughed at Franklin's scatter-brained delivery of a mediocre story. I did feel my head grow exactly 0.05 times bigger after it, though, knowing Gloria had chosen me over a rich and famous movie star.

In my younger years, I valued labels, superficial things, and was very materialistic. Ironically enough, the poorest people are many times the most materialistic. I think it's because people always yearn for what they can't have, or feel the need to put on a facade. I saw it every day walking the streets of SOS. My next-door neighbor would walk out of our apartment building wearing a mink coat and a hat with a designer logo big enough that you could see it a mile away. Mind you, where we lived was one step above living out of a box. Her wardrobe begged to differ, though. I do believe in dressing the part, but there's a fine line between reaching for your potential and just plain obnoxious.

Franklin was still driving annoyingly slow as we headed toward North of Sunset. Exhausted Franklin was not a fun experience. His erratic race car driving turned into a mere crawl as he rambled all over the place, jumping around on subjects until he'd lose his train of thought and sometimes control of the wheel.

Franklin mumbled, forgetting where he was in the story. "Anyways, when I got back to the estate to switch cars, Gloria was yelling to Mr. Fleur about Samson's pig-like behavior. Come to find out he was there to pitch a movie idea to Mr. Fleur about women's empowerment. What a scream!"

"What a hypocrite!"

Franklin replied, "That's Hollywoodland for ya. Bunch o' hypocrites. They preach peace, then get paid to kill someone on film. People don't do what they say, they do what they do. Long story short, Gloria swore up and down she'd never date an actor, and Mr. Fleur said he'd call off his business deal with O'Donell."

"Speaking of, how is the voice acting going, Frank?" I adjusted my bow tie as we entered the Fleur Estate gate.

Franklin's lighthearted smile faded away as he replied, "Ehh, it's been brushed to the side for now."

"Oh yeah? They got you working overtime here, huh?"

"I chose to."

"Just be careful if you're constantly choosing others over yourself, Frank."

"Noted." He stopped the car by the front.

"You're not going to listen to me, are you?"

"Nope."

We both chuckled as Franklin got out of the car and trudged around like a lopsided gazelle. He opened my door and grabbed my tuxedo coat, showing once again his humbling duties as a chauffeur.

As he helped my arms find the sleeves of my coat, I said, "Listen, Franklin, my father once told me you have to be selfish in this world if you want to survive. That is the only way to be. If you put others first, they'll stomp all over you."

"Not if they respect you."

"You can't be gentle and respected," I said sternly.

His face turned sour as he closed my door. "Well, that's an ugly thing to say."

I just shrugged. After all, the only way I ever got what I wanted out of life was by putting myself first. My mother was a prime example. She tried to help others and reach out her hand, but always ended up getting hurt. I closed off my emotions; people disregarded them, anyway. Nevertheless, I would've rather been cold and pragmatic than the sob story of a neglected child. I no longer felt neglected, though, thanks to Mr. Fleur.

The temperature cooled down that evening as I walked toward the front steps of the house. I knocked on the large intricate wooden door as Franklin parked the town car at the other end of the driveway. Mr. Fleur opened it and greeted me in a dark-green suit with a pink gerbera daisy in the lapel— those mean celebration and a time of cheer. Gloria must have gotten her sense of style from Mr. Fleur because he wore some of the oddest color combinations and patterns but managed to make them look smart. He led me into the foyer.

"The girls are still upstairs getting ready." Mr. Fleur rolled his eyes in the comical way old men do.

I looked around and noticed the house was empty and silent, unlike the weekdays. Monday through Friday it was like Simi Valley Airport: filled with traffic, people, and noise. Mr. Fleur and I sat down by a window that looked out on the whole front of the property as it glowed in the evening sun. Mr. Fleur explained that they gave their staff the weekends off so they could spend them with their families.

"Except Franklin, I see." As I looked out the window, he was walking across the driveway, picking at his teeth, completely alone, pacing like a lost sheep.

Mr. Fleur smiled a solemn smile and said, "Depends on the weekend for him. I always give him the option to have days off, but he chooses to work nonstop."

I laughed. "Seems like he enjoys it, though. Probably makes more money here than he would trying to survive as a voice actor."

"That's where you're wrong, son. Believe it or not, he started to become very successful. Got a contract with Microscope Pictures and was on track to make eight figures a year for a radio show."

"What happened?"

"He gave it all up. His father passed away and I needed a new driver I could trust. Franklin jumped in without a second thought."

"He just threw it all away to drive your family?"

"That's what it looks like." Mr. Fleur peered out the window. He continued, "That is one mystery I still haven't quite figured out just yet. Maybe after his father passed, he felt we were all he had left."

"I guess that makes sense. You have known him his whole life. Still, I can't comprehend why he'd give up on his dreams."

Mr. Fleur sat back in his chair and rested his arms on each side. "I think he can't help himself. He's the type of guy to give someone the shirt off his back. Who knows, maybe his dreams changed? Happens to a lot of young people."

"I don't know if young people's dreams change, but rather they give up on them. I see it all the time. My buddy Tim wanted to study marine life out on the open sea, then ended up moving to Oklahoma for some girl. Gave it all up for her."

"I did the same thing. See here, Oleander, when you find the one, it feels like you'll be giving up everything if you lose her. She becomes the dream and everything else becomes irrelevant."

"Pshhh, that's crazy. I don't think I could ever do that. I mean, I'm not sure what I want to do with my life just yet, but once I find it, I'll never let it go."

"Well, you're still green."

Moments later, Mrs. Fleur walked down the cascading staircase with Gloria slowly trailing behind. I remember looking over and seeing adoration on Mr. Fleur's face the moment he saw his wife. It was as if he were seeing her for the first time, falling in love once again. The sides of his wrinkled eyes turned upward as his teeth fought their way through his lips. Years of struggling together and rough times had all been wiped away in that moment by a subtle waltz in his direction and Italian perfume. Maybe relationships were like an automobile? You traveled long roads in it, fought over the direction you were heading, and had some accidents along the way. It required fuel and had to be serviced. The vehicle grew dirtier and more worn down the more experiences you had in it, but the rain would come one day and wash it all away. You looked over to see your partner still sitting in the passenger seat. You then remembered the reason you loved that car in all its glory, appreciated how strong it was and how strong it made you. It lasted you through life's many seasons and proved reliable when you needed it the most. So yes, maybe long-term relationships are like automobiles, and I saw the rain fall on Mr. and Mrs. Fleur's that evening.

After I watched Mr. Fleur's interaction with his wife in awe, I felt a tap on my shoulder. It was Gloria breathing down my neck, waiting for a reaction to her electric-blue satin gown.

"Ready to go?" I asked.

"Yep," she replied dryly.

I never told her she looked beautiful the moment I saw her, and I never gave her the attention she so desired. I just continued on as if it were any other day and she was any other person. I should have taken a few notes from Mr. Fleur on how to treat a woman, for they are simpler than most young men think. I was too busy caught up in my own head to take a step back and make Gloria feel special.

We walked out the front door together, while Mr. and Mrs. Fleur stayed inside, basking in each other's presence. They were going to catch a ride with the Grenadines, so Gloria and I were to ride with Franklin. The sun was low in the sky, making the land yellow before the hills turned to shadows.

As Gloria looked me up and down, she said, "You look good."

"Thank you, you too—whoa! Is that the car we are taking tonight?!" I saw Franklin standing next to a candy-apple-red convertible Peellé that cost north of $50 million.

Gloria just laughed at my excitement. "Gotta change it up every once in a while."

As we approached the vehicle, Franklin gasped. "Wow! You look stunning Gloria . . . and, Oleander, you clean up pretty nice too."

"Thanks, Frank. I was just about to tell Gloria how nice she looked."

We got in the car and slowly paraded away from the main house; dust flung from under the tires, acting as a long train for the extravagant vehicle. Dusk would soon creep in, turning the sky purple and the temperature outside seventy-nine degrees. Gloria's ruby-red lipstick turned darker as we cruised through the fortress-lined backroads of Bel Air.

Pursing her lips outward, she asked, "Why aren't you coming tonight, Frankie?"

"Ahh, well, I wouldn't fit in there. Ya know, too many fuddy-duddies."

Gloria squealed, "Don't I know it!" She then proceeded to reminisce about some old friends of theirs that would be there. The two of them swapped jokes of their heckling youth and worked themselves up to tears. As she wiped her eyes, Gloria said her stomach was hurting from how hard Franklin was making her laugh.

Once the cackling hyenas finally calmed down, I looked at my watch and asked, "Is it okay if we are late?"

"Oh yeah, we're fine," Gloria said as she continued trying to pull herself together. She then leaned in to kiss me.

I pulled back. "Wait, are you wearing lipstick?"

Gloria smiled and playfully said "Yeah" as she slowly leaned in toward me again.

"You'll get it all over my face."

"Oh yeah?" She teased as she leaned in closer, about to smooch me.

I put my hand out in front of her and sternly said, "Gloria, stop. I don't want to go in there looking like a clown."

She immediately laughed, but not the same way she had with Franklin a moment ago. I never could make Gloria laugh the way Franklin did. Not even close. When she laughed around me, it was in more of a polite way than a humorous way. Her laugh acted as a shield to something cynical I'd said. She would have nothing to contribute to the conversation and not know how else to react.

Her face turned solemn. She remained quiet the rest of the car ride as we sat awkwardly next to each other in the back seat. Franklin finally broke the painful silence.

"And we are here!"

Chapter Twenty-Three

The crimson car halted in front of a lush velvet green carpet that rolled like a brook through the front entrance. Flowers upon flowers lined the path to the beige art deco building, and people stood in groups, like lint clumping on laundry.

Franklin began to stumble out the driver's side door, but I quickly said, "I got it, Frank."

"Well then!" Franklin huffed.

I stopped him because I didn't want anyone to see him goofily walk around and open the car door. He sighed, closed his door, then remained in the seat in protest as I held the door open for Gloria to get out. I closed the back door of the car and held Gloria on my arm in a gentlemanly manner.

As we walked down the carpet, I noticed two young women standing off to the side by a photographer. They must have been fashion models, as their stature resembled those palm trees around the building, long and graceful. I stared at the women for a moment.

Hooonk!

A large car horn snapped me out of it. It was the driver waiting behind Franklin, who was still parked in front of the carpet.

Without thinking, I blurted out of anger to Gloria, "Why does that guy need to honk?! This is a beautiful place with beautiful women."

"Beautiful women, huh?" Gloria glanced over toward the two dames I'd been staring at.

I locked in on them, then back at Gloria in a panic. "A beautiful woman, I mean—you."

Gloria laughed that polite laugh, then continued to walk with me down the carpet.

I felt the silence creep up, so I said, "You're so pretty. Ugh, I am such a lucky guy."

She smiled timidly and remained quiet, displaying the hesitant softness I'd seen for the first time the night before.

"Do you know where you're going?" I asked as we walked toward the entrance.

"Yes." She looked straight ahead.

Now, I have never been the type of guy to be invited to parties, due to my bland humor and even blander lifestyle. I was normally a second-string guest, the type you'd invite just in case you were worried the room would look too empty. Although I didn't have much experience with parties, I could still guarantee that gala in late July 2125 was by far one of the most extravagant soirees California would ever see. Even I knew at twenty-four years young that I was witnessing history in the making that evening.

Gloria and I entered from the second level, which meant we had to get to the ballroom on the first floor. After walking the dark corridors of that hauntingly beautiful building, we found it. Looking down from the top of the bifurcated stairs, I saw a cornucopia of the wealthiest humans in the world. Golden chandeliers with crystals hung from the ceilings, matching the earrings on many of the older women down below. Gloria and I looked at each other, simultaneously took a deep breath in, then began walking down the marble staircase that provided a grand entrance for us.

As we slowly paraded down the stairs, I can guarantee every pair of eyes covered us as if we were the reason they were all there. Gloria's electric beauty shone through, the way it always did, and everyone gazed at her in awe. I've heard that women can be very cruel to other women out of jealousy, but that was not the case with Gloria . . . oddly enough. Her soul was so pure and so kind that it washed away any negativity anyone could feel toward her. It was as if Gloria slipped everyone around her a love potion, causing men and women alike to feel the desire to be near her. Gloria built people up, she never tore them down. That was another factor that made Gloria "Everything" Fleur not a target but a standard that all wanted to reach for.

As we continued down, Gloria didn't pay attention to the large crowd below us, she just kept gazing at me as if I were the main attraction. I looked out at all the people, listening to the whispers among the crowd as they began to dance. After making our way to the bottom of the staircase, we mixed in with the crowd like stains on a polka dot blouse. They all looked beautifully elegant, but sounded as if they were the most conniving people on earth.

"That's Milton Fleur's daughter," whispered one voice.

"I don't recognize the young man with her," responded the second.

A third guest chimed in, "Must be one of Devon's boys."

"No, he doesn't look like a Curtis to me," added another.

The guests waltzed around, tangling speculation and

stories with one another as if that were a dance as well . . .
Changing partners, changing stories, and switching tempo.

"He could be new money."

"Well, ya know Milton is new money himself."

"Pshhh, tacky," whispered a man in a silver tuxedo.

"Well, not everyone's four times great-grandfather struck
oil, Bradley," responded a woman in pink.

"Not everyone happens to marry a man that owns strip
malls, Jeanine!"

They continued dancing, their words in direct opposition
to their actions.

"Screw you," said Jeanine.

The man in the silver suit leaned over to the couple dancing next to him. "She's a lovely woman."

The pair continued dancing, loathing every minute of it.
Money must make you immune to everything, including social graces. I do have an enormous amount of respect for the
people in that champagne-filled ballroom that still conducted
themselves with utmost class. After all, money doesn't make
people greedy or selfish or generous, it just amplifies the char-
acteristics that they already have.

If Gloria were poor, I knew in my heart she would still be
kind and passionate for life. Now Charles Grenadine, on the
other hand, would be cowardly and worrisome with a hundred
dollars or a hundred million dollars in the bank. We saw his
frail figure over in the corner with a young woman and the
Fleurs. They were chatting up the attendant at the cloakroom
as they checked their hats and cover-ups. Mr. Fleur spotted us
and waved us over.

"Gloria, you remember Charles," he said.

Gloria tilted her head and shook his hand. "How do you do."

Charles replied quietly, "How do you do." Adjusting his

gold spectacles, he then turned his attention to me and introduced himself. "Charles Grenadine. How do you do."

I smiled. "Pleased to meet you, sir."

The young woman immediately turned to me and said,
"Laura. And you are?"

"Oh, Oleander."

She warmed up and said, "Lovely meeting you."

"This is my wife," Charles clarified to me.

Laura Grenadine had golden hair that twirled up at her
shoulders, delicately showcasing the diamonds that hung
heavily on her collarbone. Charles might as well have put a
name tag on her. In suit with her ice, Laura wore a strapless
white gown that had not one design or, better yet, wrinkle on
it—same went for her skin. She looked about twenty-eight . . .
Twenty-eight years old and twenty-eight years too young for
her husband. Her style conveyed swanlike purity, blending
exquisitely with her elongated features and pale eyes. I knew
it was all a costume, though—an act, if you will. Truth is,
poor girls dated rich older men—correction . . . old men. Rich
women dated wealthy young men or, more predictably, poor
young slobs like me. Laura had elbowed her way in through
sweat and grease to land a lifetime fund like Charles, playing
the part of the perfect housewife, while Gloria had ditched her
wealthy peers for "different" and "exciting" broke men. One
woman wanted to find stability while the other tried to escape it.

Mr. Fleur took the reins and said, "Oleander is working
with Gloria on the latest project."

Laura Grenadine replied, "Oh, are you being preserved?"

"Me?!"

Gloria immediately grabbed my arm and took over. "Oh,
no, the latest project for the flower company. Oleander and I
are working on the fall collection."

"Oh, how wonderful!" Laura cheered as she forced a smile. "You have grown up so much, Glory. I mean Gloria." Laura shook her head as if she were a proud aunt, genuinely believing the nonsense that she was Gloria's senior.

"You have too, Laura. Last time I saw you was at your husband's fiftieth birthday. We were in the playpen together."

"Well!" Laura huffed as Gloria grabbed my arm and strolled away.

I laughed, looking back at Laura's elegance, which was shattered on the floor. Gloria leaned her head on my shoulder as we made our way through the masses. Winning the first victory, Gloria decided to move the front closer to enemy lines. We rubbed elbows some more with the crowd.

"Ya see, I don't mind Laura. Honest I don't. I just can't stand it when someone treats me like I'm a child. I'm not incompetent. Just because I like to have fun doesn't mean I'm immature. Laura is the immature one. So you married an old guy . . . Congrats?! I don't mean this in a cruel way, Oleander, but maybe if she worked on what was up here"—Gloria pointed to her brain—"she wouldn't have to rely on her waistline. Ugh!"

"I can tell that this bothers you. Would you like to take a moment outside?" I motioned toward the courtyard out back.

"Sure. Not because I'm annoyed, but because I want to get you alone." Gloria smirked and pinched my arm.

We exited the French doors and made our way to a concrete bench nestled between two planters. The moonglow reflected on the freshly washed tiles as lavender brushed the misty air. Twinkling lamps hung from the perimeter, flickering in the stillness of the night. Inside was a world of gross conformity and exorbitance, but outside was a break for all the "free thinkers."

I wrapped my arm around Gloria. "I am truly sorry for not saying how beautiful you were right when I saw you. I thought it, I promise. I just get so distracted when it comes to cars and—"

"I understand. You're a boy." Gloria rolled her eyes and smiled. She then leaned in, her chest rising and falling slowly and heavily. "You still owe me a kiss from earlier."

"Gloria?!" a twangy voice shouted from across the courtyard.

Gloria snapped out of her trance, sat up straight, and turned around. "Oh, hi, Dr. Burton!"

He did that on purpose.

The abnormally tall man began to walk over as Gloria and I stood up, adjusting ourselves back to sugarcoated human beings. I recognized his pepper-colored hair and his deep accent from the science demonstration video I'd seen in the Fleurs' theater.

Gloria hung on my arm as she whispered to me, "That's Robert C. Burton. Brilliant scientist and third partner in the upcoming experiment."

"So your father, Charles, and Robert are the minds behind it?"

"Correct," she quietly said as Dr. Robert Burton finally reached us.

"Long time, no see. Sorry to interrupt, I was getting restless in there," he said as he hugged Gloria. I already knew I liked that guy because he acted warm and normal, unlike the rest of the cogs. As he pulled away from Gloria, he held her arms and said, "Well, you're looking healthy. I'm glad to see you're still doing well."

"Well, of course I'm doing well. Why wouldn't I be?!"

He smiled, then seemed to reel himself back in.

"Dr. Burton, this is Oleander Briggs," Gloria said as she put her arm on me.

"How do you do, sir," I sternly said as I shook his rough hand.

"Not as well as you, I see, and you can call me Burt."

"Nice to meet you."

After my polite introduction to Dr. Burton, we heard a woman shriek, "Gloria Fleur! Is that you?!"

"A moment alone." Gloria closed her eyes and whispered, "Just. One. Moment. Alone." Gloria gave me an unenthused look and said she would be back.

"Gloria, Gloria! You have to meet my niece. She's brilliant—" The stalky woman covered in fur pulled Gloria through the French doors and into the golden lagoon.

Must have been a troubling woman she knew, the kind you have a conversation with without getting a word in edgewise. Gloria stuck her head out. "Oleander studied the same type of stuff you did in college, Dr. Burton. Have at it, you two!" She blew me a kiss.

Dr. Burton laughed and said, "So where'd you go to school, Ole—"

"Oleander."

"Well, that's a unique name, ain't it?"

"Yeah. I went to Brown University and studied biological science, mainly human biology."

Dr. Burton's voice grew quieter. "Well then, somebody had to have clued ya in a little about Mr. Fleur's latest endeavor."

I laughed, making sure he knew I was aware. "Oh yeah. I have to say, it's amazing what you guys are going to accomplish with this experiment."

"It's an experiment, alrighty."

"Is that so?"

Robert Burton leaned in and whispered, "Yeah. I shouldn't be tellin' ya this, but they're all celebratin' when it is nowhere near done . . . or even stable." He looked toward the ballroom filled with drunken crowds and the balloons dancing over them, accompanied by a big band.

I matched the level of his voice. "Mr. Fleur was telling me they are still perfecting the dissolving serum. I believe the deadline is a month away."

"It has to be! That's not all that needs tunin' up. We have no clue how humans will react to this beyond twenty-five years of preservation. It's like a car with no guaranteed warranty."

"Is that why they haven't announced how long the three test subjects will be preserved for?"

Dr. Burton smiled and leaned back, acting casual again. "Well, there are multiple reasons for that, which I've signed a nondisclosure about. I'm hirin' in the fall, and you seem like a smart kid. Too smart to be wrapped up in all of this. Here's my number—"

"Miss me?!" Gloria came up behind me and grabbed my shoulders in an affectionate way.

"Welcome back," Dr. Burton said as he lifted his flute of champagne and tucked his card back into his paisley coat pocket.

Gloria leaned her chin on my shoulder. "I hope he didn't tell you too many embarrassing stories about me."

"Oh, no." I laughed.

Robert Burton smiled a crooked smile and said, "Just told him what you did to the last guy." He then motioned his head getting chopped off.

Gloria smacked him playfully. "Oh, stop!" She laughed.

"Careful ya don't get this innocent bystander killed, Miss Fleur. I like him." Burt adjusted his tie.

"And that's our cue, Oleander." Gloria grabbed me by the arm and pulled me away from Dr. Burton.

"Toodle-oo," she shouted as she waved goodbye to him.

"Toodle-oo," he said back.

"Nice meeting you, Burt!"

"Nice meeting you too, Olii-anduhh."

After my interesting conversation with Dr. Burton, the night grew longer and longer. Gloria introduced me to many influential people, but it was pointless. Every conversation went the same way with just some phrases switched around. People asked about my odd name, then asked if I was working on the human preservation experiment, then treated me like a busboy once they found out I was just working on the little flower collection. Each interaction grew more and more degrading as Gloria kept having to cover for me, replying to people's loaded questions. We all know the saying "There's a fox in the henhouse." Well, in my case, I was a hen in the foxes' den.

Gloria and I stood in a crowd that was circled around a man in a plum-colored suit with crow's-feet stepping on his temples. I heard shouts and laughs, so he must have been pretty funny.

"So I said to the chef, 'You don't have any oysters?'"

Everyone busted up at his elitist punch line to an insider joke, except Gloria. Her foot began to tap and her face grew bored. She looked like she was being suffocated by meaningless banter. Small talk was meant for people with small thoughts; the problem with Gloria was that her thoughts and notions were well beyond the size they ought to be.

As soon as the band started a new tune, Gloria pulled me away from the crowd and shouted, "I love this song! Oleander, come dance with me."

As she grabbed my arm to dance, I pulled away, quietly saying, "You know I don't dance."

"Well, I wanna dance!" she snapped at me, tired of her mind being chiseled away.

"Well, I don't! I want to talk to Dr. Burton some more. I heard he has some openings for research positions."

"Okay, okay. I saw him at the cocktail bar over there." She pointed to the bar across the room.

I began to walk toward it, then said, "You coming?"

"No, I said I wanted to dance." Gloria stood in the middle of the dance floor, throwing her arms up.

I stormed off, taking control of the situation. The next thirty minutes felt like two hours as I sat at the bar alone, drowning myself in old-fashioneds, waiting for Dr. Burton to appear. I was too self-conscious to walk through the crowd of onlookers to search for him, so I remained with my back to the dance floor. He was my last chance at networking with someone here, as everyone else had immediately written me off. My neck had started to feel the weight of my head and my eyes had begun to droop when I heard a loud sigh behind me. I turned around to see Dr. Burton out of breath and wiping the sweat off his forehead.

He took the seat next to me and said, "Man, your Gloria can really dance!"

"You were on the dance floor this whole time?!"

He laughed innocently. "Yeah, I danced with her for five songs."

I spun my barstool around to see Gloria on the dance floor, laughing with a group of men surrounding her. She made eye contact with me, then looked away, laughing once again. I felt my face grow hot with anger as my heartbeat started to get faster and faster.

Dr. Burton's words faded away as he continued, "I had to explain to her my old joints don't hold up like they used to, but she just kept on insisting . . . one more, one more!"

"Excuse me." I immediately got off my barstool and stormed toward the dance floor in a fit of rage. I noticed golden locks standing at five foot eight on the sidelines, as still as a statue. Laura Grenadine was taking in the premature loneliness of twenty-eight as she watched her "immature" peers mingle and rejoice. Charles must have been talking business with the other gentlemen in a private room somewhere. I tapped her on the shoulder, treating her like a girl her age.

"Excuse me, Laura. Would you like to dance?"

She nodded.

No wonder Mr. Grenadine was worried all the damn time, his fortune and his lady were always in cahoots to leave him instantly. I could see the sadness in her eyes melt away, though, as we began waltzing. As a matter of fact, we joyfully waltzed right into Gloria's line of sight. Looking back now, I know that was an awfully cruel thing to do, but in the moment, I wanted to spite Gloria. I relieved Laura's problem temporarily while creating a more concretized one in the woman who was supposed to trust me. I wanted to force Gloria to look at something she could never obtain, make her feel how I felt. Laura was not the way I should have gone about it.

Without hesitation, Gloria walked up to us. Calmly ignoring Laura, she looked directly at me. "I thought you said you didn't dance?" She then walked away, heading up the stairs with a swiftness that was noticeable yet subtle. I awkwardly stared at the now bland woman I was locking hands with, not knowing what to say.

Laura watched Gloria rushing up the staircase for a moment, then hesitantly said, "Go on." She motioned her head toward Gloria in disappointment. "She'll learn one day she can't have everything, but let's not make it tonight."

"Pardon me." I stumbled away and up the stairs. When I reached the top, I looked down on the once promisingly fresh crowd that now seemed expired. Like Laura, they all turned bland once you simplified their problems. They had all become rotten, and I wasn't high-class enough to entertain them. I hurried down the corridor, then outside the building. When I reached the green velvet carpeted entrance, I saw Gloria's chestnut-colored hair moving toward the red sports car.

"Hey, Gloria!"

Gloria just continued walking away from me, reenacting the dream I'd had about her where I was stuck on the music box. The rickety familiar tune began to creep softly into my mind.

"What's wrong?!" I asked.

Gloria replied without turning around. "Seriously?!"

I continued walking after her. "Well, you were dancing with Dr. Burton on purpose, then you were talking to all those guys on the dance floor and—"

"Dr. Burton?!" Gloria finally came to a complete stop, turned toward me with tears in her eyes, and said, "He asked me to dance and, yes, okay, I did milk it on purpose. I wanted to make you wait. After all, I brought you here as my date and you were just focused on Burt. As for the guys, I was just sharing some jokes. Others will gladly give me attention if you won't! You're such a pill sometimes."

That was the first time I'd heard Gloria unapologetically insult me.

"I'm sorry," I stammered. "I just thought—"

"What? That I was actually flirting with them?! I think you're getting the two of us confused."

"What are you talking about?! I haven't flirted with anyone!"

"Just danced with Laura . . . of all people!"

"That was nothing!" I brushed the hair out of my face defensively.

"Oh yeah?" An aggravated look crept across Gloria's face. "Well, what about those two dames you were gawking at when we first walked in?"

"Oh, no, I just thought I knew one of them. That's all."

Gloria sighed and walked to the car. "Uh-huh. I think it's time we go, before you run into anyone else you might know."

There it was again, the same feeling from my night terror. The music grew louder and louder. Each step I took forward, the further away Gloria was from me. I was in a tight spot, stuck between a rock and a hard place. And Gloria . . . well, she was free, walking away from me. I had to do something.

I grabbed Gloria right in front of the car door and said, "Gloria, babe. I love you."

She looked up at me, shaking. I could see the tears on her cheeks and her eyes resembled Christmas colors. The beauty of red and green.

"Really?"

"Well, of course." I smiled, knowing I'd gotten her back once again and silenced that haunting tune in my head.

She smiled and sniffled. "I love you too. Maybe that's why I get so oversensitive about these things. I've never felt like this about anyone before."

"That's understandable. It's just because you care a lot. It's a good thing, it means you love me."

"I really do!" She embraced me.

That whole time, Franklin was standing there, uncomfortably holding the car door open like a goofball. As Gloria was about to get in the car, I stopped her and brushed her face.

"Gloria, you're beautiful."

The moment I said that, a look of disdain came across Franklin's face as he watched the scene unspool. Gloria sat in the back seat, and I followed. Without saying another word, Franklin got in and began driving. He knew.

Chapter Twenty-Four

Gloria requested the top of the car be taken down so she could inhale the world. As Franklin cranked the golden lever on the dashboard, wind blew through Gloria's hair and the glow of the city lights kissed her cheeks. Her crimson lips sparkled and her dress matched the night sky. We drove on Sunset Boulevard instead of taking the side streets since it was desolate. Nothing but us, the billboards, and the extravagant buildings that looked over the city.

Franklin finally fixed his sour attitude and said, "Where to now?"

"Where to now? It's almost midnight," I responded, looking down at my watch.

Franklin turned around and asked Gloria, "Did he just say, 'Almost midnight'?"

"I think he did!"

The pair began to sing an old song from their childhood as we drove down the colorful boulevard. They laughed, belting it word for word.

Strike out a match.
Turn off the lights.
Close your eyes,
It's almost midnight.

Or turn around,
And hit the town.
Stay out till the mornin's bright.
'Cause after all,
It's only midniiigggghht!

Gloria stood up in the car, without hesitation.

"Dammit! Be careful, Gloria," I shouted.

She just laughed and threw her arms up. Her satin shawl draped around her sun-kissed shoulders as it blew in the breeze. She looked up at the towering buildings above her. Those buildings were probably the only thing that was above Gloria Fleur, them and the stars. Franklin watched her through his rearview mirror, making sure to look out for any hazards. He then proceeded to put on a record—the exact song he and Gloria had sung. The orchestral symphony continued playing as we cruised the boulevard. We laughed and cheered as we headed back to the Fleur Estate, drunk on the idea of youth.

Red sports cars and falling stars.
Catch your name on billboard signs.
Bel Air can get some clouds,
'Cause angels need somewhere to lie.

Rope the sandman in Malibu,
Or catch Sunset Boulevard's tunes.
Your love makes me feel alive.

And after all, it's only midnight,
Plus, the rest of our liiivvves!

After midnight struck on that whiskey-filled summer night, Gloria and I entered the large peach-colored house that the Fleurs called home. All had been forgotten from the gala earlier that night as Gloria walked through the quiet house, opening each door to check if her parents were back. The rose-sconce-lined walls surrounded the empty living room as we roamed the house.

"Hmm, my parents must not be home yet." Gloria sighed.

I laughed as she slammed shut another door. "They did seem like they were having a good time at the party."

"Yeah, lately they've been living like they are teenagers again!"

I smiled as I grabbed Gloria's dainty hands. "That's not necessarily a bad thing."

Gloria playfully pulled away. "Yeah, whatever makes them happy."

The house turned silent as we both stood still, not letting our footsteps make a click or a clack on the tile floor. Gloria's back was to me.

"You make me happy."

Gloria immediately turned around and a smile crept across her face. She was the sun rising, capable of extreme warmth and life, not yet shining across the land. Her eyes lifted slightly as she looked into mine. She had fallen. It looked different than the excitement of butterflies and bubbling champagne one felt in their stomach when they first locked hands. It was a stillness—a calm, deep knowing that she purely and utterly loved me.

She brushed the intense look off her face and laughed, as if she were convincing herself that her feelings were dizzy. "Well, that's a relief that I make you happy."

Gloria then told me she wanted to get out of the blue contraption that engulfed her body and change into more comfortable clothes. She asked me to grab waters from the kitchen, then meet her upstairs. In that moment, the whiskey was a solicitor and my brain was the front door. It knocked and knocked, pounding on it and insisting to be let in. I rushed over to the kitchen, groggily tripping as Gloria disappeared up the cascading staircase.

I shuffled around the kitchen, opening cabinets and looking in the pantry, trying to figure out where the water could be. I knew they had water somewhere, it was a household necessity, but it was almost impossible for me to find. Maybe it was the other liquid rushing through my brain or maybe it was the fact that it was someone else's home. Either way, my frustration grew as I left no stone unturned.

My overindulgence and lack of self-control made me process everything backward that night, checking the fridge last. I unlatched the brass handle and opened the heavy emerald doors as the fluorescent lights beamed on my face. There they stood. A fourteen-pack of glass-canned water. I heard the front door swing open and Mr. Fleur's belly laugh project throughout the quiet house. I panicked as I shuffled back and forth, not knowing what to do. I slammed the fridge door, forgetting to grab a can. His voice grew louder as he and Mrs. Fleur approached the kitchen. The door began to open, so I ducked and hid behind the cabinet in the corner. The pair stumbled into the kitchen. I immediately sat on the floor and tucked my knees into my chest, hoping not to be seen as I peeked around the corner, at eye level with their ankles.

"See, Cheryll, Charles is starting to come around." Mr.

Fleur laughed as he set a small cardboard box on the kitchen island.

"Does he really have a choice, Milton?" Mrs. Fleur rolled her eyes.

Mr. Fleur grumbled and laughed some more as he sat down. "For the paycheck, he won't let himself have a choice!" He began fussing, trying to open the box in front of him. It looked like mine wasn't the only brain that the whiskey had gotten to. Mrs. Fleur noticed the half-open refrigerator. I must have slammed the door so hard it rebounded open.

"I told Gloria to stop leaving the fridge open!" Mrs. Fleur scoffed.

"Ohhh, go easy on the gal," Mr. Fleur said contentedly as he began to eat the leftover cake in his box.

"And you need to go easy on the sweets. Remember what Dr. Hertz said?" She walked over to him, looking as if she was about to take the food away.

Mr. Fleur growled, raising his fork. "Ahh, leave me alone! In less than a month I'm gonna be confined in gold for God knows how long anyway."

My mouth fell open. I watched him eat his cake as Mrs. Fleur turned her back to him.

Her voice rang in a shaky tone. "I don't want to talk about that right now."

"Well, you are going to have to come to grips with the reality of it sooner or later." Mr. Fleur munched feverishly on his cake.

Mrs. Fleur turned around, revealing her glassy eyes. She shouted, "That's what I've been struggling to do for the past five months, Milton! It terrifies me!"

His face turned from chipper to serious as he brushed his hand across her cheek the same way young lovers do and said, "Hey, hey, look at me. You gotta have faith."

"It's just such a big risk. The odds are still slim. Even Charles and Burt say so!"

Mr. Fleur grumbled. "Well, they're pessimists anyway." He took another bite of his red velvet cake.

"How can you not be in this situation?!"

In that moment, I learned how Mr. Fleur was so good at handling Gloria—he had been dealing with her predecessor for thirty years. He remained calm as he held Mrs. Fleur and said, "We were given certain cards, Cheryll. That's a fact. I can't make my two turn into an ace, but I can learn the game inside out, study the players, and end up winning in the end, no matter my cards. It's not the cards, it's the player."

Mr. Fleur's calmness swept over his wife, and she smiled and said, "I hate that I know you're right. Sometimes I wish I doubted you more . . . My life would be so much easier!"

"Cheryll, you wouldn't let your life be easy, even if you tried! You and I both know this. You love with your whole heart and give even if there's nothing left. Gloria's your carbon copy, there's no denying that. All she got from me was the stubborn gene and a sweet tooth."

"Oh, Gloria," Mrs. Fleur blurted and began to cry some more. Her knees buckled to the floor as she put her head in her hands, wailing away. She was now at my level, but I remained crouched behind the cabinet, peering over anytime I had the opportunity to.

Mr. Fleur grabbed her arms and helped her up as he said, "No, no, no, you keep standing. Listen to me, okay? You keep standing." He grabbed Mrs. Fleur's weak arms and began to dance with her, slowly rocking side to side. He continued, "As long as you do that, the possibilities are endless. As long as you keep standing, you have the option to step, jump, run, maybe even dance . . . like we are doing right now. You see?"

Mrs. Fleur cried as she rejoiced. "Oh, I don't want this to ever stop."

"Oh, but things never stop . . . they just pause. They will eventually continue later on, that's all there is to it." Mr. Fleur stopped rocking for a moment and stood still with his hands in a waltz position. He raised his eyebrows and said, "We might pause for a while, but we will always eventually continue on. We can't help ourselves. It's only human nature, and soon we will be together again. Just like this. With faith, we will all re-unite and dance again . . . just North of Sunset."

He grabbed her hand as she stood there looking emotion-ally drained. I held my breath when they passed by the cabinet I was hiding behind. Mr. Fleur led her out of the kitchen and said, "Come on, time to rest your eyes. Remember when you wake to get ready for all the opportunities that lie ahead."

Once the pair left the kitchen, I waited an hour or so be-fore going to the fridge, grabbing a water, then booking it to the nearest exit. My bottom was sore from sitting on the cold checkered tile for so long, and my mind was reeling. There was no chance of going upstairs to Gloria at that point, so I figured I'd better head home. I reached the front steps and gazed at the empty driveway. Franklin must have gone home, assuming I was spending the night because of how long I'd kept him wait-ing. It was two o'clock in the morning and I was stranded out front of the Fleur Estate.

Chapter Twenty-Five

Out front of the Fleur Estate, the crickets chirped loudly, as if everyone got the punch line but me. The whiskey began to wear off, and I decided I had to walk home. I couldn't go back inside to call a cab, and public transportation didn't run that far north of the boulevard, so walking was all I could do. My head pounded with toxic liquids and even more toxic thoughts after that tumultuous gala. As I walked the empty streets of Bel Air, the yellow lamps lit the foggy road, and the tall hedges served as fortresses to keep nightwalkers out. I shuffled my feet on the pavement.

I can't believe Mr. Fleur is the one being preserved. That's why Gloria was saying all that nonsense about people volunteering their bodies for science. She was defending her father. I get that he is older, but he still has quite a few good years left in him. So, if he's one of the three, then who are the other two?

In that moment I remembered when Gloria had introduced me to Dr. Burton earlier that night. She'd said he was the third partner in the experiment.

There's the answer.

I mumbled to myself, "Robert Burton, Charles Grenadine, and of course . . . Mr. Fleur." I then remembered Laura asking me if I was being preserved.

Maybe she thought she could run to me after Charles is gone? Maybe get back at Gloria—with all the "chaperones" gone. Celebrating a death wish. These people are sick and truly macabre. I know the saying 'Geniuses are never appreciated until they are dead,' but this is taking it to a whole other level. Talk about overachievers!

As the web they'd weaved so well began to untangle in my mind, it was already three in the morning. I had been walking for an hour and hadn't even realized it. My mind was racing and my feet were keeping up. I passed over a large concrete bridge that arced through the mountains. I could see the outskirts of South of Sunset, in all its lifelessness, far away. I paused for a moment in the iridescent color, letting the view consume me, then continued walking as my thoughts grew wilder.

Ahh, man, then there's Gloria. I'm gonna have to stick around and comfort her because her father decided to turn into a human Oscar. I love her and all, but that's going to be a pain in my ass. I know my life is already lousy, but I am still young. Last thing I need is to get involved with a widow's daughter. Whether the experiment works or not, she's still going to be without a father for God knows how long. That selfless, selfish bastard! Fathers always leave.

I'd thought Mr. Fleur was going to show me the ropes and guide me to be as successful as he was. I now know that's not at all how that works and you have to do the work on your own. You drive down your own path, and every now and then someone will pay to fill the air in your tires. That's how success actually works.

I felt discouraged knowing that Mr. Fleur wasn't going to

be around to see the flowers Gloria and I picked for the fall collection become a success either. I almost didn't want to return to North of Sunset. I wanted to forget everything I'd heard and disappear, away from the malarkey, but that wouldn't be the right decision. After another hour of reckless thinking passed, I finally glimpsed light at the end of the tunnel. I knew I had reached the outskirts of SOS as soon as I saw the black wrought iron gates that read *South of Sunset.* Behind the gates stood the colorless world I knew so well, even as the fog blurred out everything around me.

"Aren't you a scene for a sinner?" I stared up at the shabby fence running alongside the gates.

On top of the gate, the *t* at the end of *Sunset* swung crooked as a raven flew off it. I walked through the entrance, and in that moment, I finally understood what they mean when they say something goes south.

The next thing I remember was waking up to the sound of ringing. It buzzed repeatedly in my head as the vibrations grew stronger. At first, I thought it was my friend old-fashioned, reminding me of the brain cells he'd taken, so I just shut my eyes and let the ringing fade away. I fell asleep once more in my dull apartment, still wearing my suit from the night before.

Brrring! Brrring!

There it was again. This time I knew it wasn't in my head, it was the telephone that was hung strategically on the opposite end of the room. I rose in a panic, unsticking my sweaty face from the hot pillowcase. My brass clock read 3:02. My head pounded as I stood up out of bed and regrettably proceeded toward the agonizing, nonstop ringing. If anything, that ringing made my head hurt more than the whiskey. I felt the white sun beat down into my square living area as if it were an artificial UV light, my apartment the cage, and I the reptile.

I answered the phone.

"Gloria?!"

"Hey, hey, buddy!"

"Oh, hi, James."

"Don't get too excited now."

"Sorry, I just woke up."

"Ahhh, boy! I was going to ask if you wanted to waste the rest of your Sunday with me, but seems like you don't need my help."

I grumbled under my breath. "Yeah, I'm in no shape to go out. Sorry, James."

"You shouldn't be! Sounds like you had a pretty wild night out last night. I guess Ms. Fleur is not a bore after all. I'm just tooling around at home, living the complete opposite. Was hoping you'd be my excuse to escape the old lamp at home."

"You asshole!" I could hear Elsie, James's fiancée, screaming in the background.

They were a funny pair, James and Elsie. He aggravated her and she aggravated him, but they loved each other dearly. I think they put on a show in front of others, not letting anyone else know how deeply they respected one another. People try to ruin beautiful things and they seemed to know that. Like I said, a funny pair. I was just happy they hadn't killed each other yet. I fell back asleep to *Science's Latest Discoveries* that night, as the city remained fairly quiet. While Fridays were like dry martinis and Wednesdays like apple juice, Sundays were the water of the week: boring and necessary.

The following morning, I stood in front of the factory at eight thirty, like any other Monday, and waited for Franklin to pick me up. I read my book on the steps while my old coworkers passed me by, exchanging sour glances, until the town car pulled up around nine.

I walked up to the vehicle and said, "Franklin, you're late—"

"Good morning," replied a warm voice.

It was Mr. Fleur. He immediately got out of the car, towering over my measly self.

I softly replied, "Good morning, sir," hoping he hadn't taken offense to my previous remark.

"Just because those people are wealthy, doesn't mean you should act like them. I've seen kings make fools of themselves in front of jesters." He looked down and noticed the book in my hand. It was a textbook that spoke of the different theories of life preservation, which I'd picked up at the library on my way in. It was too large to hide, so I just did my best to keep my hand still and not cause a row.

"You're curious about the experiment, aren't you?"

I shifted my eyes down. "Well, sir . . . it really is none of my business."

A ticked-off smile crept across his face as he asked, "Is that so?"

"Yes, sir."

He began to walk up the steps and into the front entrance of the Fleur Industries factory. He motioned for me to follow. "Then you must not take a fancy to hiding behind cabinets either?" He continued down the long rose-lined hallway as I grew more frightened by his words. "And you're a man whose character condemns eavesdropping as well, right? And—"

"Okay, okay." I finally cracked. "I'm sorry, sir. I did not mean to listen in on your conversation with Mrs. Fleur. I was just grabbing water, then I panicked when I heard the door—"

He raised his hand to get me to stop blabbering. Mr. Fleur looked me in the eyes and laughed. "Why didn't you just say hello?"

"Well, I didn't know if you wanted me to be a part of your conversation. Also, it was so late, and I was still there," I reasoned, trying to avoid the uncomfortable.

"Oleander, listen to me, son. Stop being ashamed of your

decisions. Live your life as if everything you say and do is to be put on a billboard in quotes with your name underneath it."

"Like the ones on Sunset." I smiled.

"Exactly, son. If you own up to what you do, you now hold the cards. Remember, on carpet, bleach stains can be worse than brandy."

I looked down. "I will keep that in mind, sir. Again, my apologies."

Without looking at me, he just said, "Don't apologize. Do better."

I wanted to crawl in a hole and die, but instead, I said, "I'm relieved of my duties here, aren't I?"

"Oh, no, my boy. Not yet." Mr. Fleur pulled the cage door to the elevator open. "I can tell you are fascinated by what we are doing. Enthusiasm is one of the most valued assets in an employee. Time to feed your curiosity, Oleander."

The elevator rose quickly, leaving my stomach behind, and then came to a complete stop on the twelfth floor.

"Isn't there a saying that goes 'Curiosity killed the cat'?"

"Yes, but then all the other cats decided to kill curiosity due to their fear of it. Never be afraid to question things, Oleander. Knowledge is power."

"Oh, but ignorance is bliss."

"Well, enjoy your last bit of bliss because I'm going to answer any question you have regarding this experiment," Mr. Fleur announced.

The elevator door opened, revealing a black hallway with one grand door at the end. I slowly trailed him down that ominous hall, staring at the blank walls. Once we arrived at the single door, Mr. Fleur pulled a large key out of his pocket and opened it. Inside was one of the most fascinating rooms I had ever seen. We stepped inside that two-thousand-square-foot room with emerald-green walls covered in molding and brass gadgets sprawled around like an art exhibit. The machines looked like original prototypes to who knows what. Some stood eight feet tall with pulley systems and buckets resembling waterfalls. Some were short and stumpy, compactly square, resembling an oven. These oddly shaped machines were all part of the attempts that had led to Fleur's success. Turns out they were all prototypes for the smelting systems we had in the factories.

Engulfed in the sea of shiny brass contraptions was a black desk covered in gold trim with a sitting area in front of it. Mr. Fleur and I sat down simultaneously. I watched him squirm a bit as he got comfy in his chair.

"Okay, Oleander, ask away, my boy."

"Where do I even start?" I chuckled, looking around the glittering room. "How'd you get to be this rich?"

"I cured cancer." He shrugged.

I cracked up.

Mr. Fleur smiled. "Well, you don't think I became the third-richest man in the world from flowers, do you?"

He wasn't kidding.

"Medicine. I was the man that discovered the cure for cancer, Oleander. Well, in the United States at least. Turns out we had it all along, but health isn't as profitable as sickness. I started my own independent pharmaceutical company that was outside federal regulations. With enough proof and believers, we skyrocketed to the point the public had to be made aware. Others took credit of course." He looked off as he pulled a cigar from his drawer. "Everything followed suit. The gold, the flowers. It all started with Fleur Industries' medical advancements."

We talked for hours, everything from how he discovered life preservation to the formulas and equations used to make it possible. Mr. Fleur even mentioned all the machines he'd invented for the experiment and their exact locations. He went into detail about how he'd physically prepped his body to undergo the experiment too. We got off subject sometimes, talking about his past and even mine.

"And I haven't spoken to my mother since the day I left for college." I sighed.

"Now, son, that seems like a very harsh punishment, don't you think?"

"I think it's merciful. She made my father leave."

"Made him? A true man can't be made to do anything. This may be hard to hear, but everything in life is a choice, directly or indirectly. From the story you just told me, sounds like he did it of his own accord."

"He wouldn't have chosen to leave, if my mother hadn't—"

"Hadn't what? Pissed him off, Oleander? Painted a fence? Not changed for him? Put food on the table, even if your father wasn't there to eat it? Pretend he would come back so you learned the importance of faith? Overcompensated by acting silly, despite what others thought, so you wouldn't lose your childlike wonder for life? Loved you dearly?"

I sat there in silence.

Maybe I should have brought an old smock with me rather than a university sweater.

One wearer created while the other destroyed.

As each question progressed in that office, so did the length of our answers and the depth of the conversation. Little did I know, that was something I had genuinely missed. Valued, interesting conversation. The action of speaking to someone who listens to what you have to say or, even better, actually wanting to hear their rebuttal. Mr. Fleur was the most interesting man I have ever met, still to this day. Fifty years later, I remember the conversation I had with him. I was the type of guy that got the same thrill being told any question I have could be answered as a kid being told they could have any toy they wanted. I mean, who wouldn't be thrilled by that?

Feeling completely comfortable, I asked, "So what will happen to the company once you, Grenadine, and Burton are frozen?"

Mr. Fleur looked confused, an expression I hadn't seen on him before, as he said, "Pardon me?"

"Oh, I'm sorry if that question was too—"

"No, no." He shook his head. "I must have misunderstood you. Repeat it again."

I slowly and calmly asked, "Once you, Charles Grenadine, and Robert Burton are preserved, who will run Fleur Industries?"

He looked puzzled for a moment, then light came back into his blue eyes. "Where did you get the idea that Charles and Burt are being preserved with me?"

After that question, I quickly became the confused one. "Well . . . three subjects, three partners. I already know you're in for sure, so that left two. Process of elimination."

Mr. Fleur rubbed his chin in contemplation as he replied, "Yes, that does leave two."

In that moment we both heard a knock on the door, and Mr. Fleur shouted, "Come in." It was Mr. Walter, my old boss. It was nice to see him in all his neurotic glory; it gave me a sense of comfort knowing not everything changes. He told Mr. Fleur that Cheryll was on the phone asking if he would be home for dinner.

"Tell her I'll be home shortly," he replied.

Mr. Walter relayed the message to her, then asked, "She wants to know if Oleander will be joining?"

Mr. Fleur looked at Mr. Walter, then back at me. "No. Tell her it'll be just us three tonight. Me, her, and Gloria."

I felt my heart drop to my stomach like an unattached elevator as everything clicked into place.

Chapter Twenty-Six

I remember staying up that whole night, thinking and thinking. I wondered how I could have missed the obvious and if that was what my dream in the library had been all about. I was stuck inside the box, not realizing the answer was to think outside of it. Then I wondered if I was even supposed to be looking for the answer. Did Mr. Fleur want me to find out or did he think I was oblivious to it? After all, I was a well-oiled machine, focused on the tasks assigned to me. I was determined not to get distracted by anything. I guess that was expected of me. Steady like a rock, that's what I told myself. I decided it was best not to let them know that I knew, since I was armed with classified information. I had to be just as strategic as they were in that twisted game. It was like Texas Hold'em: I was holding the aces, but I had to keep it a secret from my opponent.

I worked alone on Tuesday while Gloria was apparently in and out of meetings. This gave me a full day to let a very elaborate plan of attack brew inside of me. I vowed to myself that I'd stay vigilant, calm, and unassuming, like any good stoic, and let Gloria lose her cool. Boy, did that go out the window. It's funny what you think you can accomplish when you're sitting alone in a calm, quiet room, unbothered by outside factors, versus what actually happens when it comes time to act in front of others. While I thought up that foolproof plan, I forgot the most important factor that played into the strategy . . . human nature. The moment I saw Gloria, I caved.

It happened Wednesday morning, the first day of August. In my life, monumental events always coincidentally occurred on the first day of a new month. I don't know why, and I don't know how, but maybe the universe thought it fit. I was fonder of the idea of change over the reality of it, so the fact that it would come on schedule maybe made it easier for my detail-oriented personality to grasp. Sometimes the scariest type of change is not external, but within one's mind. I thought I knew the situation I was in, but a cloth had been tied over my eyes.

When I walked into the greenhouse, I noticed something. The plants outside that glass building looked less vibrant as their season started to come to an end along with mine. Gloria cheerfully greeted me and went in for a kiss. I involuntarily turned my head, letting her lips fall upon my cheek. That was my first mistake in giving away my position.

"I'm not wearing lipstick today, no need to worry."

"Oh, that's good." I drifted away from her.

"I heard you spent all day with my father Monday." Gloria walked closer to me.

I nodded.

"What's wrong?"

"Nothing." I sat down on the ledge.

She shrugged and said, "Okay."

The room was silent for five whole minutes as Gloria went about reading her book. She knew exactly how to get inside my head, letting her insincere carelessness torment me. I finally cracked—my emotions couldn't bear it.

"Why didn't you tell me you're going to be frozen?!"

Gloria turned to me with a look of shock. "How did you find out?!"

"Doesn't take a rocket scientist to put it all together!"

Gloria immediately stood up and walked toward the hydrangeas that were hanging along a glass wall. I could hear a soft whimper emerge from her. Her body twitched a bit as her breath became shallow and short. Her hand delicately touched the hydrangeas as she tapped her foot in distress.

"It's so funny that hydrangeas can stand for heartfeltness, but when put in a certain location, like indoors, they mean bad luck," Gloria said. She then turned around to face me, her cheeks splotched with tears.

"You realize I was already opposed to your father doing this," I said. "He's still got quite a few good years left in him. Even Charles and Burt say it's a death wish!"

"He should have never told you! You weren't supposed to find out!"

"Till when? All of a sudden you disappear, and I get a telegram? What the hell, Gloria?! It's suicide."

Her spirit came back into her face as she said, "Well, think about if we succeed! We will save so many lives beyond ours."

"And if you don't?"

Gloria's face turned serious as she sat back down next to me. "Don't succeed? We already have by the incredible advances we've made with this new technology."

I sighed in frustration. "Okay, let me rephrase that . . . Not succeed, but survive."

Gloria laughed and her tone lightened as she said, "Well, everyone dies eventually! No one is ready to, but—you still think you're immortal, don't you?"

"No, but I'm young," I countered.

"And?"

I realized Gloria's point and that no argument I could make would suffice, for she was regrettably right. Doesn't matter if you're young, death works on its own clock. Like I've said before, Gloria was very wise beyond her years. She figured it was a noble cause to risk her life in hopes of helping others. After all, we risk our lives every day whether we know it or not.

I grabbed her hand, ignoring all the alarms that sounded in my head, and said, "I'm just not naturally brave like you."

She smiled. "Brave? I'm nothing of the sort. I think people become brave when they're handed a situation where there's nothing else to be."

"Well, I personally don't want to be in a situation where I have to be."

"Neither did I." Gloria sighed.

In that moment, the alarms turned back on in my head like faulty smoke detectors.

"So, what is this . . . a fling to you?" I snapped at Gloria.

"What?!"

"Well, you're going to be gone soon, so—"

"Preserved." She lifted her finger.

I sighed. "We aren't going to be together much longer."

Gloria's face turned panic stricken. "But you said you loved me?"

"And?"

Gloria stood up. "Love creates miracles and knows no boundaries!"

I tilted my head and looked at her in disbelief. "So what do you expect to happen?"

Gloria paced back and forth. "I don't know! I just love you. That's all. I just want to be with you. I didn't plan on this."

"Plan on being preserved or taking a liking to me?"

"Well, both. But both are out of my control at this point!"

She sat down on the opposite end of the greenhouse and began to cry heavier and louder. The sleeves of her lavender-colored dress got wet as she covered her eyes in the most tragically humble way. I could feel the pain radiating off her as I watched from afar, like watching a bad traffic accident. Other people's extreme emotions made me very uncomfortable, so I had to act fast. I walked over to her as I thought about what I could say to stop her episode. I tried to channel my inner Mr. Fleur because he knew how to handle Gloria, but my mind was blank. She sobbed about how it was all out of her control, so I figured a good response would be, "Well, not mine."

Gloria's red-and-green eyes looked up at me in disbelief.

I grabbed Gloria's shaky hands and said, "Maybe I'll be brave for you. Four is a better number, anyway."

"What? No," she replied.

I smiled and nodded as if I were on autopilot. I don't think I understood the gravity of what I'd just agreed to. In the moment, I'd just wanted to create a short-term solution to the ear-aching problem I had in front of me. As soon as Gloria rejoiced, hugging and kissing me all over, my consciousness came back into my body like a virus. A sense of dread surrounded me as I realized what I'd signed up for. I had just sealed my own fate.

Chapter Twenty-Seven

T here is the boy wonder," Franklin shouted as he threw a football to Jimmy, one of the three landscapers I'd come to know.

It was Friday morning, and all the men of Fleur Estate were in high spirits, scattered around the lawn, warming up for a football game. Chef coats draped on garden chairs, butler sleeves rolled up, jumpsuits tied around waists, and wallets and keys in a pile on a table set the scene for a typical summer game with the staff.

"Heard you're in," Franklin said to me as Jimmy chucked the football back.

"I had no clue there was going to be a football game. I would have brought better shoes," I replied as I walked over.

"No." Franklin smirked. "The other game . . . the big one."

"The killer one," Scott added as he pulled the gun from his holster and placed it on the table like it was another set of keys.

Word traveled fast at the Fleur Estate. I'd spontaneously told Gloria on Wednesday that I'd volunteer with her for the experiment, and by Friday, the chauffeur and security guard were already bidding me adieu.

Mr. Fleur came around the corner, rubbing his hands on his stomach, then clapping them together, as if his shirt were chalk. "Mornin', fellas."

An assembly of waves rose and fell with a few "Morning, sirs," as he integrated into the group of ten or so.

"Ready to have a limp in your other leg too?" Scott remarked to Franklin, rolling his neck around.

"Believe it or not, I get mistaken for a famous football player all the time. So the gag's on you."

Laughter erupted over the grassy lawn.

"That's ludicrous!" Scott shook his head.

"It's true. In the appropriate attire, I'm a ringer for Hardy Lockwood."

All the foxes got a kick out of that.

"Too bad you don't have the uniform on. If we saw it, we might believe you," Mr. Fleur said as he nudged me, winking.

"Uniform or not, you'd still look like a jackass, Frank," Scott interjected.

"That's where you are all wrong!" Franklin puffed his chest out as the men continued laughing.

"Oh, wait!" A devilish smile reached Mr. Fleur's face. "I do have an old football uniform inside. Why don't you go put it on?" Mr. Fleur shooed him. "I bet you'll look more like a bowling pin than Lockwood, though."

"You're on." Franklin enthusiastically jogged away.

Keep in mind, Franklin was about a foot taller than Mr. Fleur.

Mr. Fleur whispered in my ear, "Let me confide in you, son. That uniform is from when I was a young boy."

About fifteen minutes passed before we heard rustling in the bushes nearby.

"Are you ready to see the finest Russian racehorse there ever was?!"

The crowd fell silent.

The moment Franklin jumped out of the bush, all the men collapsed with laughter, rolling around on the ground like a bunch of heckling hyenas. Here is the visual: Imagine a six-foot-something lanky man with a mustache in a child's football uniform. The red-and-white shirt was a crop top on him, causing his love handles to spill out the sides and exposing his hairy belly button to everyone. The pants barely made it up his legs, leaving him to walk like a penguin. And lastly, the helmet didn't fit on his head all the way and pinched into his temples, resembling a cone. So yes, he did look like a human bowling pin.

"Ya know what?" Mr. Fleur reached into his pocket. "Here's the money. You won just out of sheer comedic relief."

"Oh, keep it." Franklin waved his hand. "I don't gamble. I do it for the people." He began to pose, flexing his muscles in the most disturbing way. The men continued laughing, and he even got a giggle out of me.

"What in—" Gloria walked up, and all the men grew quiet. Franklin immediately wiggled his shirt down a bit to try and cover up his exposed navel. Gloria burst out laughing.

"Oleander, you working with me today or playing dress-up too?"

"Dress-up seems like the better option," Franklin responded as he posed some more.

"I guess we are cutting it pretty close. I'll see you guys later." I waved goodbye.

Gloria was still laughing to herself about Franklin's ensemble. "He's a character, isn't he?" She looked back at Franklin.

"Yeah. If that's a good thing, I don't know," I replied, feeling a little jealous.

"I think it is. Heck, we all are! Might as well embrace it." Gloria squeezed my hand as we made our way to the workstation. We ended early that day, as we'd spent it mainly thinking about how to market the new collection. It was harder to convince people to buy flowers for a friend rather than a lover. We had yet to figure out our angle.

After calling it quits for the day, we spent the afternoon in the far end of the garden by the pond, shaded by willows. We brought with us a gingham blanket and a bottle of sweet wine. I don't remember the name of it, but Gloria said Chef Anthony had slipped it to her the other night when her father wasn't around, as a gift.

"He said I should save it for a rainy day, but we don't have time for that." She looked up at the bluebird sky peeking through the trees.

"Summer rain regrettably dislikes August in California." I peeled the top off the bottle. "Did you bring a bottle opener?"

"Oh, I didn't even think about it." Gloria laughed and shook her head.

We didn't have a sip of anything that afternoon; once we began talking, everything else faded away. Gloria asked me about my views on politics, religion, and all the other serious questions that are important to know about the person you are with.

"Oleander, I've been thinking a lot lately. Too much, actually. I know everything happens for a reason, but . . . well, do you believe in God?"

"Yeah. Why?"

"What do you think He is like?"

"I think God is cynical."

"What makes you say that?" She laughed.

"God made man in His own image, didn't He?"

Gloria fell silent. She looked flabbergasted. We watched

the ducks swim around the pond a few more times before Franklin came over.

"I'm heading out, are you ready to go home?"

"Oh, no. Please stay, sweetie." Gloria grabbed my arm and held it tight.

"Sweetie can stay. I just need to know if I should head out with or without him," Franklin replied.

"I should head home. It's past five." I got up from the blanket, brushing my pants straight.

Franklin already had his back to us, walking away, when I gave Gloria a kiss. I followed him to the car, running a bit to catch up to him.

"Franklin, do you think God is cynical?"

"Odd question," he remarked as we got into the car. "No, I can't say that I do."

"Well then, what do you think?"

"I don't know. You see a lot of terrible things in the world, but there are also miracles that happen right under our noses."

"That's why I think He is a cynic."

"Or a psychopath. Psychopaths can create some of the most ingenious, miraculous things, but they also let the most unimaginably horrific things happen without remorse. Maybe that's it."

"That's ridiculous, Frank."

"This whole conversation is ridiculous. Since when did you get so deep?"

"Since her."

"Well, why don't you ask her about her thoughts on the subject?"

"I did. We talked about it for quite some time."

"Well, if God is all-knowing, all-powerful, and all-good . . . why do terrible things happen? Did you ask your sweetie that?"

"Yes," I responded calmly. I could tell I'd struck a nerve with Franklin. "She said she saw Him more like a parent. He is all three of those things. Being all-good doesn't mean preventing bad things from happening. A good parent teaches their children life lessons, but also has to take a step back and let them learn. She said that, like a good parent, He is a 'good God.'"

We both laughed.

"More for humankind than for individuals, you think?"

"I don't know," I replied. "They are one and the same, I guess."

"I guess you're right. Hey, you're not all that bad, Ollie."

"Was I ever?"

"How would I know?" Franklin smiled.

"You're right."

He dropped me off at the factory, relieving me from the Fleurs' tight grasp for the weekend. I decided to go out that night to a picture show, since it had been so long. I typically would've called James up on a Friday night to hit the town, but I felt like being alone—taking a break from people. I asked the usher which film was the best and she recommended a Samson O'Donell vehicle. I nodded, then proceeded to buy a ticket to a lesser-known picture, one without Samson and one without a crowd. It was a film about a knight who had been wrongfully accused of stealing from the king and sentenced to death. I wept quietly in the empty theater as the black-and-white film rolled on, cutting from scene to scene.

"Forgive me, for I am innocent." The knight prayed alone in his hay-filled cell the night before his execution. "I am a young man who has yet to save a maiden, yet to fall in love, yet to conquer lands and lead armies into victory. I am a young man who has yet to live."

An old beggar woman in the cell across from him, looking tattered and frail, replied, "Yet to live? What have you been doing all this time?"

I got up and left the theater early because of my "runny nose." I didn't make it to the end to see if the innocent man escaped death.

Chapter Twenty-Eight

Since I'd volunteered to be another unfortunate test subject with the Fleur family on their risky experiment, Gloria hadn't mentioned a thing about it when we worked together. Maybe she didn't want to think about it or maybe she wanted me to bring it up. Maybe she thought if she kept me out of the loop, I couldn't go through with it. Either way, I was relieved to be in the clear as Gloria and I tenderly embraced being together. The days grew hotter and windier as the finish line for the fall flower collection started to come into view. All was calm again at the Fleur Estate, until one night, out of the blue, I was personally invited to dinner by Mr. Fleur.

As Gloria, Mrs. Fleur, Mr. Fleur, and I sat at that fifteen-foot wooden dining table that evening, Mr. Fleur raised his glass for a toast.

"I would like to congratulate Oleander here on his bravery to move forward in the life preservation experiment."

My blood circulated through my veins at double time.

"Gloria told me about your decision, and I have to say that I am pleasantly surprised. Choosing to do this, whether it's in the name of science or love"—he looked over at Gloria then back to me—"is a commitment to the greater good."

There's that phrase again.

"To a special night with even more special people."

We all clinked glasses and drank the champagne in full gulps. I wanted to hide under the table, but played along, smiling and celebrating. After we all feasted on pheasants and souffle, Mrs. Fleur pulled me aside while Gloria and Mr. Fleur threw darts in the parlor.

"Dear, you know you don't have to do this," she whispered.

"I promised Gloria, ma'am."

"Well, do you intend to keep it? No one expects you to go through with this. There is no reason for you to."

"I have to now."

"Think it through. The rest of us have no choice, but you— well, you're a young man, dear. I advise against it, but Milton is a romantic and he'll let you kill yourself for our daughter. Don't let him bully you into it."

I smiled, appreciative that someone understood my position.

"Or me bully you out of it, I guess. If this is what you truly want to do." She shrugged and threw her white gloves to the side nonchalantly.

"Thank you."

"Oleander, I am not a good judge of character, but it looks to me as if you already know what you are going to do and the rest of us will just have to sit back and watch it play out. I must say, I am sitting on the edge of my seat." She walked away, her red satin dress swaying as she shouted, "Milton, darling! Let me have a go of it."

She and Gloria nudged each other playfully as they took ten synchronized paces back and began to throw the lethal points at the board.

"Come into my office, Oleander. I've got a two-hundred-year-old cabernet with your name on it. Well, of course not literally," Mr. Fleur said as he hung his arm over my shoulder like an old pal.

Because of that summer, I grew to love expensive wine and even more expensive people; everything else after it seemed dull in comparison. I graciously accepted his offer as we entered his handsome office.

"I have some forms for you to sign," he said as he pulled a stack of papers from his filing cabinet. He slapped them on the desk, then began rummaging through a bottom drawer. "Aha!" He pulled out a bottle of wine and put it directly next to the papers as if he were pairing it with them like a charcuterie board.

"Remember, you must keep this experiment a secret. The press is starting to get too nosy. Word is getting out to the general public, but they don't care too much about it. Sounds like another boring scientific experiment to them. They don't know it is me who is being preserved or my family. Tabloids would drag our names through the mud if they found out. I am worth too much to disappear quietly. Many people will try to stop me. I know you don't speak with your parents anymore, but is there anyone else important in your life you'd want to say goodbye to?"

I thought long and hard. The only person that came to mind was James, but he was a social fella with many friends. I saw him as my only best friend, but to him, I was probably the outcast he felt bad for. If I disappeared one day, he wouldn't realize it till a year or so later.

"No, sir. No one."

He opened the bottle of wine, not even acknowledging my answer as he began to pour the burgundy liquid into two glasses. He sniffed it and swished it around in his glass. After taking a long sip, he pointed to the top page.

"I'm going to need you to sign this release of liability form first. Basically, it states you can't sue us if something goes wrong."

"All due respect, sir, but if something goes wrong, I won't be able to sue either way, will I?"

"Thanks for reminding me," he joyfully shouted as he walked to another cabinet. "Do you have a will?"

"A will? No, sir. I don't even have a car or a mortgage."

"Do you want those things or is it a nomadic choice?"

I laughed. I'm sure Mr. Fleur was used to eccentrics turning their backs on capitalism just to make a point. But I was poor and couldn't afford to make a political statement.

"I would love those things one day."

"You do understand that one day might not—ooof!" Mr. Fleur swung his arm wide, knocking over his wine glass. "Dammit." The potent liquid spilled all over the stack of papers, smudging the ink and leaving the paper smelling of berries. It was a soggy mess.

"Go run and grab a towel for me, son." Mr. Fleur pointed to the door.

"Yes, sir." I ran out and got one from the kitchen. The white rag was luckily sitting on the counter, conveniently in plain sight. By the time I got back, all the papers were in the trash and the desktop was covered in wine.

"Thanks, my boy!" Mr. Fleur began feverishly wiping up his cherrywood desk. "We'll have to finish this discussion another time. Have some fun tonight. Go out, cause some trouble." He roared and swatted me away. "Not too much, though. I don't want to have to kill you for Glory."

"You're gonna kill me either way." I laughed and shrugged as I walked out of his office.

"I'm much more forgiving than you think."

Mr. Fleur's voice stuck with me; I got the sense that he was well aware of where my head was at. Once I finally shook off the false rattle he caused within me, my days were filled with leisure again. I met Gloria's dearest friends at garden parties and developed a tan from afternoons filled with croquet. Gloria's socialites welcomed me with open arms, as they were just as happy that I shared the same love they felt for Gloria. She even patched things up with Laura Grenadine, letting her win at croquet.

As the days grew shorter, I made sure to keep up with my own research for the fall collection, and my hobbies South of Sunset, which included golfing with James 10 percent of the time and seeing if he was free the other 90 percent. Gloria and I stopped working together for a while as the family spent a lot of their time prepping for the experiment happening at the end of the month. I worked from home as they grew busier, engulfed in all that the experiment entailed. We were like a bunch of snakes slithering around with our heads chopped off, rushing to go nowhere. In the chaos, I realized I had missed multiple phone calls from Gloria letting me know I'd skipped another doctor's appointment for the experiment. She thankfully didn't come from a place of suspicion, but concern.

"I gave the test facility your number, so they'll call you directly," Gloria stated over the phone.

"Thanks. Sorry I missed your calls. Been working out of the house, studying at the public library."

The only ally I had was procrastination of the inevitable, for the experiment was in just over a week. After Gloria's calls, I began putting off the calls from the actual test facility asking when I was available to reschedule. There was a lot of preparation to be done before the human preservation date and I figured if I kept delaying it, I physically wouldn't be able to go through with it. It wouldn't be my fault on purpose . . . it would just be poor planning.

A few days later, I finally decided I should answer the phone or else I'd be out of a job. It was Gloria. I said hello, pretending it was the first call I'd gotten from her.

"Have you received any of my calls or heard anything from the test facility?!"

I said "No" in a surprised tone. I went on to explain that my telephone must need to be serviced or something.

The hesitation in her voice showed a glimpse of skepticism, then she just played it off with an "Oh, okay."

We went on pretending like everything was alright, and she said she was ready to get back to work on the new flower collection.

The following morning, when Franklin drove me to the house, there was a shift in our dynamic. It was either from the August winds or the fact that no matter how hard they blew, I was still around. He didn't talk much to me; I had finally infiltrated the castle of secrets. Franklin glared at me through the rearview mirror as I avoided eye contact. I could feel his forest eyes pierce me like a Damascus sword. Technically, I'd done nothing wrong, but Franklin looked at me as if I were the gum stuck on the bottom of his shoe.

"I didn't see you the other day at the testing facility," Franklin said, finally breaking the silence.

I made sure to stick to my story. "Oh yeah. My phone wasn't working, so I had no clue I was supposed to be there last week."

Franklin nodded. "It's a pretty cool place inside."

I couldn't tell if he was making small talk or trying to get information. Either way, I decided it was best to turn the conversation around on him. "You went inside?"

He smiled and chuckled a bit, lightening the tone as he said, "I walked the family inside, carrying some items for them. I left my jacket in there and had to run back. Gave me a chance to explore a bit."

I nodded, letting the conversation die.

There was definitely a strange feeling in the air that day at the Fleur Estate, as if the gusty weather was making everyone hot and antsy. Gloria was struggling to focus on marketing as she paced around the greenhouse, complaining about anything she could complain about, from micro things, like the unsavory weather, to things on a macro scale, like her feeling stuck, unable to travel and see the world.

All the complaints came to a complete stop when I asked Gloria if she wanted to call it quits for the day. I could tell she was looking for any excuse to get out of working that morning and just needed me to back her up on it. A part of me still suspects that Gloria was so in tune with nature that her emotions affected her surroundings. For once she calmed down, and so did the fire-prone air.

Gloria and I spent the rest of the day playing cards on the balcony attached to her bedroom. It must have been ninety-two degrees outside, and the sky was a deep, hazy blue. We drank raspberry iced tea and switched the game we would play every few hands, filling the void of our empty conversations fueled by boredom. Gloria and I honestly knew we had nothing in common except the fact that we were in the same place at the same time. The truth was so obvious as it stared both of us in the face and filled the air between our sentences. Being young, we chose to ignore it.

"So, I gotta be honest with you," Gloria said casually. "My father thinks you're bluffing."

"Bluffing? About what?"

"You know," Gloria whispered as she looked down at her cards.

My voice raised a few notches as I said, "Tell your father I'm a man of my word!"

Gloria smiled at me. "He doesn't see that you love me."

"He doesn't think I care about you?" I asked, nervously bending the cards in my clammy hands.

Gloria's eyes shifted in contemplation, as if that subject had been on her mind for a while. She hesitantly said, "Well, he finds it odd that I have never seen your house . . . or met your friends. Maybe like you're trying to hide something? Maybe hide me?"

"From what?"

"The real you."

I stood up immediately and pushed my chair back. I walked into her bedroom from the bright balcony and said, "That's it! I'm phoning my best friend, James. We are going to South of Sunset tomorrow so you can see my world!"

Gloria ran over and hugged me. She acted excited and pleasantly surprised by my statement, as if it was all for her and not for Mr. Fleur. I grabbed her hand and ran over to the brass telephone hanging on her wall. After speaking with the mumbly operator, I got James on the line. Gloria stood over my shoulder as I leaned casually on one arm.

"James, ol' boy, clear your schedule tomorrow night! I'm bringing Gloria Fleur to dinner and bowling."

James's staticky voice responded, "The princess herself!"

I heard Gloria laugh behind me as she listened in on the conversation.

"Don't forget to bring your princess too, James," Gloria shouted toward the phone.

James grumbled. "Ahhh, Elsie's just a peasant compared

to you, Gloria." After James's comment, we heard a woman scream and yell profanities in the background.

"Sounds like you did it this time! Best of luck, sarge," I calmly said.

James shouted, "Ay, ay. Seven o'clock," then hung up.

The moment I hung the phone back up, Gloria slipped her shoes on and ran around her room in excitement. She sighed. "I've got to hurry and go shopping for this special occasion!"

"Oh, you don't have to. It's very casual," I said, hoping Gloria wouldn't go overboard.

Gloria smiled and held my hand. "I have to make a good first impression with your friends."

I gave her a kiss as she rushed out the door. This was going to be a whole new exciting experience for her. She had never seen my world. "Show me your friends and I'll show you who you are" had never made its way into our conversations until this point. I knew she was beyond curious, at the very least, to meet the people I was subconsciously influenced by. I was nervous once I realized the gravity of the situation. Our polar opposite worlds were going to collide vice versa this time, and there was no way I could protect Gloria from it.

Gloria Fleur going to South of Sunset . . . This only makes my situation worse.

Chapter Twenty-Nine

Humans overestimate and underestimate our powers in all the wrong ways. We always think we are worth more than what we are paid for, and we always think our words are worthless, even though they can change a life—possibly many. If I had known the effect I had on others, I would've acted much differently that summer—hell, that night. That night. That one pitiful night where the dam finally broke and the raging water came out, crashing and destroying all that had been delicately built.

It was the night I took Gloria to South of Sunset to see my world. I now realize she'd just needed to see it, not live it. Going to North of Sunset, I wore my nicest suits and did my best to blend into my new surroundings. Gloria didn't change, she didn't waver. Gloria was just as much herself whether in California or in Europe or on Mars. When I knocked on her bedroom door that evening, she was just finishing getting ready.

"You ready?" I shouted, then pressed my ear to the door.

"Yes, hold on!"

Gloria opened the door and then walked back to the center of her room. She stood there and posed with her arms on her waist and her foot in a bevel position. Green. The first thing I saw when I walked in was her bright emerald-green dress. Her lipstickless lips smiled as she waited for an immediate reaction from me. I felt my blood pressure rise as I thought about how extravagant her outfit was. Gloria looked almost too beautiful for South of Sunset. We would stick out like a sore thumb if I took her over there dressed like that.

"Are you comfy in that?"

Gloria's smile faded. "Yes, why?"

I rubbed my face and said quietly, "Well, it's very . . . out there."

"Not really." Gloria giggled. "It's how I dress any other day."

I grabbed Gloria's arms gently. "I think you would look so pretty if you put on a long skirt and blazer or—"

"You want me to change?"

I sighed, trying to figure out what to say without upsetting her. I calmly replied, "Well, no, it's just—"

"You don't like it?" I could see Gloria's heart drop as she grew more worried.

"No, no, no. Not at all! It's just . . . your shoes don't go with your dress."

Gloria smirked at me. "Well, I can change my shoes, Oleander."

I jumped. "No, I like the shoes."

I really had no evidence or validation for the case I was trying to make, so I proceeded with action to avoid going back and forth with Gloria. I went over to her closet and pulled out a long black pencil skirt and a blazer that were hanging in the far left corner.

I held it up on the hanger and said, "What about this? This is very cute."

Gloria's face turned confused and sour. "That old thing?! I'm fine with the dress I'm wearing. I really am."

I handed Gloria the jet-black ensemble with a matching hat. "Just try it! You should see if you like it."

Gloria looked up at me with the clothes in her hands and quietly said, "But it's not me."

"Just try," I pushed.

A look of defeat swept across Gloria's face as she headed to the bathroom to change. Her posture shifted as she walked back out in the drab outfit that hung over her unenthused frame. I could see she was visibly uncomfortable as she fussed with her sleeves and pulled down the tight skirt a few times.

I ignored her clues. "Ahh, look at that. You look great. Ready to go?"

Gloria said nothing as she passed by her vanity covered ironically in coral amaryllis flowers. We both walked out of the room and down the stairs. I tried to remain cheery, though I felt Gloria's silence shame me. We saw Mrs. Fleur, who looked at Gloria strangely. She fixed her face, the same way Gloria did.

She smiled and said, "Gloria! Wow, look at that outfit. Very different."

"Doesn't she look great?" I asked, trying to convince Gloria of my decision.

"Yes, very pretty," Mrs. Fleur responded, her face displaying something much deeper. Being a good parent, as Gloria always said, she stepped aside and let us handle it ourselves as we walked out the front door.

We made our way down the front steps extra slowly since Gloria's skirt wrapped her legs together like a rubber band. Franklin was waiting by the car with the back door open. His face was so animated, you could see his reaction from a mile away.

"Woah, I didn't recognize you for a second, Gloria!"

I smiled at Franklin. "South of Sunset, please, Franklin."

"Yes, sir," he replied with an underlying tone of disrespect.

We drove for about three minutes before Franklin blurted out, "I'm sorry, Glor, but I must ask . . . What's the deal with the outfit? You guys going to a funeral?"

"Could be the death of something, that's for sure," Gloria grumbled under her breath as she looked at me. I could feel the resentment growing within her like a disease, spreading slowly and dangerously.

I quickly said, "Franklin, you wanna put on some tunes?"

When we entered SOS, Gloria's black pressroom-looking hat cast harsh shadows on her face, blending her right into the world outside our windows. Franklin pulled up to the front of my apartment building as the white sun began to set, illuminating the side of that concrete structure. Gloria and I stepped out of the Peellé and began to walk toward the glass front doors. I noticed she wasn't wearing her hat, so I asked her where it was. Everyone wore a hat outdoors South of Sunset.

"Oh, I left it in the car." She ran back to the vehicle.

I saw Franklin run around and grab it out of the back seat. He met her in the middle of the sidewalk and she grabbed it from him in a flustered manner.

"Thank you, Frankie!"

Franklin's voice grew quieter. He murmured to Gloria, "I don't know what is going on, Glor, but I want to let you know I think you are just as beautiful in a ball gown as you are in a paper sack. Don't let anyone make you feel otherwise."

Gloria smiled politely, looked at me awkwardly, then back to Franklin. "You're a good soul," she said to him as she put her hat on and ran back to me.

My apartment's elevator was broken, which was a normal occurrence, so we walked up the spiraling wrought iron stairs for quite a while. My room was high up, so it was no easy task—especially for Gloria in her constricting outfit. The pale sunbeams shone through the windows that ran along the side of the building, revealing the dust particles floating in the dense air. When we finally reached my floor, we were both exhausted. My itchy clothes clung to my sweaty frame, and I could see a sweat stain on Gloria's lower back. Nevertheless, she seemed excited to see my humble abode.

I opened all the locks on my front door, adjusted my sticky arms, and said, "It's no palace, but—"

"It's lovely!" Gloria twirled around my one-room apartment. Amid her wandering, she stopped and noticed the dried-up sunflower sitting on my desk. It was the one she'd given me the first day we met. She looked at me and smiled as her eyes grew sentimental.

"Growing up, I always dreamed of raising a family in a small home. Less space, fewer walls to separate us. When something went wrong, you couldn't just run to another room. You'd have to talk about it. Communicate. I always thought there was something so special about being able to experience every moment together. No secrets. Ya know," Gloria said softly.

Being hot and uncomfortable, I sighed. "So, rich people aren't happy with what they have either."

Gloria laughed. "No, I am very happy with what I got. No matter the troubles, I am still thankful for my situation."

"You rich people and your troubles, ha! You must go out and almost kill yourself to get some sort of a thrill!"

Gloria looked put off. "You really have no clue what the hell you're talking about!"

I gasped. "Oh my goodness! Ladies and gentlemen . . . the esteemed, perfect Gloria Fleur has just spoken an obscenity. She has said the word . . . 'hell.'"

"Well, that's where you can go!" Gloria paused, then turned to me. "Ya know what, I am not going to apologize or feel bad for what I've been given in life, okay?! And I am not going to let you, of all people, make me feel bad!"

"Wow, you really are self-righteous!"

"And you really play the victim!"

The phone rang—a fortunate interruption. I knew it was probably James calling to see where we were, it was already fifteen minutes past seven.

I turned to Gloria. "Ya know what, this can wait. We've really got to get going." I grabbed her arm and hat. "Come on."

Gloria and I walked in silence to the bowling alley where we were meeting Elsie and James. The sun had set, making it far away from the moon, just like Gloria and me. I could hear the familiar tune from my nightmare play in the back of my mind as Gloria walked ahead of me. She had to stop every few paces and angrily wait for me because she had no clue where we were going.

Once we finally arrived at the swanky venue, I sighed. "Better late than never!"

Sweat glistened around Gloria's hairline as she took her hat off to wipe her forehead. My hair felt greasy as well, from all the walking up stairs earlier. Gloria tugged on her skirt, unsticking it from the back of her legs as we walked in. The glowing white sign flickered, revealing a packed joint. A band was performing on a small stage lit up with one overhead light. That place was beyond overstimulating with riffraff. I feared Gloria would be overwhelmed. I watched her look around at the people bowling and drinking. The women were dressed identical to her in all-black ensembles and the men in shabby suits.

"Ah, look at that. Aren't you glad I made you change out of that loud dress?"

Gloria looked at me with disgust. "So I can look like everyone else?"

I nodded, trying to remain positive to avoid confrontation. I spotted James and Elsie sitting at a lane, joking with one another. James had his coat off and his sleeves rolled up, his shirt already a wrinkled mess, and Elsie wasn't that much better. She wore a smart-looking black-striped dress that hung on her gangly frame, similar to a scarecrow, and her matching black hair was chopped right below her ears, curving in to cover her sharp cheekbones. The pair were a pathetic display of two people who'd quit trying, almost as pathetic as the brassy instruments and hums of voices that filled the smoky air. When we walked over, I could see them stand up, Elsie being a few inches taller than James.

"Gloria, this is Elsie and James."

Gloria shook Elsie's hand enthusiastically and said, "So nice to meet you. You are absolutely beautiful!"

Elsie gave Gloria an odd look, shocked by her kindness. Her chapped lips then smiled, thanking Gloria.

Avoiding a handshake, James shouted, "Come here! I feel like we're already family." He grabbed Gloria and hugged her so tightly, her feet lifted a few inches off the floor. Gloria squealed a little, caught off guard. I could tell James was already a few beers deep.

"So, how was the drive?" James asked.

"It was fairly quick. Gloria never realized how close South of Sunset was," I said as we all sat down in the lane's booth.

"I find it unfathomable how just a few miles up the road is an entirely different world," he responded.

Gloria added, "It is even more unfathomable how the person right next to you could be living an entirely different life." She looked over at me in discontent.

I huffed. "Well—"

"That's the beauty of perspective," Elsie stated, saving the conversation.

"Elsie teaches at the School of Fine Arts, East of Sunset. A few years ago, she was famous," James proudly announced.

"Let's not lead Gloria on. One of my paintings was. Only for a moment—but yeah. I got burnt out." Elsie threw her arm up as she lit a pipe.

"Elsie now harnesses her talents teaching children how to turn their art into a sustainable business," James remarked as he motioned to the waiter for another beer.

"It's basically babysitting brats with paintbrushes." Elsie coughed out some smoke.

"I got in trouble for painting as a kid," I replied.

"Boo-hoo," Elsie whined.

"I think it's very important, what you do, Elsie. To be taught at a very young age how to prosper financially off your dreams, that's incredible. For example: If my child took an interest in cameras, they would be sent to a school that prioritized photography. Not only would they learn all the technical aspects of the camera, like correct focal lengths and how to develop film, but they would also learn how to survive off their skill. Don't get me wrong, of course they would be taught basic math and reading and language and all that other stuff, but it would be taught in context. Math learned through invoicing clients, other financial tasks, and so on," Gloria said.

Elsie and James both looked at each other, then laughed under their breaths.

"Honey," I said, putting a hand on her knee. "That only works if you got money."

Gloria's mouth opened a bit and her eyes shifted, as if they were searching for her response somewhere in the air.

"Well, my parents believed in the traditional schooling system and colleges," I said.

"And look where that got you, bud." James slapped me on the arm. "Elsie never went to college and look at her now! Teaching kiddos. It's all a racket to me anyhow." James gulped his caramel-colored liquid.

"It's all so ridiculous, no offense, Elsie," I responded.

"College is a thing of the past, Oleander. Embrace the new age or die with the old one," Elsie replied. "All those Ivy League cats are stuck in alleys nowadays."

The waiter came back with another beer for James before the rest of us had a chance to get water, and Elsie continued berating me. "Your unwavering faith in the system is outdated. You could be in no debt and have researched everything yourself, no degree necessary. How much did your education cost?"

"Els, don't get personal," James interjected.

"No, no. He's a big boy, Jamesy. He can tell me if I'm making him uncomfortable. Oleander, am I making you uncomfortable?"

No wonder she and James fought like fish; Elsie had a talent for public belittling.

"No. You're fine. I went to Brown on scholarship. My parents saved a small fund when I was a kid, so I'm not in debt."

"Well, there you go!" Elsie threw up her toothpick arms. "Your day of reckoning will come later. Not from paying off debt, but from finding out degrees mean zilch."

Gloria laughed under her breath.

"Do you find this funny?" I turned to her as my face grew hot.

Gloria straightened her mouth and looked down, remaining quiet.

The waiter returned, finally bringing the water. As he began to walk away, I stopped him. "Hey, you said your name is Ralph, right?"

"Yes, sir," he politely replied, with the empty tray in his hand.

"Oleander," Gloria said as she put her hand on my arm, gently trying to stop me. She could tell I was elevated.

"Well, Ralphie," I said, tittering. "Can I ask you a question, son?"

"Yes, sir."

"Did you go to college?"

"Yes, sir."

"Ha! Where?"

"Harvard."

Our group fell silent as a pitiful sigh came from Gloria.

"Why do you ask, sir?"

"Oh, no reason, thank you," Gloria interjected, slipping him a cash tip.

"Careful, Oleander," Elsie warned. "A chip on your shoulder can quickly turn into a gash."

"Ollie, have a beer. Relax. Anyhoo, I've got exciting news for all you clowns," James said as he got up to bowl.

"Tell 'em, James!" Elsie turned likable again.

"Hold on, my little raven, let me bowl."

James pretended to throw in the direction of the pinsetter in the lane over, laughing at the scared kid. He turned back to our lane, let go of the large wooden bowling wheel, and knocked over all the pins in one fell swoop. Cause and effect perfectly executed by one choice and one quick movement that night. I grinned involuntarily as I stared at the knocked-over bowling pins, picturing Franklin's dopey face in the miniature football uniform. James was the type of guy that was naturally good at everything without putting too much effort in. After walking back to us three like nothing had happened, James sat down and told us his exciting news.

"Looks like we are both moving on to bigger and better things, bud! I got offered a job as a docent at the historic Museum of Decline."

James had been collecting lost smartphones since he was a kid, so he was extremely enthused that he would be working in the screen sedatives exhibit. He decided he was going to take the job since it paid better than the factory and was at least something that sparked his interest. The way James would go on about history was a spectacle within itself, he switched topics like a cook flipped flapjacks.

Standing up enthusiastically, James ranted on. "Hell, that was the government for ya, legalizing all that is bad and banning all that is good." He held up his glass and talked to it. "Let's hope they never get rid of you again, little buddy." He paced around the lane. "And that's why cows are extinct. The government deemed the amount of methane gas they produced to be harmful to the environment."

"He never stops talking about bullshit," Elsie joked. She then leaned into Gloria and whispered, "James loves history more than he loves me." Elsie got up to bowl.

"I can't confirm nor deny it," James blurted out, then gave her a kiss.

"After all, history is his first love, and I can't compete with that." Elsie swiftly took her turn, then sat back down. She whispered to Gloria, blowing smoke in her face, "You know how men are."

By that point in the night, every lane was filled up, the bar had earned itself a crowd around it, and the music was louder than ever. A man in a gray suit with a camera was walking around the joint, asking people if they wanted their picture taken. When he approached us, I could feel Gloria become suspicious. She asked him why, and he looked at her oddly. Gloria was not exposed to scrappers North of Sunset, so it was hard for her to understand that people would go to a crowded place and try to earn a few bucks doing odd jobs.

Once we all explained to Gloria that it was okay and he was just offering, she finally agreed. He snapped our photo, handed us all four copies, and said it would be $275. Without hesitation, James handed him the cash and Gloria went on gabbing about how that was unlike anything she had ever seen.

We all sat back down, and James asked what everyone was ordering for dinner. As he and Elsie bantered about how they would share a bunch of appetizers, the band caught my attention. It was a young woman accompanied by a saxophone player, and they were phenomenal. I found myself caught in a trance by the singer's devilish talent and larger-than-life stage presence. Her light shoulder-length hair caught the gray glow of the spotlight as her dark lips continued casting a spell on the audience of drunk bowlers and hungry diners. The vibrato in her voice rumbled lowly, enticing me to stay locked in. The saxophone was played by an old man with much more talent, but less appeal—to put it subtly.

I noticed her bare shoulders as she turned to face my direction. *Maybe she's noticed me?* It felt as if the jazz singer began singing the lyrics directly to me from across the room as the saxophone grew louder. Amid my shameless staring, I felt a tap on my shoulder. I found out that it was now the third time Gloria had asked me what I was getting for dinner. I murmured in a panic and quickly looked at the menu.

"She's got nice pipes, huh, Oleander?" Elsie remarked, throwing gasoline on the fire.

Gloria looked down without saying a word.

"Dammit, Elsie, can you ever shut up?" James snapped as he stood up.

"What?" Elsie casually laughed as she motioned to Gloria. "The woman's not a moron."

"You are, you—"

"James, it's alright," Gloria said as she calmed the pair down. "I'm not so hungry. I'm gonna call Franklin. Oleander, you ready to go home? If you want to stay longer, you can."

"No. I'll go with you."

Not kissing me before she walked away, Gloria headed straight to the phone booth in the corner.

Chapter Thirty

You've heard of a New York minute, but what about a Los Angeles minute? From personal experience, it means ten minutes feels like sixty. The car ride from the bowling alley back to the estate was ten Los Angeles minutes long. Boy, oh boy. Gloria remained silent as Franklin drove through the pitch-black night. I went to grab the hand that was resting on her knee. The moment I was in close proximity to that lifeless extremity, it resurrected itself, moving to scratch her shoulder. I felt the anxiety brew inside me while Gloria kept her knees faced away and stared out the car window. I knew she was upset, but my patience and arrogance were tired of her tumultuous mood swings. I sighed, frustrated by her poor attitude and Franklin's bothersome face.

"So, Franklin, what made you turn down your big break?" I poked.

He looked at me confused through the rearview mirror and mumbled, "Sorry?"

I felt like stirring the pot. "Well, I heard you got offered a multimillion-dollar contract for a radio show. I've been racking

my brain, trying to figure out why anyone in their right mind
would turn down an opportunity like that."

Franklin's eyes shifted from me to Gloria, who was
slouched in the corner of the car, deep in thought. He replied
in a wobbly tone, "Ohhh, but I'm not in my right mind! Don't
you know I'm a madman!" Franklin began swerving the car
through the streets of Bel Air, earning a giggle from Gloria.

"Oh yeah? You think that's funny, you two?!"

Both Gloria and Franklin turned quiet again as they
chuckled to themselves. I knew they were happy about upsetting me. I just knew it.

Once we arrived back at the Fleur Estate, the lush green
plants and golden lamps leaned forward, waiting for what was
to happen next. Even the stars eavesdropped—they were just
as unsure as me. Franklin parked the car in front and Gloria
opened up her own door quicker than the speed of light. She
didn't wait for either of us, like she usually did, she just rushed
out of the car.

As I followed her out of the vehicle, she said, "It's easy to
fall in love with beautiful strangers, isn't it?"

There it was. I already knew the lyrics, but I finally heard
the music. I threw my hands up. "Here we go!"

"Here we go?! Ya know what?! If that's how you're gonna
act . . . I'm done talking!" Gloria stormed into the house, like
the hurricane she was, and I followed, trying to act as the Red
Cross.

"Gloria, whatever it is, you're blowing it out of proportion!"

"Ya know, when you talk like that, it makes me feel crazy!
You know that, right?!"

"You sure are playing the part pretty well!"

That comment set her off. She huffed loudly, then stomped
up the spiraling marble staircase.

I followed her. "What has got you all upset this time? Did something happen?"

Gloria replied, "Uh-huh," as she continued up the stairs.

"I told you James and Elsie were rough around the edges and South of Sunset is a terrible place. I already warned you."

"No, no, no!" Gloria stopped at the top of the staircase. "South of Sunset is beautiful! Vibrant neon signs, bright, colorful buildings, bustling streets, and your friends . . . they were nothing but kind to me. It's you, you're the problem!"

"What?! Oh, is it because of that dame onstage?"

Gloria angrily headed down the long hallway. "No, I don't give a damn about her. You're the one who was staring!"

I followed her, staying back at a safe distance. "Staring? She was up on a stage singing! I enjoy music! So now I can't even look at other people? I can't watch a concert. Is that it?"

Gloria stopped in front of her bedroom door. "You weren't just staring, you were gawking! One second later and drool would've started coming out of your mouth!"

"Now you really are being insane."

As we entered the bedroom, Gloria threw her hat on the dresser and shouted, "You ignored me!"

"Gloria, you are being insecure."

Gloria took off her blazer. "I know, and I never was before you!"

I threw my hands up and paced around the room. "So now it's my fault that you're insecure?!"

Gloria sat down in front of her flower-covered vanity and just stared at herself, tears in her eyes.

"Ya know what, you've been in a mood since the moment I picked you up. I'm going home and you can just sleep it off." I went over to the intercom on her wall and paged Franklin.

A quiet whisper came from Gloria's lips as her shoulders

caved forward in the most tragic way. "You made me change," she mumbled to herself.

"Huh?"

Pure rage swept across Gloria's face as she stood up. She turned around and pointed at me like I was a monster. Tears were streaming down her scarlet cheeks. "You made me change!" Gloria walked toward me. I was shocked by the volume and power in her voice.

I stood up and calmly laughed. "Your outfit? That's what this is all about?"

"No, it's not just about clothes! It's so much greater than that, and you know it, so stop pretending. You made me change! You made me turn into some-something I'm not. Truth is you can't accept me for what I am! Do you know I spent hours getting ready just so I could get some sort of reaction out of you?! Do you know that?! Do you know I spent a whole day looking for a green dress, just because one time you told me that green made my eyes glow?"

Gloria sat down next to me, and I wiped a tear from her face. I didn't know what to say just yet, so I remained silent as she continued on.

"And today, you looked at me in distaste. I love you, so I changed. We get to the bowling alley, and you ignore me, gazing hopelessly at the woman on stage who is wearing something identical to me and everyone else in the joint! I know you're not just watching a show, because the way you looked at her was the way you used to look at me! I've seen that look before, so stop treating me like I'm stupid. I know what I saw, and I've come to the conclusion that it's not my clothes, it's me!"

"Oh, Gloria."

She began crying harder again as I tried to hug her. She surprisingly pulled away, rejecting my attempt at physical affection. "It's true," she remarked. "I did everything I could, and

I still wasn't good enough for you . . . and I love you." Her knees buckled to the floor and she covered her face in agony.

Gloria looked up at me and said, "I'd do anything for you, that's the worst part of it all. I'd change. I'd cut my hair. I only have eyes for you, Oleander. I only want to be with you. Do you know how much it kills me inside to watch your eyes dreaming of someone else's? I know you don't love me as much as I love you."

I opened my mouth to speak, but Gloria interjected, "No, don't even try to make up a lie this time. That's just the way it is."

I grabbed her hand and pulled her up off the floor. "But, Gloria, I do love you."

Gloria looked at me head-on. "Do you remember the first time you said you loved me?"

A wave of concern engulfed me as my face turned solemn. "At the ball?" I mumbled, unsure of where this was going.

"Yeah, after I stormed off because you refused to dance with me but then you danced with Laura. Remember that?"

A knot rose in my throat as my heart dropped.

I looked down as Gloria said, "Pretty lousy, huh?"

She began to walk away.

"I had to say something!"

"You had to say something?!"

"I didn't want to lose you."

"Lose me or the benefits?" Gloria sniffled and wiped her face. Her green-and-red eyes looked up to the ceiling, making the most earnest effort not to cry. She murmured, "Now the truth comes out! People always talk about not wanting to know the truth, but I knew it all along. I knew it! But hearing it . . . Ohhh, that feeling is one I hope you never experience. It's sickening."

"Gloria, I really do love you now."

"Now?!" Gloria jerked her arm away and gave me a sharp look. Remember how I mentioned that Gloria loved things with her whole heart? Well, that night, she hated me with it. I felt an amount of shame and negativity thrown at me that would take a person a long time to recover from.

"I am done being manipulated by you!"

"Manipulated?! So now I'm the bad guy, huh? I love you! What more do you want from me, Gloria?! Why is it that I always do something wrong? We were having such a great night and now you have to go and ruin it—"

"I was called?" A head peered in. It was Franklin. He must have been standing by the door that whole damn time, watching the unfortunate events transpire. He hesitantly asked, "Is everything alright?"

I looked over at him. "This doesn't concern you, Franklin. Why didn't you wait by the damn car?"

Gloria immediately began crying again as she sat back down in front of her vanity, overwhelmed. Franklin stormed in, ignoring what I'd told him, and walked over to Gloria. We both stood over her like good and bad consciences, crowding her with our presence, thinking the other belonged on the devil's side of her shoulder.

As the three of us stayed in that position like a bad soap opera, a butler knocked on the door.

"What now?!" I blurted out.

"Oh, um," the butler stuttered. "Mr. Fleur has requested I see if you gentlemen want to join him and the other guests downstairs for a game of poker. Mr. Grenadine, Dr. Burton, and the other members of the board are here."

Franklin responded without hesitation, "Tell Mr. Fleur I am sorry, but I have something more important going on right now."

I looked over at Franklin in disapproval. "Well, you can tell Mr. Fleur I'll be right down. I wouldn't be so rude as to turn down his invitation."

The butler nodded timidly and walked out. Gloria was still upset; she just sat there with her hands over her eyes, breathing heavily. I glanced at the door, then back at her, contemplating what to do.

I hurt Gloria, but if I turn down Mr. Fleur, I will hurt myself. All his most important colleagues are here. Who knows what opportunities could arise? I'll just swoon Gloria another day and she'll be fine.

I headed for the door and hollered to Franklin, "You're missing out."

Franklin glared at me and said, "I don't gamble."

Gloria turned to Franklin. "Are you sure you don't want to play?"

Franklin rolled his eyes. "Yeah." That was his typical pious response, acting as if he disliked everything I valued. As I walked out, I heard Gloria ask Franklin why he'd turned down that big contract, and his response was, "It's not my number one priority."

I headed down the hallway, aggravated by all that had occurred. Looking back, I want to smack myself for being an arrogant little prick, but in that moment, I was on autopilot, acting how I saw fit. After leaving Gloria's bedroom, I heard footsteps behind me. I turned around to see Franklin following me down the corridor.

As he approached, I shouted, "Fear of missing out, eh?"

Franklin grabbed me by my shoulders and pinned me to the wall. His voice growled in the most terrifying tone. "Listen to me . . . if you ever hurt that woman again, I will put the fear of God in you." He let go, throwing me to the side as if I were a weak maggot. He then slowly walked away. "I hope He's a psychopath to you," Franklin mumbled under his breath as he rolled up his sleeves and disappeared.

That floppy-eared Irish setter I thought I knew so well turned into a hellhound that night . . . tracking down his next victim.

Chapter Thirty-One

"Oleander! Come on in!"

The vibrations of chatter and occasional coughs filled the smoky room of old men. As I entered the parlor, Mr. Fleur greeted me. Charles Grenadine, Burt, and a few other familiar faces from the gala presented themselves. The gold chandelier that hung over the center of the poker table lit up all the men's faces in the most dubious way, as if they were members of an underground coalition. The smoke from their expensive cigars matched the dark-gray color of the walls, and the green poker table matched the stacks the men pulled from their satin-lined pockets.

A lump rose in my throat as Mr. Fleur encouraged me to sit down at the table with the foxes. I felt a sense of angst stir within me as I noticed the only chair available was directly across from the boss man himself. I could tell every other man there had made a conscious decision not to sit in that doomed chair. Even Burt and Charles Grenadine were to the right and left of it. I slowly proceeded, hands starting to sweat. I didn't have Gloria as my buffer that night, for I'd left her upstairs to lick the wounds I'd made.

Being truly alone, I timidly took my seat among the intimidating older men. Grenadine, on my left, gave me a stale nod, letting me know that he remembered me—whether from our formal introductions or the very mention of my name coming from his wife's angry lips. On my right was Robert Burton, or Burt as I called him. Contrary to Grenadine, Burt loudly acknowledged me, letting everyone else know that he remembered me.

"Good to see ya, Oleandjeshjhssss . . ."

Well, it was the effort that counted. I smiled back at Burt, forgiving him for his humiliating name butchering. The table grew quiet as I reached for my wallet. Mr. Fleur shook his hand, signaling for me to put my money away. I humbly stuffed it back into my coat pocket and noticed the disgusting amount of funds these men were gambling with. My hundred-dollar bill couldn't even buy me a seat at that game of Texas Hold'em. Luckily for me, I was in with the house.

"Do . . . do you know how to play, Oleander?" Charles asked.

"I think so."

Truth was yes. Yes, I very much knew how to play that game. I had been playing that game for over fifteen years. On thunder-filled nights in Cleveland, the rain would slap against the windows so hard, it felt as if someone were pleading to come in. When my father was still home, I never got scared or, at least, never admitted to it. I would pull the covers over my head and shiver myself to sleep. But when it was just my mother and me, I became a bolting, cry-happy wimp. She'd spend nights like those teaching me poker, which worked very well to distract me until I'd fall asleep with my head on the foldout table. Any other time, when I'd have a hard day at school due to kids being unnecessarily cruel, or when I was just missing my dad, she'd pull out the table, shuffle the cards, and we'd play until our crying came from a place of joy rather than solemnity. Looking back, maybe I cried because I didn't want someone to be let in. My father had forced structure into my life, while my mother embraced the fact that life has no structure.

Instead of a spritely five-foot-two woman with tawny hair, there was an older, more shy man with white hair who dealt me in that night. His name was Keith or Mike, I don't quite remember. I met so many important people that summer, they all began to blend together. That was why the Fleur family was so magical. No matter how many years passed by or how many faces I came across, they were truly unforgettable.

As the night grew long, my mediocre hands were barely keeping me in the game. I felt the stakes start to rise as each man slowly got eliminated one by one. It almost felt unfair to be playing with other people's money, let alone to win with it. I felt the torment build within me, watching the pots worth $50,000 being blown like a coffee left on the hood of a car. To these men, that money meant nothing, but for me, it meant a better way of life and possibly a car.

Mr. Fleur had annihilated the whole group except me. He tinkered with his fort made of poker chips, while I refused to stare at my measly pile. The few rounds before, I'd gotten some very lousy hands, but I'd played conservatively, which had led me to this predicament. The dealer, Mike or Keith, slowly handed us our final two cards. This was it.

Burt gave me a cigar and lit it in honor of him pledging his loyalty to my side. He always struck me as the type to root for the underdog. I swiftly looked at my cards . . . a two and a seven, damn. At least they were both spades. With my astounding $5,000 as the big blind, I hoped for a miracle.

"Here we go, gentlemen." Keith/Mike sighed as he laid the three cards on the table.

A ten of spades, a three of hearts, and a queen of spades. I heard the whole table groan. That wasn't the prettiest flop. The men began peeking and whispering to one another as half of them crowded behind Mr. Fleur and the other half behind me. I felt the tension rise as I had four spades that could possibly turn into five. If I got a flush, that would put the odds in my favor.

I checked, waiting to see what the turn had in store. In that moment, clunky footsteps passed by the door, causing Mr. Fleur to raise his head.

I flinched as he shouted, "No poker tonight, Frank?"

Franklin peered his head in and said, "I'm sorry, sir, but I'm still on the clock."

My blood boiled as I watched Mr. Fleur's eyebrows lift and his mouth pinch into a smile. The other men nodded out of respect and went on asking Mr. Fleur about the holier-than-thou driver. I looked down at my cards, not saying a word, as I puffed away. The dealer stood still as the men continued conversing. Once silence appeared in the room, the dealer turned his focus back to acting as fate.

"Dammit," Mr. Fleur groaned as an eight of clubs revealed itself on the turn.

He took the words right out of my mouth, and I checked again, waiting on edge and praying for another spade to appear on the river. My measly two and seven needed a miracle to make them a winning hand. I felt things could turn in my favor. In life we have those few instances where we feel the world turn and we feel ourselves turn in sync with it. We aren't in tune with the earth, but rather, the earth is in tune with us— that's what I think luck is. You know in that case that fortune is yours and nothing can halt it or let it slip out of your hands . . .

Click clack, click clack.

All the men's heads turned away from that ugly eight of clubs lying desperately on the table like an old hooker with some city miles on her. As the door swung open, I delayed my reaction, for I knew the volatile personality those footsteps belonged to. I glanced in the mirror in front of me and saw a tight black gown, crimson-red lips, dark-green velvet gloves, and slick dark hair poison the room with incontestable beauty, floating in my direction. I remained with my back to the alluring creature, fighting not to react.

Burt broke the silence. "My, don't you look lovely, Gloria!"

Mr. Fleur suspiciously followed with, "It's ten o'clock, where are you heading off to?"

"Out," Gloria replied numbly.

Mr. Fleur leveled his gaze at me, waiting for a response, and I felt Gloria's green laser eyes pierce my back. I puffed away on my cigar, still staring at my two and seven.

After ten seconds of silence, Mr. Fleur cheerfully said, "Okay, have fun!"

I jolted my head in shock as I gaped up at the bold man across from me.

"Thanks, Dad!" Gloria smiled.

I saw the dark-green velvet gloves reach around me and delicately grab the cigar out of my hand. The crimson-red lips wrapped around it and blew out a smoke cloud, just so it could rain over my head. Those lips had been the same color the night of the gala, probably made with the blood of all the other guys she'd tortured. The black gown then turned around and slowly strolled away with my cigar as a hostage.

"Hey," I shouted.

Gloria immediately walked back to the table and smiled.

"Oh! I'm sorry, hun." She leaned toward me and gave me a big wet kiss right on the cheek. She then turned to all the men at the table, rolled her eyes, and sighed. "You know how he gets. Can't leave without a kiss."

My face turned red hot, blending in with that obnoxious mark on my cheek. The old men snickered. The black dress and green gloves disappeared out the door, but the crimson-red lipstick stuck around. Everyone and their mother could tell Gloria was loaded for bear as she took out publicly on me all the hurt I had placed upon her. Charles Grenadine walked out from behind Mr. Fleur and circled around to my end of the table. For once his voice wasn't timid as he quietly spoke in my ear. "If that were my lady, I'd already be halfway out the door in a panic by now."

Everyone was caught up in the turmoil Gloria and I had created, except the dealer. Keith/Mike put down the river without saying a word. He was probably my favorite guy in the room, not because he suppressed his opinion of my romantic endeavors, but because he put down a spade . . . a jack of spades, baby. All the men at the table smiled—on my side and Mr. Fleur's side.

Mr. Fleur immediately looked up and said, "You can go after her, son. We won't be mad if you don't finish this hand."

I felt my foot start to fidget because I knew that was his final attempt to dethrone my flush . . . or was it? I'd broken Gloria's heart, and her bold move was her last resort to stir up some kind of reaction in me. Problem was, she knew the art of timing—poor timing, that is. I knew it was a test, I knew she wanted to see if I would chase after her. She wanted to see if I loved her as much as I claimed to. If the roles were reversed, Gloria would have been clutching my arm, never letting me go out on my own. Poor Gloria was probably waiting right out front, crying to herself or, worse, Franklin, as she coughed up the cigar. As I sat at the table I could hear her voice in my head, bawling, "He didn't even chase after me!"

"I'm still in."

I got up from the table as torment stirred within me and rushed to the front door of the house. The large door was wide open, which was odd. Maybe she was so torn up, she'd forgotten to close it? I slowly headed toward the open door. I stopped at the door as I heard Franklin shout, "What the hell are you doing with this?"

"Having a good time. Can't you tell?"

I stepped to the side of the door and peered out the window. Tears ran down Gloria's cheeks. I didn't want my vision to be obstructed, but I wanted to make sure theirs was. I watched him rip the cigar right out of Gloria's mouth as he scolded her. "You and I both know you shouldn't be smoking this with your condition."

"Condition, schmission," Gloria mocked in that old New York gangster accent.

Franklin cracked up and replied in the same accent, "Condition, schmission. Myah, myah."

"Myah, myah," Gloria grumbled back playfully.

Seeing those red lips reminded me of all the aggravation and embarrassment they'd caused. They even reminded me of the time she'd said Mr. Fleur thought I was bluffing about everything. I swiftly turned around and walked back to the poker room.

When I entered, the men were all standing around and conversing.

Keith/Mike noticed me and asked, "Ready?"

The men got quiet as I replied, "Yes, sir."

Mr. Fleur and I took our seats as Burt said, "I didn't reckon' you was comin' back."

"I always finish what I start." I made eye contact with Mr. Fleur.

"And that's why I hired ya," he replied.

Being numb to the gravity of everything around me, I pushed all my chips into the center and said, "I'm all in."

I felt the crowd take a deep breath as Mr. Fleur pushed his chips in without a beat missed. The men behind him were laughing to themselves and gloating, but I was very confident in my hand. Unless Mr. Fleur had a king and ace of spades in his hand, giving him an unbelievable royal flush, he couldn't have beaten me.

The dealer said robustly, "Okay, men, time to show 'em!"

I slapped my cards down and yelped, "Flush!"

My smile turned a tinge less enthusiastic as smirks and jitters crept across Mr. Fleur's side of the table. *Does he have the royal flush? Impossible!*

I watched Mr. Fleur immediately stand and throw his arms up. "Well, damn, my boy! You have me beat! I have nothing."

Confusion and silence swept across his entourage as Mr. Fleur scrounged all the cards together in a pile. Next to the messy pile of cards was an even messier pile of chips worth $100,000. The best part of it was that it was all mine.

Mr. Fleur and I shook hands as the men congratulated me. I never saw his cards, and sure enough, the dealer had grabbed them all. *Should I have asked?* Either way, I felt I already knew the answer.

Mr. Fleur humbly said, "Good game."

"You too, sir."

"Eh, you win some and you lose some."

With my bag of cash and a sleepy suspicion, I wished everyone a good night and walked out the front door. The town car was gone, the driveway was empty, the land was silent, and it was just me and my winnings in hand. The one person

I wanted to share my great news with was absent. I'd let her go. Gloria had walked away, right out of my life, as I remained shackled by the machine. The system Gloria was placed upon in the beginning had looked beautiful and shiny, so I'd switched roles with her, as I'd wanted what she had—status and money. I'd put myself in the box. As soon as I felt my feet stuck on top of the expensive machine that I'd so helplessly craved, it was no longer a symbol of luxury but of imprisonment.

As I stood there alone, with only my life's dream in hand and my night's dream in mind, Mr. Fleur's words rang in my head, stinging like alcohol on a burn.

"You win some and you lose some."

I had won some . . . and I had lost something much greater.

Chapter Thirty-Two

As the clock struck eleven, I began to walk into the dead night, passing fortress after fortress surrounded by stone walls or hedges. I was carrying a canvas bag filled with wads of cash from the poker game, the last thing I wanted was to be robbed. The rectangular bricks were protruding, showing their shape through the material.

Screeech!

I jumped back as a brown Peellé automobile came to a halt in front of me. I grabbed the bag tightly to my chest, but the driver paid me no mind as he pulled straight up to a gate with a large cursive *H* written on it. Every estate had a decadent gate, as if it were a stamp of approval saying the residents inside belonged—belonged to a neighborhood filled with secrets and unspoken codes of ethics and false benevolence and greed disguised as charity and ignorant righteousness and, not to mention, disloyal drunkenness.

"Come, ah, Laura," slurred a man as he spilled out of the chauffeured vehicle. He was wearing a tuxedo that was as dark as the night, and his crisp white teeth reflected the same color of his undershirt. He looked no older than thirty and rich, the kind of rich that comes from bloodline rather than wits.

"I'm hurrying," responded the woman as she stumbled out of the vehicle.

I knew right away those short golden locks and gangly frame. Laura Grenadine's white-gloved hands were holding the stranger's as they struggled to buzz the gate. She was wearing a smart white dress—her signature—and the color had become ironic.

"Come on, let me in! Dammit," scolded the man in the suit as he bent over the buzzer.

"Don't get all fussy. Your guard is probably napping." Laura adjusted the string of pearls wrapped around her neck as she looked around.

Realizing I had been staring, I began to slowly walk past, hoping they wouldn't see me.

"Who's there?" The man puffed his chest out and walked around the vehicle.

"Oh. I was just out for a walk. I'm heading home," I replied as I continued to try and slink away, hiding my face and the bag from Laura.

"You live close by, pal?"

"Well—"

Laura's suspicious face lit up. "No, he doesn't! You dirty dog! My darling, it is so wonderful to see you." Laura gave me a heavy hug, draping her arms over me like a mink. She pulled away and motioned to the gentleman next to her. "Oleander, this is . . . uh, he's an old friend. We're just catching up."

"And who are you?" asked the man with no name as he put his hand on Laura's waist.

"An old friend too," I replied, gazing at the pair with discontent.

The man immediately removed his arm and went on pushing the buttons on the buzzer like a frustrated toddler.

"I better get going." I began to walk away.

"Hold on. Do you have a long walk ahead?" Laura asked.

"Well, yeah, but—"

"Let my chauffeur drive you home!"

"You mean Charles's chauffeur?"

"Quit pretending you're innocent. You and me . . . we're two cats of the same color."

"Not even close."

"What's that bag in your hands?" Laura reached for the canvas bag tucked behind my back.

"Stop!" As I pulled it away, a stack of hundreds fell to the ground. I swiftly picked it up and stuffed it back into the sack.

"Came from the Fleurs', didn't you?" Laura had a sick grin on her face. "I won't tell if you don't."

"I didn't rob them, Mrs. Grenadine." I made sure to emphasize the *Mrs.*

"Whatever you say." Laura walked to the driver's door and motioned for the chauffeur to roll down his window. "Henry, take Oleander here wherever he needs to go." Henry nodded as if talking to Laura would make him an accomplice rather than just an innocent witness.

I hopped in the back seat with my bag slouched over my lap. Laura leaned in and gave me a kiss on the ear. "Feels good to milk them dry, doesn't it?"

My stomach sank. *Is this how everyone sees me?*

She slammed the door and poetically walked through the finally open gate with that night's mystery man. On the silent drive home, I looked out my window and watched the glamour fade away as we crossed the border into dreary South of Sunset.

I rode the elevator up to my empty apartment. The moon

bled through the slits in my blinds differently than it had the night I'd kissed Gloria. Maybe it was a different moon? Maybe astronomers had been lying to me this whole time? The remnants of the dried-up sunflower remained on my desk—it was a miracle it had lasted as long as it had that summer. I sat down on the edge of my bed and stared long and hard as the liquid that coated my eyes blurred the room. In that moment, I felt like one of those gold-dipped roses Fleur proudly mass-produced. My exterior unbreakable, shining in gold, but I still wondered if I was empty or dead inside. I didn't know. Maybe there was a living thing in there, whether a delicate rose or a fragile soul. Sometimes I wished the truth was that there was nothing inside . . . sometimes.

I laid my head down and slept like I had never slept before—as if there was no reason to wake up. The stillness of the night overpowered my body as feelings of peacefulness and subtle melancholy rose within me. I didn't dream of Gloria, my dreams were just black—no tinny music, no haunting ballroom, and no one to lose.

Chapter Thirty-Three

The next morning, I tried to distract my mind from the war that had raged between Gloria and me within the Fleur Estate the night before. It was a Saturday, the most gruesome kind, the type of Saturday that felt like a Sunday. The air was calm as I felt responsibility creep up on me, holding me by the shoulders. I ignored the dread I felt that late-August morning as I decided to achieve a milestone I had long awaited. I purchased my first ever automobile that day, a brand new 2125 base model Peellé. Looking back now, the salesman didn't even ask for a driver's license when I pulled out the wad of cash from the night before. Hell—I didn't even *have* a license.

The vehicle I chose was stark black with flakes of silver. I didn't care that it had no emblem on the front hood; I was just happy I got to be inside the water-powered machine I used to pine for. I drove around the city, almost killing a few unaware pedestrians as I swerved and braked. I had the euphoric feeling of surpassing my feet's limitations as I turned off the radio to hear the engine roar. It clanked and thudded, matching my heartbeat. Driving for the first time was an experience I will never forget and one that I had conquered alone. In the back of my mind, I did think about Mr. Fleur and how I wished he was there, pointing me in the right direction. Nevertheless, I knew I was okay on my own, driving down my own path to success with the passenger seat empty.

After cruising around all morning, I arrived back at my small, discomforting apartment. I parked right in front, since the curb was empty due to all the poor walkers in that area. I grew to appreciate that building—it was the only thing in my life that didn't change drastically.

Anyways, when I looked up at my apartment building, I could feel it tip more than an inch, like an unbalanced boat, as everyone rushed to their windows to see me, Oleander Briggs, lock my own automobile. I jogged to the elevator and headed straight for my scratched-up writing desk. After working for two months on the new flower collection, racking my brain on which ones to pick out of fifty thousand, it hit me.

Once I stepped away from everything and turned my focus toward life's other pleasures, that's when it all came together. All my hard work, all those years of knowledge, all my failed attempts, all those distractions coalesced in my subconscious like a symphony. I sat down while my adrenaline told me what to do, as if I'd known it all along. I smiled softly as I pulled out a fresh piece of paper and filled my pen with ink.

"Sunflower," I whispered to myself as I looked deeply at the dried-up one on my desk.

I thought of the day I first met Gloria Fleur and her world filled with everything exactly exciting on earth. I pictured her dainty hand wrapped around the sunflower, sharing her happiness with me. I should have never taken it that day; I'd drained her, along with that sunflower, of their joy and warmth. I'd dried them out as their beauty dissipated in my hands. Happiness comes and goes, but if we can eternalize the idea of it within us, it will never die. I began writing again.

"Cosmo." I laughed to myself as I remembered the day I tried to kiss Gloria and she threw me for a curve.

Later that day, I uncovered that she'd fallen victim to loving me . . . poor gal. It was like a game of cat and mouse in the dawn of us. It never lasts, because either the mouse wises up and runs away for good or the cat eats it, quickly and mercilessly. I don't know who was which animal, but nevertheless, the idea remained. I looked at the definition of a cosmo and felt the remembrance of a flutter I'd never had. I'd told her she was like a cosmo, pretty and resilient, but that had all been forgotten now. *Cosmo* in floriography means order and harmony, which I once believed everyone longed for, but now I know it's the opposite. They fit the bill physically and emotionally, and they meant something much more to me.

I took a deep breath in as I prolonged writing the last flower species, for that was the one closest to my heart. I'd rushed and rushed that entire summer to find which three flowers were best suited to be preserved, and now that I had the answers, I wanted nothing more than to unlearn them. For it's never finishing the goal that makes one's soul fulfilled, it's the search for the answer. Once I knew the search was about to end, I had the dreaded notion that so were the people involved in it.

After reading "sunflower" and then "cosmo" once more to myself, I clenched my black steel pen with the silver tip, knowing I could no longer procrastinate living my life. I watched the ink dye my bleached paper as I traced two straight vertical lines. My hand moved in slow motion, connecting two diagonal lines to the former. As I lifted my wrist from what appeared to be the letter *M*, a vibration filled the empty room, alarming my already heightened senses.

Brrring! Brrring!

My loudmouth telephone hollered and hollered, forcing me to drop my pen on my impatient sheet of tree. I ran across the room, tripping over my black scuffed-up shoes that I had thrown on the dusty floor. My heart rose in my throat and my palms sweat as anticipation brewed within me. Once I reached the telephone, my hands began to fidget. To be quite frank, I was about as still as a wind chime in Antarctica. The two gold bells on the front of that telephone stared at me as if they were the eyes to that empty wooden box. I stared back, letting the fear of what it had to say paralyze my very being.

Brrring! Brrring! Brrring!

I closed my eyes real tight, clenched my jaw, grabbed the receiver, and quietly held it to my ear. In a hesitant tone I said, "Hello?"

"Hi," replied the soft voice of a woman I had come to know. I smiled and sighed. "Oh, hi, Gloria."

A brief moment of silence held us both by the back of our necks as we waited with a phone grasped closely to our minds. I took a deep breath in to begin speaking the standard small talk I knew by heart. Gloria cut to the chase.

"So, the experiment is in six days . . . and I think we need to talk."

I tilted my chin down toward my collarbone. "I agree."

"Can you be over in an hour?"

"Of course."

I remember that phone conversation feeling completely different than the rest of our encounters; it was cordial. The calmer Gloria was, the more worrisome. The night before, I'd arranged my own symphony filled with crescendos and tears. I knew after that call that I had to face the music I'd created . . . the avaricious, disparaging music.

Chapter Thirty-Four

An hour after my phone call with Gloria, I made my way over to her residence. As the sun began to drop closer to the horizon, I felt the road under my wheels turn from choppy asphalt to glass. My brain was soundless—there was no use torturing myself over how I'd acted the night before. I just continued steering toward the location I knew by heart. I stopped at the gate and swiftly pressed the buzzer. Scott answered, not recognizing the vehicle.

"How may I help you?"

"Scott, it's Oleander."

Static raged in the speaker as Scott laughed. "Oh, hey there, moneybags. Glad to see you finally put your big-boy pants on and drove yourself . . . Pansy."

"Careful, Scott. I took Franklin's job, you might be next," I joked with him.

"You couldn't protect yourself down a measly hallway, let alone an estate," he jabbed. "Anyways, you'd have to pry the security badge out of my cold, dead hand!"

"Well, you are already a hundred, so it shouldn't be too long."

Scott guffawed. "I really don't like you, but you've grown on me. At first, I thought you were a mole I'd have to remove, but you've turned out to be benign."

"Just a friendly little freckle, I am."

Scott scoffed. "Well, I wouldn't go that far. Go in before I change my mind, asshole."

"Asshole," I replied as I entered the gates.

Scott and I couldn't get along, even if our lives depended on it. I stood for everything he hated in this world, academia and intellect, and he prioritized violence and strength. I did grow to respect him—at least he was consistent with his beliefs. I, on the other hand, was as wishy-washy as buttons are triangular.

I pulled up right behind the town car, which was parked on the decomposed granite driveway. I didn't see Franklin. He must have been tooling around the property. I walked to the gardens, breathing in the fresh air that the landscape produced. My lips twitched, curling up a bit as I looked over at the fountain that had acquired a sum of pebbles at the bottom of it. I strolled with ease through the yew hedge maze that I'd frantically gotten lost in on my first day at the estate. I knew the property inside out at that point, which was bittersweet. As I've said before, the searching is much more exciting than the knowing.

The wind whistled through the cottonwood trees as I reached the nook where the faded greenhouse stood. There she was, sitting inside, as fragile as a porcelain statue. When I walked in, Gloria and I shared a sincere, yet uncomfortable, smile. I thought I could maybe convince her one last time to change her mind, though I knew Gloria was stubborn—I had to approach the situation delicately. I sat down next to her. Not a book in sight. Her sage-green dress had small matching buttons that ran all the way up to her neck, framing her solemn face, and her boots were ivory. Her chestnut-colored hair was pulled off her forehead.

"I'm sorry about what I put you through last night . . . with the singer and the clothes and the poker and—"

Gloria calmly interrupted. "That's okay. You can't make it up to me and I no longer have time to waste. I just want to lay everything out on the line." That was so Gloria Fleur, nothing ever sugarcoated and always straight to the point. "I know you're not being preserved."

"Uhh, well," I stuttered.

Gloria lifted her hand, the same way her father did, to stop me. "And that's okay." She stood up and began walking toward some flowerets across the room. "I don't expect you to sacrifice your life for me. I don't expect anyone to. I hope you know that."

"Sacrifice their life . . . for you? Isn't this a group effort? Like you said, for the greater good of science," I pressed.

"Yes and no." She watered some gardenias. "My part in this hasn't been entirely unselfish."

"Gloria?"

She turned around, showing her eyes that looked like lily pads in two ponds. "Oleander. I'm sick."

My insides were kicked out. There was much more gravity to the situation than I'd thought. It was in fact life and death. Gloria sat down as she comforted me—ironically enough.

"Five months ago, the doctors discovered a rare, fatal disease in me when I lost all feeling in my fingertips. It is unlike anything they've ever seen before. They're not exactly sure what will happen, but they estimated I had about five months before the disease started to take its toll, deteriorating me from within."

"So that's why there was a rush and the experiment had to be done in five months."

Gloria nodded. "The moment we got the news, I was ready to give up, accept my fate. Remember the room with the lavender piano?"

"I sure do."

"Well, after we got home from the doctor's office, I sat on the floor in there for a week straight, with the curtains drawn and the lights turned off, sobbing. My father finally came in. I figure he'd needed time to pull himself together too. He told me we would get through this. I shouted and screamed at him, 'It's hopeless!' He told me to have faith in him. I calmed down and made him promise that I was going to be okay. I was just as scared as he was." Gloria shrugged. "Well, he promised."

I watched the tears run down Gloria's cheeks, as if they were draining the fountain of youth from inside her. I thought about the first day I met Mr. Fleur, when he'd come to the factory, and how he'd bragged about his daughter. "Oh, no, I'm the lucky one," he'd boasted. "You boys will understand someday when you have kids of your own. You will do anything in your power to make them feel better. To take away their pain, give them peace of mind. You'd give them your arm and your leg if you could. They become your whole world."

My eyes began to catch the contagious rainstorm that Gloria's had. I finally understood the meaning and depth of love a father could have for his child. I was bewildered by Mr. Fleur as Gloria explained to me all that he'd sacrificed. After he made his promise to Gloria, he immediately went to work. Mr. Fleur spent every day and night in his laboratory, running tests and experiments, trying to use the technology he'd created for flowers on humans. Modern medicine didn't know enough about the disease to cure it, and he wouldn't let Gloria be the one they tested a new cure on, anyway.

"My father burned so many bridges doing this. He pitched his idea to thirty-five different councils and boards, but everyone called him irrational. The last thing all those people wanted was blood on their hands. Being good friends, Robert Burton and Charles Grenadine finally approached my dad, asking what all the malarkey was about. He told them I was fatally ill," Gloria shakily said.

I understood. Mr. Fleur didn't need funding, he just needed other people with his level of knowledge to help him tackle the problem. Burt and Charles loved Mr. Fleur like a brother and Gloria like a daughter, so I'm sure they'd felt ethically obligated to help.

"I remember the day he told my mom and me." Gloria laughed. "You should've seen the look on her face. My father said he had a solution, but there was a catch to it. My mom's face turned as white as a ghost and the silverware in her hand began clanking like an old teapot. She looked terrified! To be honest, I was disheartened when he said he hadn't found a cure, but hey! He discovered a way to buy time. A cure could be found in five years."

"Or fifty," I snapped back.

"Well, either way, my parents decided to stay by my side through it all, and Charles was not happy about that."

"Charles is not happy about anything."

As we both laughed, I remembered the argument Charles had had with Mr. Fleur on my first day at the estate. I'd assumed he was upset about the new flower collection. Boy, how things had changed. I pictured Mr. Fleur agonizing over the pressure he'd put upon himself, all for an unsure outcome. I understood where Charles was coming from as well, but love takes sacrifice—sometimes in small habits and sometimes in life-changing decisions. I could see the gratitude in Gloria's eyes as she went on and on about her father. She would have to stop every few sentences to get her tears under control, then she'd continue on.

"I've tried to convince my parents not to be preserved with me. I really have, but they can't handle the idea of never seeing me again. If a cure is found long after they're gone—I've thought about all the outcomes, and sometimes think it'd be easier if—" Gloria's mouth quivered as tears began to flow more rapidly. She held her fist to her lips as if she were trying to prevent them from finishing the sentence. She took a deep breath in, composing herself. "Do you have a pen?"

"Oh, um, yeah." I immediately rummaged through my coat and found one in the pocket.

Gloria grabbed the pen, satisfied, then a worried look swept across her face. "Do you have paper, as well? I just need something to write on."

I stumbled through my pockets again, hoping a sheet of tree would magically appear. I jingled my car keys. *I have car keys!* Then I felt my wallet. I opened it and found a crumpled receipt from coffee. "Will this work?"

"Perfect!" Gloria took the receipt, examined my fifty-dollar coffee order with a faint hint of judgment, turned it over, and began writing *Fleur Atom Immunizing Technological Health*.

"Not the best name." She laughed as she underlined the first letter of each word, creating the acronym *FAITH*. "And that's what my father gave me. Whether the experiment works or not, I'll always have that."

FAITH. It's what they used in the flowers, the people, it was Mr. Fleur's highly respectable formula. Faith. Had it been a scam this whole time? Was the formula, ironically enough, formulated? Mr. Fleur was a clever man; I know every decision he made was a tactical one. If you gave faith a scientific name, maybe people would question it less—maybe Gloria would. As she was alluding, maybe it would be easier if she were dead. Morbidly enough. Gloria's fate was either one of unknown decay and suffering or one of dying quickly, full of ignorance and hope. I guessed the latter was a better option. *Shame on Mr. Fleur. Will he and his wife actually go through with this suicide mission, or are they just telling Gloria that to ease her mind?*

"So, when you go on about how you envy everything I have, do you now?" Gloria grabbed my hand.

I wouldn't say my answer to that, but we both knew it. The next words she spoke still shake me to my core today, reminding me how much older her mind was. "Ohhh, I don't feel bad, it's really alright. You lack the one thing I take for granted . . . living in luxury. I lack the one thing you take for granted . . . the luxury of living."

My face grew hot as tears infected my eyes. I thought of my mother and our nights playing poker when I'd felt exactly this way. "Oleander, my duckling," she'd say. "If everyone in the world put their problems in a jar and you had to pick one . . . you'd pick your own." It wasn't until that moment with Gloria that I finally understood what she'd meant.

Gloria's tears dried up, grown used to escaping the pit of despair. "So, I just wanted to say a proper farewell. Even if we had all the time in the world or met under more fortunate circumstances, we aren't meant for each other."

"The truth stings, doesn't it."

"Well, I think now is the time to tell the truth. You once told me life is pretty black and white, very straight and angular. I believe it's a beautiful, soft place." She lifted her hand, making a swooping motion. "Pastel tones filled with constant curves and arcs."

My face stood still, flinching ever so slightly as I let her continue to beat the dead horse.

"Last night when I went for a drive, I started to see the world in black and white . . . and that scared me, Oleander. More so than being preserved in gold! The violet orchids turned gray, and the golden moon turned silver. Life looked drab, a way it has never looked before. That's when everything became clear."

"I'm sorry." I looked down at my freshly pressed black suit.

"But you see, it's not your fault!"

But I knew it was, deep down, I just knew it was. I never realize the house is on fire until every room is scorched, there are no survivors, and the snap of a flame finally hits my own flesh.

"Don't feel bad," she continued. "It's who you are and how you think. And I just think differently. I became bitter and resentful, when I have no right to try and change you and vice versa. Both of us are right in our own way and we're built for different things."

"Just not built for each other, I guess."

"Correct."

"I would try to bargain to get you back—"

Gloria raised her hand. "There's no use. Just so we can be together for a few more days? That doesn't make sense. We both know how it ends."

"Who cares about what makes sense?"

In our twenties, we all have the same job title: a bunch of incompetent contractors, building plans on faulty foundations we know are bound to fall apart sooner or later. All for the dream of a skyscraper.

I loved Gloria and will always love her, but not to the depth she needed. I couldn't give my life for her; I didn't want to. Even if the experiment didn't exist and we were in a normal, non-life-threatening scenario, I still don't think I could have given her my life. I don't think at that age I could have given it to anyone. When all is said and done, that's what love is ... giving someone your life, whether literally or metaphorically. They own your mind, body, soul, and actions. What you choose to do with each other's lives determines the outcome, of course.

I slapped my hands on my knees and took a deep breath in, falling back into what I was trained to do. "Let's finalize the three flowers while I'm here."

Gloria cheered with excitement. Her job to serve as a guide was finally over, in all aspects. "Let me hear 'em."

"Sunflowers, cosmos, and last but not least—"

As I named the last flower, Gloria hugged me. She did in fact love things with her whole heart. I felt it. That upcoming collection had now gained her twentieth whole heart thanks to me. It became more than just another idea to make money for the company, the new collection became about eternalizing my time there.

Mr. Fleur will be so ecstatic when he hears—Mr. Fleur. Wait till he hears a piece of my mind. I don't know if I despise him or want to give him a pat on the back for his (not so little) white lie. He's capable of fooling his customers ... why not his daughter? But is it my place to say?

Chapter Thirty-Five

Knowing it would be my last afternoon at the Fleur Estate, I strolled down the lane of dirt slowly and methodically, stopping a few times just to stare. Nostalgia for the present swirled in my head, swooping around, keeping track of my every move. It is such a strange feeling to be somewhere you know is in the past. As if I were living in a photograph: My premonition told me that I'd never see this place, untouched by the rest of the world, in the future.

Some bushes up ahead on my right rustled, and as I came closer, two voices grumbled to each other in the courtyard on the other side.

"So what happened last night? Finally give that guy a piece of your mind?" Scott's voice presented itself.

I peered through a thin spot and saw Scott put Franklin in a headlock. Who knows what those two were doing . . . a couple of eccentrics, I tell ya.

"I just don't get it." Franklin grunted as he maneuvered out of Scott's grasp.

Scott then held his hand toward Franklin, making a finger gun. The two men stood still as Franklin paused in thought.

Scott said, "Remember to grab the barrel and cut."

Scott was teaching Franklin tactical maneuvers, for they kept up to date on the curriculum of the school of hard knocks. Each year in life was just another test for them. Franklin made his hand into a blade and chopped at Scott's wrist, causing his arm to go limp.

"Ouch! Good job," Scott shouted.

Franklin didn't even react to Scott's words of encouragement as he threw his hands up in frustration. He began to walk away from Scott as I continued to stare through the shrubs. I found Franklin's lost composure intriguing. The past few days it had been slipping away more and more, snowballing out of control.

Franklin clasped his hands together on the back of his head as he bellowed, "Why?!"

"Well, you hit the nerve endings. You did a good job. If I was a robber and I held you up at—"

"No! Why him?"

"Who?" Scott asked. "Ohhh. No guts, no Glory." He strolled away in his indisputably blunt fashion.

I walked over to the opening to see Franklin standing there, his face red, glaring at me. I knew the ball was in my court—I could either add fuel to the fire that Franklin had brewing inside him or de-escalate the situation. I saw the pain on Franklin's face, and then I finally knew the weight he bore.

"You were right." I smiled as I approached him.

I felt the defeat, the same kind every other fool he drove around wore.

"Got more than you bargained for, huh?"

"Yeah, we decided to throw in the towel."

Franklin grinned as he rubbed his mouth. "More like raise the white flag."

We both laughed the same way young boys did after they beat the living daylights out of each other. Blood dripping, cheeks flushed, knuckles burned, and smiling from ear to ear.

"Yeah, I'm about to head over to give Mr. Fleur a piece of my mind before the big send-off."

"You need a lift later?"

"Oh, no thanks. I feel like driving myself today." I turned around, ready to walk away, but my feet stood still, urging me not to leave anything unsaid. I raised my hand, my finger pointing to the sky. I kept my back to Franklin as I blurted out, "Oh, Frank, I have one more question before I go." I turned around, showcasing my solemness.

Franklin's eyebrows raised and he nodded, motioning to me that I had the floor.

"How did you know? I mean . . . that it wasn't going to work between Gloria and me."

Franklin smiled. "I told you the day we met."

I tried to recollect that day.

He continued, "The way someone says 'beautiful' is the ultimate telltale sign. The tone of the word, how they say it. The way you described that breathtaking young woman was the same way you described that cold factory the first day I picked you up."

"Beautiful," I sarcastically said.

"Beautiful," Franklin graciously replied.

"Some pill I was, huh? I messed up, didn't I?"

Franklin sighed. "Oh, but a mess-up is nothing more than a knowledge bump."

"And a multimillion-dollar contract is nothing more than an obstacle between you and the woman you love."

"Yes. Yes, it is," he admitted.

I walked to the house for the last time, the horizon blurry as the sun illuminated the grounds, gold falling over the Fleur Estate. Autumn was right around the corner, lowering its heavy head down into the atmosphere. I just hoped my next season in life would give me the same fulfillment. When everything is about to end, our first response is to go back to square one, the person that started it all. I wanted to let Mr. Fleur know the fall collection was prepared. I also wanted to finally pry the truth out of him . . . which was a difficult task. He knew exactly how to switch subjects and avoid direct answers, as if that was what he'd majored in in college.

Knock, knock!

"Come on in!"

I walked through the office doors to see him sitting at his desk, all his papers put away as if he'd been expecting me.

"Sit down, Oleander."

I sat down without even a "Hello" or "How are you?" All I said was, "Are you really going to be following through with this death sentence, or are you just telling Gloria that?"

He took a deep breath in as he adjusted his position in the chair. "Always with the charm, Oleander," he cracked. "You really do think that's what it is, don't you? You have such little faith in—"

"Gloria told me all about FAITH, and I must say, it is very clever on your part. To trick her into going peacefully . . . Is that humane or cruel? I'm not sure yet. But anyways, we finished the flower collection, so I'm assuming I'm going to be starting back at the factory, like how it was before."

"Do you know my reason for visiting the South of Sunset factory two months ago?"

"To survey the machines or motivate the employees, I guess." I tried to push the conversation along.

"No." Mr. Fleur smirked. "It was to find the person that will run the company while I'm away."

I froze.

Mr. Fleur then continued, "All the employees I met were chatting with one another about their hobbies or loved ones, laughing away. When I saw you, your face struck a chord with me. You were expressionless in a way that was well past solemn. You reminded me . . . well, of me when I was a young man. I was poor and had to fend for myself South of Sunset. I spent many years doing so, not letting myself get distracted by anyone or anything. I noticed you were the only person that was concerned about being behind on production when I visited the factory. I asked Mr. Walter about you, and he said all he knew was that you'd never missed a day of work. Once I spoke with you, that sealed the deal. You were impersonal and, frankly, it was like talking to a dead fish. You had no light in your eyes and pined for motivation."

"Wow." I laughed. "Thanks."

Mr. Fleur laughed back. "You have come out of your shell a lot since then, thank the heavens! You still have a long way to go, my boy. I know a tortured soul when I see one because I was the same way. If I'd met Cheryll in my twenties, she would have had nothing to do with me. My head was in a constant state of stress over the future, my future. Deep down inside me, I knew I was destined for something much greater, and I see the same in you, Oleander. You're hardworking and get the job done, not because you want to, but because you need to. It'll chip away at you like a brain-eating bacterium if you aren't constantly propelling forward."

I'd never known how to put my feelings into words before, but Mr. Fleur understood me. He gave my life the purpose I so craved. That is one of the biggest struggles with young men, no matter the era . . . We all have no sense of direction. Mr. Fleur, on that hot summer evening, August 25, 2125, crowned me the chief executive officer of Fleur Industries. He then ensured that Grenadine and Burton would mentor me in the beginning if I had any questions. I knew my first order of business would be speech lessons for old Burt to teach him how to pronounce his new boss's name.

Without hesitation, I hugged Mr. Fleur goodbye. I wanted to ask him more about the experiment, but I was so bewildered; I don't even remember if I told him "Thank you." If Mr. Fleur was as good at reading people as he seemed to be, I know he saw an enormous "Thank you" in my eyes. There was no hiding it. As I left the office, Gloria came up to me. Before she headed in, she pulled me aside and hugged me once more.

"Oleander, don't you worry about me. Don't you worry about anything you can't control. It's too exhausting!"

"Well, it's easier said than done."

The last words Gloria spoke to me were, "If it was your last night on earth, and above you were stars and twisters: Would you try to grab a constellation or run and hide?" She walked away, into the office, leaving the door open—a bad habit of hers.

I heard Mr. Fleur greet her. "I would say, 'Mornin', Glory,' but it's afternoon. What are you up to?"

"I just wanted to give you a flower because I gotta make up for all the days we are going to miss." I peeked through the door as Gloria continued talking to her father. She handed him a Canterbury bell, which means gratitude in floriography. Mr. Fleur grabbed Gloria and hugged her tightly, as if his arms were the jaws of life. I watched tears stream down his cheeks, his head resting on her shoulder. That was the first time I had ever seen Mr. Fleur cry—it was sobering.

Gloria whimpered as she pulled away. "You are making the ultimate sacrifice; you're giving your life for me."

"I already agreed to that the day you were born. That's part of the job description." Mr. Fleur sniffled as he wiped his eyes with a handkerchief.

"I love you, Dad."

"I love you, sweetheart." Mr. Fleur then proceeded to tell Gloria that they were all set for the experiment.

"Really?"

Mr. Fleur nodded. "Four molds ready to go."

"Four? Did I not tell you? Oleander won't be joining us."

"I know. He would've had to show up for the tests to even participate."

"Wait, why didn't you say anything if you knew?! Who else is being preserved?!"

Mr. Fleur sat back down at his desk and began working. "Some things in life you'll have to figure out for yourself."

Chapter Thirty-Six

I walked out of the Fleur household for the last time that evening, finally thankful to be in the scuffed-up shoes I was in. My financial worries were soon to be over. I looked forward to what life had in store for me for the first time. The lamps on the driveway shone like a tunnel, pointing me to the great wide open. Franklin was sitting on the hood of the town car, mumbling to himself in torment, as I drove away.

When I pulled up to the automatic gate to leave, it didn't move. I backed up and drove over the sensor many times, but still no movement. I got out of my car and walked over to the security command post to get some assistance. It was empty. Scott was probably in his "office." I sat down for a moment to watch the screens. I had picked up the sick habit of eavesdropping that summer. One screen came into view that was particularly intriguing. I watched Franklin pace around the driveway in a frenzy. He looked as if he was contemplating something. I thought about what Mr. Fleur had said to Gloria back in the office, about four people being preserved—*no*.

I remembered Franklin mentioning to me how nice the

testing facility was inside; it made perfect sense. When Gloria had stood on the table underneath that willow tree, I'd hid, embarrassed by her, but Franklin had just laughed. Thinking about it, he'd always admired her, and she'd reciprocated, whether she knew it or not, giggling at his jokes and conversing freely. Franklin's humor made Gloria's eyes light up, whereas I blew out her candle; his warmth was as genuine as a hundred bonfires, whereas I turned a room stone cold. My heart ached to realize the truth, but I knew what was meant to be. Franklin had always loved Gloria with his whole heart in a way I was incapable of. As I slouched over in the chair, watching Franklin agonize over professing his love to Gloria, I thought about all that I lacked. I wasn't even jealous or passionate or possessive, I was just . . . eh. Deprived of feeling and lost within myself, once again. Gloria could never love me the way she could Franklin.

As I watched Gloria appear on the screen, I sat up and leaned forward in my chair—the nauseating feeling of being only a spectator in your own story. She stood on the front steps of the house as Franklin looked up at her with the dopey demeanor he so humbly owned. Franklin's mouth didn't move, he just shrugged at Gloria as if, in that moment, he had accepted everything.

Scott came rushing into the security room with a bag of corn nuts in his hand. "Move, move, move," he said as he rolled my chair to the left of him.

He reached toward the screens and pressed the button that belonged to square number one in the middle, where Franklin and Gloria were shown. Static filled the air as crickets and frogs became audible. Scott was the MVP for turning the volume up. He pulled up a chair next to me and patted me on the back, congratulating me on my new position. We watched the screen as Gloria ran to Franklin, her sage dress ruffling like seafoam. No words were exchanged, she just rushed over to him as if she had been gone for a long time, on vacation or back from her fifth tour. The pair held each other close as they engaged in the kiss that had been waiting for them. It was not the desperate kiss of goodbye; it was the tender kiss of coming home.

"Finally, you two!" Scott shouted at the screen as if he were watching a football game.

I scanned the other screens and saw movement: The three landscapers watched from behind the bushes, hugging each other in celebration; Mr. Fleur smiled to himself as he looked down from his window; the butler shook his head and chuckled as he threw out the trash on the side of the house; and lastly, there was me. I saw the love they had for one another, and it gave me hope, melting away my discontent. All was healed at the Fleur Estate, at least within our minds. I rejoiced that Gloria had someone willing to experience the incomprehensible with her. That kind of love is the kind you wish upon anyone once it is found, and shame on those that try to destroy it; I could never be the person to do that. Gloria gave her heart openly and purely and she'd finally found her mirror image. *I will miss Gloria and Franklin, and I know the world will miss them just as terribly.*

"Why are you risking your life?" Gloria asked Franklin as she put her head on his shoulder.

"Well, I love you," he replied, so matter-of-factly.

Tears began to consume Gloria's eyes. "How could you stand it?! Stand seeing me with other—if I were you, I would've walked out of this place a long time ago."

Franklin laughed as he hugged Gloria tighter, brushing the top of her dark hair. "I thought about it many times, but the problem is . . . I'll never stop loving you. Not having you in my life is much worse than you not being mine."

Gloria pulled back and looked at him with astonishment.

"Glory, you have my whole heart."

Gloria began to cry some more. "I don't know what I would do without you."

"Well, we don't have to talk that way, because I will always be here for you, through thick and thin. No matter what."

"The experiment isn't guaranteed, you know that, right?"

Franklin nodded as Gloria stood there in disbelief.

"I thought you said you don't gamble?"

"I don't gamble. If I don't do this, I would have to live without you. That's a guaranteed loss. If anything, I just want to get the opportunity to love you."

"So do I." Gloria squeezed Franklin. "Will you still give me that chance?"

"Forever."

My mother once told me that it's not about the person you can live with, it's about the one you can't live without. Franklin and Gloria had been a part of each other's lives for such a long time, and it wasn't until time posed a threat that they noticed. I think they assumed if they always had time, they always had each other.

"I will always love you and I will never make you question it, no matter what our future holds."

"I am in love with you, Franklin."

Franklin smiled. "You always have been."

Gloria playfully nudged him as the pair sat down on the front steps, ready to rediscover everything they already knew about one another. I felt at ease as Scott walked outside with me to fix the gate. Once we got it working, I reluctantly headed home, not wanting to leave but not wanting to stay either, belonging nowhere. I watched the large castle of secrets fade away in my rearview mirror, into the starless night, hoping everyone in there was going to be okay.

Chapter Thirty-Seven

A week after I privately got confirmation that the Fleurs and Franklin Petacki had been "preserved," the announcement was made that I would be taking over the company. Fleur Industries' board was apparently in charge of their bodies, making the corporation the designated holder. The board also had ownership of the Fleur Estate until they "got back." A part of me felt guilty for lying to all my old co-workers, saying Mr. Fleur had retired, but I was obligated to say that—legally and morally. Although James transferred to work at the Museum of Decline and remained my best friend, I stayed consistent with my dishonest story to everyone. If the truth ever got out, Mr. Fleur's name would be dragged through the mud for orchestrating a suicide pact. Either way, it would not be good for the company, or anyone involved.

The strangest feeling was having my first meeting with all the employees at the South of Sunset factory—the same room where Mr. Fleur had lectured us on the day I met him. I stood there behind the podium, looking down on all the unenthused familiar faces of my peers. I felt my hands shake, not from nerves, but from emotion. Everything was moving forward so quickly, except my feelings . . . those moved slowly and painfully.

I began to speak into the rickety microphone as employees whispered to one another. "I present to you the three new flowers for this season's collection." The three banners behind me unraveled, displaying beautiful paintings of each species. In front of me were three glass cases covered by black velvet cloth. I pulled the cover off the first case and revealed a gold-dipped sunflower. I heard the crowd awe with astonishment as the metal sunflower shone under the stage light.

"Sunflower, bringing customers joy and happiness."

I pulled the cloth off the second flower, revealing a gold-dipped cosmo.

"Cosmo, bringing customers resilience and harmony in a time of hardship."

I watched the employees tap each other on the shoulders, smiling to one another. Enthusiasm brewed within that room, for it had been hibernating for a long time. I had the crowd in the palm of my hand as I announced the third and final flower for the fall collection.

"Lastly, my personal favorite"—I uncloaked the last case, the flower glistening in the spotlight, temporarily blinding the audience—"a morning glory." I thought of Gloria Fleur and how her name fit her as mine did. "This flower resembles human life. They wake up in the morning and fall asleep at night. Although they do die each evening, they are reborn again the next day, symbolizing hope and how precious life is. With their ability to grow in challenging situations, this flower embodies the fleeting nature of love and life. They bloom brightly and fully, unapologetic of their fate. And lastly, before I bore everyone to death . . ."

The crowd laughed at my lighthearted statement. My

smile dissipated as I mustered up the strength to finish my speech.

"The morning glory reminds us of one important thing . . . Take nothing for granted. Our life, our loved ones, our health, our wealth, and our abilities at this moment in time."

That was the speech that assured the employees my position in the company was rightfully deserved. It's also safe to say my first collection was a hit. After the release, days went by, then weeks, then years. As I tackled my new career running a major corporation, time flew by like a hot-air balloon. It floated with ease, and for once in my life, I knew my purpose, my direction. While I enjoyed spending my days surveying machines or crunching numbers in the factory, nothing compared to Gloria and me brainstorming together in a colorful greenhouse, hidden away in a garden, when we were young. Nothing compared to Gloria.

"Oleander, we got somethin' to show ya," Burt said as he knocked on my office door. He slowly led me down a hallway, using a cane to make his way. He took me into a small, private room toward the back of the factory, where Charles Grenadine was waiting. They had set up a demonstration. There was a gold-dipped rose on the table along with a bunch of different medical supplies. Grenadine performed the process of removing the coating and dissolving the FAITH from its system, as Burton narrated the science behind it.

"We wanted to make sure you were doing well here for a few years before we showed you," Charles stated.

For the first time, I saw the process with my own eyes and felt like a fool when Burt handed me the beautiful fresh rose, fragrant with life.

"Excuse me, gentlemen." I calmly left the room and retreated into my office, rose in hand.

Once I reached the room, my knees buckled under me. I

broke down. After all, I was full of life inside, just as much as the flowers here. Whenever I felt like this, I couldn't play cards with my mother anymore, all I could do was cry. I hate memories. A wave of them doesn't flood over me, like most people. They pester me. Unlike Noah's Ark, two by two, memories enter me one by one, wearing me down. As if that single number is all I'm capable of taking care of. One memory will tap on my head and stay there long enough for me to forget, and another one pops up right after, ready to take its place. They do it on purpose, saving themselves, trying to last longer throughout my life. I envy those who get flooded with memories. Take me down in one blow, don't just keep adding one pound to my dumbbell each day. But when I do have hard days, when my legs don't want to work due to the never-ending weight of melancholy, I think about the words Mr. Fleur spoke that one fateful night in the kitchen.

"You keep standing."

Mr. Fleur's conversation with Mrs. Fleur has continued playing in my head for fifty years now, and I keep telling myself, "Oh, but things never stop, they just pause. They will eventually continue later on, that's all there is to it." I can picture everyone's faces at the Fleur Estate, laughing, crying, and loving one another as Mr. Fleur's sentences continue in my head.

"Soon we will be together again, just like this. With faith, we will all reunite and dance again . . . just North of Sunset."

Every once in a while, I'll drive past the Fleur Estate and peek through the large iron gates to see if anyone is inside. It's always empty now, as the castle of secrets has no more lies to tell. The property is decrepit; that's what happens when a conglomerate tries homemaking. Dead leaves cover the decomposed granite driveway, the bright-peach-colored house is now a light salmon, and the flowers are all withered.

Once when I was driving by in my early thirties, I passed

Scott, who was locking up. He was moving slowly, still filled with gusto, of course. A little girl who was with him had the same eyes and taste buds. They split a bag of corn nuts as he explained to me that he was showing his granddaughter, Aster, the property before closing it off for good. He informed me that statues were made in honor of the Fleurs and Franklin out of twenty-four-karat gold. We shared a good laugh—that seemed fitting for their extravagant departure.

"You can hop the fence and take a look at them. I won't stop you anymore, asshole. I'm too old for that shit."

I looked down at the little girl standing next to Scott, not even blinking twice at his profanity. She looked up at me defensively, as if her expression said, "Try me, asshole." I nodded as they turned away and began to wander down the lane. Once they were no longer in sight, I stuck my foot against the iron and hiked my leg over the rose gate. Jumping down, my feet resolutely hit against the decomposed granite, creating no echo—just one loud, hearty crunch.

Making my way through the desolate grounds, they looked as if Mother Nature hadn't necessarily neglected them but rather scorned them. As if the property were once the golden child but had stopped listening to what was best for them, going against God's will. Passing the empty fountain, now with a cracked swan, I saw large glistening figures in the distance, scattered among the grass. When I reached them, I stared up at the four figures posing Greek-like. I laughed as my eyes watered at their tragic opulence. A gold plaque stood in the brittle grass reading *Grab a constellation.*

I reached out to hold Gloria's statue hand, the woman made of stars, but it was cold—lifeless and cold. A shiver ran through me, and anger brewed inside me. I stared up at Mr. Fleur—the man who could stop time. I couldn't even imagine how they'd felt the day of their departure, willingly throwing away the greatest gift given to man. I still torment myself over my complacency with it all. A shit hand is a shit hand, no matter what Mr. F says. Feeling kills, but thinking tortures.

Fifty years later, I'm still in this crummy little office, staring down on the colorless factory I've spent my lifetime in. Many summers have come and gone, but none have measured up to that one fifty years ago. No one ever talks about how magical the first summer of adulthood is. You work all day to survive while the rest of your peers lounge around in the heat. You are faced with new challenges and opportunities that all the other seasons could never offer. You are on the precipice of change. You make new friends and have serious relationships that go nowhere because life is moving too fast for all of you. It is a truly unprecedented time in a young person's life. Twenty-four years old, that's a blip. My age is now seventy-four.

Age. What a weird word. *A-G-E, age.* What a weird concept.

The definition is the time a person has lived, or a thing has existed. Society labels us by this number, but it doesn't take into account leap years, the day you actually gain consciousness, or lastly, people like me . . . who are seventy-four years old and haven't started living. The number is factually incorrect, so why does society label us by it?

Well, age helps us keep track of what we are ready for in life as well as what we aren't just yet. For example: our milestones, our mental capacity, and our physical abilities. It tells us things we must accomplish today versus things we shouldn't even sweat about till far in the future. Age is the measuring cup of life, and I used to wholeheartedly believe that . . . We all did. Whether we would like to admit it or not, everyone uses this system. From crooked politicians on the East Coast, conjuring up laws with age requirements, to the out-of-touch studio heads on the West Coast, using age for their market research and target demographic nonsense to sell their latest plant-free cookies. In all honesty, we don't truly measure or remember life by exact age, but by moments, phases, people, places, and events.

It's all a bunch of malarkey, it is. That is why I am finally leaving the flower business after fifty years. This retirement form will be the key to my freedom. A world unknown for me to search, hoping never to be jaded by the act of discovery. It is time for me to pass down the torch to another lost youngster. I have accomplished more than I could have ever imagined in my career and am satisfied with the strides I have made within this company. I just wish I could bring back cars and telephones and good people. At least we still have radio. I turn up the volume and a man's staticky voice projects off my gray walls.

"Tonight's episode of *Science's Latest Discoveries* is brought to you by the Citizen's Blue Project. Save our water source, turn in your vehicles. With a worldwide shortage of water, disaster is imminent. Turn in your automobiles. Water-powered vehicles are dangerous to society, not to mention how much healthier walking is! Don't be 'that guy,' visit our automobile buyback center located on the corner of Sunset and Crescent to do your part in saving humankind."

"Ha!"

I look at the rain crashing outside the window and the people stomping in puddles filled with horse crap. You get to an age where you see it from a mile away. They pray for us all to die off so they can repeat the same tactics as before. I still enjoy this program. It gives me a sense of stability—being around for over fifty years, and all.

"This week on *SLD*, we have breaking news: The first person ever has been cured from a rare disease that first popped up in the United States in the '20s. A private company has successfully diminished the fatal components of the disease, now known as alchronicea, in an unidentified twenty-year-old woman, who is from right here in Southern California! This is a historic moment for America and for the whole world. We will be bringing you live updates. It is a day of celebration for many."

Could it be?!

I feel my heart warm up, causing condensation to leak from my wrinkled eyes as I look around my office. My office. My beautiful, ebbing and flowing office. The place that has been my home. I look over at the photograph of James, Elsie, Gloria, and me in the bowling alley. I walk to my office window that looks out on the whole factory and all the workers. The faces of a thousand pasts and a million futures, the faces that have the possibility to reach for the constellations. The blissful youth of America, unaware that the sun can set on any of them at any moment in time. To see a sunset: shades of raspberry and lemon, harmonizing with one another in a give-and-take of sweet and bitter. The perfect summary of life. This factory, the perfect summary of my life: large shining brass pots pouring glistening, piping hot gold over vibrant, colorful flowers as the smell of machines and burning leaves fills the air. A cornucopia of color here South of Sunset, just like North. Correction—I am seventy-four years old and didn't start living till this afternoon. I have heard people talk about how heavenly it is here, but I finally believe it. Heaven is always North of Sunset and South and wherever you can see it. In her green eyes and in his kind words, in a field of roses or a café covered in dirt, in an insult to ignorance or a push of truth, in life forcing you to do the things you never would otherwise do. To find North of Sunset, one must be willing to look up, above the stinging blindness that burns their face. One must look up.

Some may call it a love story, others . . . a warning. It may be about having strong family values, or it may be about the children that didn't. It could be about truth or it could be about hope. It all comes down to perspective. After all . . . it just may be a tale of redemption.

Acknowledgments

I would like to start by thanking Mom, Dad, Mimi, PopPop, Casey, and Wyatt for their love, generosity, and unwavering faith in me. I am eternally blessed to have a family like you and be able to pass on the morals you instilled in me as a child.

Next, I would like to give a special thanks to Kevin Anderson and Associates. To Jaime Levine—if it weren't for your incredible expertise and fearless expression of truth, this story would still be a sloppy manuscript sitting on my computer. And to Mark Weinstein—I had my arrow drawn back for a long time, and thanks to your guidance, you pointed me in the right direction to aim. Thank you both for your crucial help in making this dream achievable.

I would also like to acknowledge my publisher, Girl Friday Productions. Your team of remarkable women has turned this terrifying process into a wonderful experience. Thank you, Kim Kent, for keeping me level-headed, always staying one step ahead of my worries, and making it all happen. You are a force to be reckoned with. Thank you, Adria Batt, for your keen eye and honesty when it came to strategic decisions. Thank you,

Kylee Hayes, for your attention to detail and patience with me during the editing phase. I am beyond grateful for all of your enthusiasm and hard work on this project—a mountain far too large for me to climb alone.

C.M.P., you were the first person to hear this story, and if it weren't for you, it would have remained a half-written screenplay in my doubtful mind. I will forever cherish the memories of coming home and reading a newly written chapter to you. Thank you for existing.

Lastly, I was not alone while writing this. Thank you, God. I felt your love in every page.

About the Author

© Arian Mahboubian

Haley Ahern, born and raised in Southern California, has been immersed in the entertainment industry from an early age. From performing as a professional dancer on Hollywood sets to founding her own production company, Ahern's passion for storytelling and classic cinema has always been at the heart of her career. With over twenty film awards as a director, screenwriter, and camera operator, she channels her cinematic experience into her writing, blending the charm of Old Hollywood with the fresh perspective of Gen Z. When not crafting stories, Ahern enjoys classic cars and keeping up with her chaotic German shepherd, Comet.

www.ingramcontent.com/pod-product-compliance
Lightning Source LLC
Jackson TN
JSHW030022130625
86001JS00002B/9